THE RIVER

of

LOST SOULS

D.L. CALVIN

ISBN-10: 0988840200
EAN-13: 9780988840201

1

Ж Ж Ж

LARGE SCARLET, HYACINTH AND RED WING macaws screamed at the marauding Tamarind monkeys for invading their space. Matching the macaws' persistence, the primates taunted the birds while gibbering at themselves, as they held fast to the newly claimed territory. The reason for the disturbance was becoming clearer by the second—the stench of death was overpowering, as a rotting corpse of a young Squirrel monkey lay close.

Captain Zack Steele sat motionless on his coiled legs, his binoculars seemingly glued to his eyes as he intently watched workers building a large oversized hacienda that resembled a fortress. Sweat dripped off his nose and fell unnoticed onto his chest, making small rivulets, as the drops meandered down his emaciated body and disappeared under the waistband of his pants that were secured by a handmade rope. Of course being covered by his ghillie suit did not keep him from sweating. However, it did manage to keep the afternoon rain from soaking him while it camouflaged him from the observation planes, and security helicopters, that flew over quite frequently. In case the helicopters were so equipped, his ghillie suite reduced his infrared signature. In fact, he was damn near invisible against the jungle flora.

He had learned that the hard way when one morning a female Fer-de-lance Viper had slithered over his ghillie sack, looking for a warm place to nest. Since he was not discernible from his surroundings, his body had been perfect for the mother to be and she had coiled her length between his legs. Steele knew she needed little provocation to strike, and her bite was deadly. It would be an agonizingly slow, painful death, as his life ebbed away from massive internal hemorrhaging. However, fortune had smiled upon him; the viper decided to move on, leaving Steele to his job.

That job was to gather information and report his findings to his superior in Bogotá. There the information would be reviewed and analyzed by the DEA and the DOD, who in turn would pass his findings on to someone in the State Department. After that, the information would sit on somebody's desk while nothing would be done. This was because the people who needed the information would have to wait for the perpetual motion machine, called "bureaucracy," to decide who was worthy enough to see the information in Washington. In the meantime, the Julio Mendoza Cartel would get richer and more powerful while Zack Steele continued to sit in the stinking jungle with the birds and the damn monkeys for company, watching and waiting for the day that he could help destroy, or even kill Julio Mendoza and his empire of human misery.

He had been in the field for ninety-two days instead of the originally assigned twenty days. He needed medical attention; his supplies were exhausted, and had received no orders since he got here. His condition was untenable, forcing him do something that was personally distasteful to him¾he deserted his post. During the past three months he had lost weight, his shoes would no longer stay on his feet. His pants had become so loose he had fashioned a rope from jungle vines in order to make a belt to keep his pants in place. Another discouraging point had been the lack of communication from his counterparts in over three months. Not only was he physically in a bad way, but emotionally and mentally as well. He had hit the wall, which simply meant he had reached his maximum endurance. A positive was that he was angry; an essential human element if he wanted to survive. For ninety days, he had been living like an animal. *Fuck'em*, he thought. *I have had enough and I want out!*

He wrapped his ghillie sack into a ball burying it where he could find it again, if the need arose. Pulling the drawstring snug on his hat, he filled his two canteens with stored rainwater, looked around to be sure he was unobserved, then stealthily headed down the mountain towards the river.

2

Ж Ж Ж

LOST IN THOUGHT, COLONEL Ryan Mc Bride walked into his office. Recently, McBride had been put in charge of Operation Cadence. As the State Department, DEA, and the Pentagon had all thoroughly briefed him about his new assignment, he was quite aware not only of his new duties and his responsibilities, but also the dangers they entailed.

He felt naked without his uniform. Wearing civilian clothes is what he did on the golf course, but to actually go work in them was still just a bit hard for him to accept. Another adjustment he was told to make was to let his hair grow long and to grow a beard. These ploys were intended to help him look nothing like the neat and clean-shaven colonel he really was. As of now, by virtue of the DEA and the CIA, he was a coffee and sugar broker from Gringo-land. Both agencies had put him into their systems as a documented, "person of interest." Thus, the Costa Rican Police in San Jose` had a file on him, as did the police in Mexico City. Like it or not, Ryan Ryan Mc Bride was now, officially, a covert operative. With a few strokes of a computer board, his military rank was no longer valid. From now on, Ryan Mc Bride was labeled as "a bad dude" someone in whom the Mendoza Cartel would be interested in. All Ryan had to do was stay alive and wait.¾The sacrificial lamb staked out as bait.

Ryan Mc Bride was a big man, standing well over six feet tall. He was tall and lean, with a long, narrow face, and deep-set hazel eyes that some might call beady. Though officially his hair was red, upon closer look, gray could be seen making definite inroads into the bright mop of hair. As happens when maturing, his moustache and beard were now mostly gray, but with enough of a red tinge that it gave him a distinguished look.

A graduate of West Point, Ryan spoke Spanish, French, some Turkish and a little bit of Arabic. Since the day he had graduated from West Point, he had been married to Sally, a nurse specializing in cardiopulmonary and urgent care. Early on in their marriage, she had declared she would not be a camp follower. Therefore, they bought a beautiful home while he was stationed at Fort Carson and that is where she stayed. He was free to roam the world and when he got tired, he was free to come home. It was what a discreet person would call an open and loveless marriage.

Over the years, Ryan had become an expert in karate; although he had never used this skill to kill anyone, he was capable of doing so. If his predecessor had been capable of better defending himself, he might still be alive and Ryan would be somewhere else enjoying himself.

As Ryan sipped his hot coffee, he stared out his office window, recalling what he had been told about his predecessor. Ryan thought his name had been Adam Smith. Appears Smith had just disappeared off the face of the earth. One minute he had been buying a pack of smokes and in the next, two men walked up behind him, a car screeches to a halt, and Smith is grabbed and tossed into the back seat of a black sedan. Smith had never heard from again. With him went all the codes and signals of the field operatives. Ryan did not know who they were or where they were. In fact, he didn't know if they were even still alive. *So much for a grass-roots operation with central control,* Ryan thought to himself, dunking his toast.

3

Ж Ж Ж

ROSSI READ THE INTEL REPORT FROM the Bureau Chief at the State Department in Bogotá. Sadly, it was not good news. Operation Cadence was in shambles. *What makes these guys think they are invisible?* Rossi thought. *The drug cartels have spy networks as good, if not better than ours. In addition, like us, they share their knowledge.*

Personally, Rossi felt that Colonel Smith was a bad choice from the get go. His cover was that of a Spanish Padre yet he did not look Spanish, nor did he even speak Spanish. Neither was he very convincing as a priest, probably because he wasn't Catholic. That might have had something to do with things. On the other hand, possibly, it might have been because Smitty had never been to a mass in his life, let alone conduct a mass. That had to have been a dead give away to anyone observing his actions.

Upon finishing reading the report, Rossi concluded that Operation Cadence had been an ill-conceived idea from the start and was as fucked up as Hogan's goat.

So far, millions of dollars have been spent on intelligence and setting up surveillance sites. Columbia is the hinge pin of the drug cartels and responsible for shipping out annually approximately seventy tons of cocaine by land, sea and air. Moreover, that data was two years old. The National Oceanographic and Atmospheric Administration (NOAA) and DOD satellites constantly took pictures of the terrain, trying to locate coca fields, processing plants and even donkey trails. Still, the best and most reliable method of gathering intelligence was bribery.

Rossi threw down the report and picked up the phone. This operation was not going to fail, and as the Operations Chief changes were going to be made, and quickly.

Ж Ж Ж

General Seth Hatfield hung up the phone. A grimace crossed his face as he tried to control his emotions. He was upset that he had not been briefed about Colonel Smith's murder and to hear about it from the Operations Chief was an insult. However, it did tell the story and he had to agree with Rossi. The Cadence Operation was a fucking nightmare. If he had his way, he would just go in, drop a few well-placed nuclear bombs, and be done with it.

However, that was not an option for him, nor would it ever be an option. Now, the general had found out that the State Department, the DEA and the Secretary of the Army had chosen Ryan Mc Bride to replace Smith. He was aware that McBride was a Green Beret, had been a brigade commander and was actually in line for a star¾that is until now. Now his ass was hanging out there, surrounded by drug lords who had bad tempers, very short attention spans, did not like spies, and loved to torture and kill spies in order to satisfy their lust for power and above all, to gain information.

Hatfield sat there and idly thought about the whole situation: *I wonder what Smith told his torturers and which drug lord had killed him... probably Senor Mendoza or rather, Don Julio Mendoza, as he likes to be called. That would make sense, as Mendoza is an oddity at best.*

Then General Hatfield found himself going over the facts that were known about Mendoza: *We know he is well educated and his family pedigree very impressive. His father was a well-respected doctor who turned to politics, while his mother had been an opera singer. That probably explains why Don Julio loves theatrics of any kind. In fact, he usually dresses in Edwardian coats made of velvet or silk with pants that are rather large, like the ones worn in old movies where they showed royalty in pantaloons. Of course, his shirts all have lace at the cuffs that stick out from his coat sleeves. Not to forget his shoes which always match his outfits? Then to complete his outfits, he always wears a large, orange cummerbund and carries a hickory walking stick. It sure is not hard to miss Julio, as he always looks the part he portrays—that of royalty. I wonder if the way he dresses is a way for him to draw attention away from his short and rather stocky build. Then for dramatic effect, he wears his hair long and usually pulls it back into a ponytail. To complete the ensemble and add a dash of flair, he sports a large diamond earring in one ear and adorns his fingers with rubies and emeralds. Julio may be comical to look at but no one should ever underestimate his deadly persona. Did Smitty underestimate him?*

One thing that added to Mendoza's charm and mystic was that he *was a chameleon. He funded schools and hospitals and even had a* bridge built so the peons of his native village could have access to the schools and hospitals. Before the bridge, the villagers used to have to climb the old mountain trail, and then take a canoe to the river road and finally a bus into town. Now, they just merely walked across the bridge and took the bus into town.

Julio always made sure that his good deeds were reported to both his family and the public. However, Julio Mendoza had a hidden agenda that was pure evil. He was Satan incarnate, with a desire to seduce politicians and judges and control them through blackmail, intimidation, and cocaine usage.

He would have his security force raid the villages up and down the rivers and along the coastal towns, in order to take the young boys and girls from their families. Then he would personally inspect each child; separating the pretty girls from the not so pretty girls and he did the same with the boys.

The ugly children were sent to his processing plants where they would walk up and down in big steel tubs, macerating the coca leaves with their bare feet while men wearing surgical masks would dampen the leaves with water. Then these faceless strangers would dust the broken leaves with lime. When the leaves had been pulverized to the correct texture, they would pour kerosene into the tubs while the children marched up and down stomping the leaves. The sharp edges of the coca leaves cut the soft, tender flesh of the children's small and delicate feet to ribbons and each innocent child's blood was incorporated into the wet and slippery green mush.

Naturally, when the kerosene was added, it would burn the children's flesh as it slowly entered their bodies through the cuts and gashes on their feet, causing the children to cry out in pain. Their cries were ignored while the masked men added more kerosene, continuing the process until a white paste began to form. Then the children's cries of pain slowly gave way to euphoria as the cocaine entered their young bodies through the cuts and into their blood. Soon they would beg for more and more. Obliging souls to the last, the faceless, nameless men would put them into another tub and again the children would march and stomp up and down, waiting for the wonderful feeling to return. When the ugly children's bodies were used up they were taken into the jungle and let go. There were no survivors.

The pretty children he sent to schools and educated in the humanities and sciences. Also, they were taught French and English, even Chinese. They were able to do what their parents could not do—read and write. Along with their studies, they were taught table manners, proper decorum and how to bow and curtsey. Though they did not know it, all this training and education was slowly grooming them to be "escorts," better known as on-call whores.

When they became of age, Julio had them introduced to sex— man-to-woman, man-to-man and woman-to-woman. Whatever sexual perversion Julio's clients preferred, Julio would see that they got it. His client's wishes were his to fulfill. If by chance one of the young people rebelled (and some did, although not often) Julio would simply send them to one of his processing plants until they could be controlled. When his female protégées were used up and could no longer perform, he had them dropped off in cities around the world. They had no real names, no birth certificates and no identities. They were just broken-down hookers with a cocaine habit and no supplier or money.

When replacements were required Julio sent for another bunch of youngsters and the process would be repeated. Unless bought by a client, the boys were sent to a processing plant, where they were rewarded with a constant euphoric high, and ultimately death. Their broken lifeless bodies would be tossed into one of the many lakes for the piranha to feast upon. In that way, there were no clues, no names, and no person's just very fat piranha.

4

※ ※ ※

ZACK STEEL SAT IN HIS CANOE and watched the river that would take him back to civilization. Idly he dabbed Mercurochrome on his grass cuts. Mentally and physically he was exhausted and in dire need of a woman. However, before he could fulfill this urgent need, he had to find a dentist as one of his teeth had become abscessed. Once the tooth was treated, he planned to take a hot shower and then have a long, hard sleep. His plan included eating a steak with fries and a tall, cold beer. Then for dessert, he wanted to find a beautiful whore to satisfy his lust.

All in good time though, as his immediate need now was rest. His body needed to recover its strength before he could begin to tackle the river currents downstream. The trek down the mountain had been long, arduous, and fraught with danger. Twice he had almost been discovered by the security patrols that worked for Mendoza.

Though Mendoza was a great one for security, the problem was he hired young, illiterate boys who were ill trained and ill equipped. The

boys did not understand that if they failed in protecting Julio or notifying him something was amiss in the jungle, they would become his
mules and be forced to carry heavy coca sacks on their backs over the
Andes Mountains from Peru, the only other country that grew excellent
coca. As mules, their life expectancy would be short, as the tempera-
tures fell below zero in the mountain passes and most were ill clothed,
wearing whatever they had on when "hired." Thus cold and often high
on cocaine, their death was a certainty.

Steele watched intently as the sentry dog led the young and very
bored security guard through the dense jungle. The dog's immaturity
and constant barking caused the Howler monkeys to erupt into a violent,
deafening chatter. As the Howler monkeys chattering and screeching
became painful to the young boy's ears, Steele watched him grab his
machine pistol. The young boy pointed his pistol at the monkeys and
squeezed off a short burst. For a brief moment in time, the jungle was
quiet. Then without warning, the giant macaws began to sound the danger alarm and the monkeys followed with one long deafening wail of
grief. The young man's burst had been deadly, killing three, maybe four
adult monkeys and a baby. With one deafening scream, the monkeys
seemed to explode in unison as they pointed at the pathetic creature
holding the leash and screamed their contempt.

Steele thought to himself, *if monkeys could wonder, they would be
wondering how long this two-legged animal had to live…*

Ж Ж Ж

"Rossi, get in here!" boomed the voice belonging to Don McGee,
the Under Secretary of State, who reported directly to the Secretary of

State. Don McGee was a very experienced diplomat who clearly understood the immensity of Operation Cadence. He also understood the political wrangling and arm-twisting necessary to achieve the desired results—the *complete* eradication of illicit drugs into the United States. Everyone, but the president knew this was nothing, but an idealistic pipe dream.

Rossi walked into Don's office to find the under secretary leaning forward on his desk, his hand supporting his chin. Seeing the suit Ryan et draped over the back of his chair, Rossi knew that Don's administrative assistant, Ethel, had not gotten to his Don's jacket yet. Whenever Don was not looking, she would whisk his jacket away and hang it up properly. Now he was intently reading something. It was the same intelligence report from Bogotá that Rossi had already read and Don would want to know what was being done about it. Don McGee never wanted to know names or dates—just results. He could care less how the results were obtained.

Looking up the under secretary quipped, "Rossi, Operation Cadence is a mess! I see here that one of your people, a Colonel Adam Smith, has been kidnapped off the street and is presumed dead. General Hatfield has informed me that a Colonel Ryan Mc Bride was selected by the Secretary of the Army to replace Smith. In addition to all this bullshit, I have been told that McBride has no idea who or where his people are and has no way to get in touch with them. Now, Rossi, this is bullshit! You hear me, Rossi? Bullshit! You leave brave men out there to be captured, tortured and murdered. What kind of fucking operations chief are you anyway?"

"Sir that was done on purpose for security reasons each man operating independently of the other, reporting his intelligence information only to Smith. And sir, he was the only one who knew each man by name and by sight," Rossi responded in a very forceful, if not disrespectful tone.

Putnam looked defiantly at his subordinate. "Okay, Rossi, tell me what in the Sam hill you are going to do next? Nothing seems to work against this Mendoza fellow."

"Well, sir, we know for sure that Mendoza is old school. He processes his cocaine by the old traditional methods. Meaning, sir, that he does not use acids to process his cocaine. Instead, he still uses the old steel tubs or plastic swimming pools that can be inflated at one location then deflated and moved to another.

In addition, he kidnaps women and children from the neighboring villages up and down the rivers. He takes them to an indoctrination center where he sorts them by age, size, and beauty. The ugly women and children are sent to the processing sites which, because of their flexibility, can be almost anywhere in Columbia. Pretty women and young girls he educates and turns into prostitutes, controlling them by intimidation and/or drugs. When finished with them, he turns them loose in various cities around the world to 'blend in and never be heard from again,' that's if their lucky. However, since they have no real names or birth certificates, they cannot prove who they are or where they are from. Since Mendoza has robbed them of their culture and heritage, they can no longer speak their native language. They are citizens of nowhere. If they speak only French, they would be dropped off in New Delhi or maybe Tokyo. They would also be cocaine addicts with no money and no supplier.

"Mendoza uses only the coca leaves from Peru or Columbia. He simply walks the leaves over the mountains, using human mules or maybe an airdrop. He is smart and has the police, judges and the politicians in his employ. He has created mistrust and indecision within the country and he fuels it with lies or half-truths and great public relations.

We wanted to initiate "Operation Interdiction' but have been told to wait. Therefore, sir, we wait. Meanwhile, Mendoza keeps producing his cocaine and innocent women and children are cruelly yoked to slavery in order to satisfy the lust and power of a drug lord."

"Rossi, get off your fucking soapbox!"Don McGee growled. I asked you what you were going to do about Mendoza,"Don McGee said, looking at a satellite-imaging photo from NOAA.

Glancing at the photo, Rossi knew that Don did not understand the map, but he was acting if he did. Obviously trying to impress somebody the question was What was Don doing with it? The National Oceanographic Atmospheric Administration is the nation's weather watcher so everybody in the world uses the information gathered by NOAA. Therefore, what did the NOAA have to do with the DEA and the State Department?

"Don, I'm going to take Mendoza and his cartel down and if need be, I will have him killed along with the rest of his sleazy ilk," Rossi stated.

Putnam said nothing Pissed off, Rossi got up and left.

Ж Ж Ж

Rossi sat at a break table lost in thought, drinking coffee and smoking a cigarette. The break area was not large, considering the number of people who worked in the State Department building. It was done in a courtyard style with little alcove areas surrounded by fir trees or oleanders trimmed with pansies, petunias and multi-colored impatiens. In spite of the idea, it was designed to hold as few people as possible. Most of the State Department employees were non-smokers and they either went for walks around the complex or sat in the cafeteria where the air conditioning caused their nipples to harden and their lips to turn blue. However, there were still a few smokers left who enjoyed sinning with one another, drinking coffee and swapping stories.

Paying no particular attention to anything or anybody, Rossi was suddenly startled back to the present when someone walked up to the table. "Yes?" Rossi asked.

"I was wondering if I might sit with you, as all the other tables are occupied."

Rossi looked up into the face of a very attractive woman. "Of course you can," Rossi said, standing up so the woman could squeeze by.

Rossi sat back down and took a long, slow drag on the cigarette, slowly exhaling the obnoxious smoke into the face of the woman. Rossi then leaned over and slowly ground the cigarette into the concrete and dumped the butt into the coffee cup, engrossed in thought, trying to figure out why Don McGee had been trying to read a satellite thermal image photo with a NOAA stamp on the back.

"Do you come out here often?" Once again, Rossi was brought up short by the soft southern drawl of the stranger's voice. "No, I don't," Rossi replied. This is actually my first time outside. Normally I just get a cup of coffee and bagel and go back to my office. And you?" Rossi said, smiling for the first time all day.

"This is my first day of work here at the State Department. I'm a bit overwhelmed, really."

Rossi smiled, "What is it that you will be doing here?"

"Well, I'm not exactly sure. You see, I am presently enrolled at American University in their Doctorial Program. I was working at the National Oceanographic Atmospheric Administration in Maryland where I did thermal imaging analysis on pollution. I monitored pollution around the world and wrote reports. Then on Friday, my boss called me into his office, handed me two, large envelopes and told me I have been re-assigned to the State Department, he was unclear what I would be doing, but he was told it would be top secret. This morning I handed the two envelopes to a Mr. Don McGee. When I did, he just smiled, said 'Thank you, and walked back into his office with my envelopes. Turning, he told me to get coffee and that he would talk to me later."

Rossi began to laugh. "What's your name?"

"Shirley Lamb," the woman replied.

"Where do you come from, Shirley Lamb?"

"Atlanta," she said, taking a sip of coffee.

"Have you been assigned to a department yet?" Rossi asked.

"I think I will be working for Mr.Don McGee," Shirley replied, as she tried to cut her bagel in half, using one of those useless, white, plastic knifes.

"Shirley, almost everybody at the State Department works for Don McGee. He's the under secretary of state," Rossi said, smiling. She continued to smile, got up and left Shirley Lamb to her coffee and bagel. Rossi had now put it all together.

By pure happenstance, Shirley Lamb had asked to sit down and by pure luck; she had mentioned Don and the two envelopes containing satellite imaging of environmental pollution. She was an environmental scientist working on her doctorate from American University.

Rossi knew that on Friday, Shirley had been working for NOAA and on Monday, she was with the State Department and yet, unassigned. However, by this afternoon, Shirley Lamb of Atlanta, Georgia would be working for Rossi.

Shirley's job would be looking at satellite images of every river and stream in Columbia. The sulfuric acid used in the processing of cocaine pollutes the water and kills the vegetation when poured into one of a thousand streams. By simply following the path of pollution where the dead vegetation begins, one could find where the cocaine was being processed. Shirley would be empowered to relay her findings to General Hatfield's office. He would then dispatch a strike team to investigate and if need be, they would eradicate the site and arrest or kill the workers...simple!

5

※ ※ ※

UNFORTUNATELY, THE RAINY SEASON HAD NOT yet started. Therefore, Zack Steele had to work hard as he paddled his canoe down a river that moved like molasses, since there was hardly any current. Slowly, he paddled, maintaining a straight and determined course to avoid the jagged rocks that could rip his canoe to shreds. He was following one of the many rivers that had no name. All he knew was that it flowed south and east towards the Putumayo River.

With luck, he would be back in Miami before Christmas. Not that it mattered much, as he had no family to speak of. His mom had died when he was a boy, and he never knew his dad. His aunt and uncle that raised him, were good to him, teaching him Christian love and right from wrong. Still, a deep anger burned in Zack's belly the kind of anger that festers and no matter what will not go away. His Uncle Tom had been a karate instructor and had taught young Zachary how to defend himself at an early age. However, what was more important, Tom had taught him that karate was the only sport that would make him a better person. Eventually, as happens to every boy, little Zachary grew into manhood. His friends just called him Steele. By the time, he entered college he was an expert in the martial arts allowing him to pay his way through college.

Though Steele was now a captain, he often wondered what his Uncle Tom and Aunt Kitty would think of him. The point was moot however, as he would never know. Both his aunt and uncle were killed during the blizzard of 1978. Eighteen at the time, he had inherited the land and money, but it had left him cold and devoid of any personal satisfaction. Though he had become rich in the death of the two people, he had loved the most, he would have much rather had his family.

The sun was just starting to break over the trees. Looking at his watch, Steel realized he had been rowing for hours. He was thirsty, tired, hungry, and he had to pee. He steered the canoe towards shore and pulled it out of the water. He grabbed his canteen and proceeded to unzip his fly, quenching his thirst as he peed. When finished, he sat down in the tall grass along the river's edge, partially hiding himself from view from both the air and land. Opening a MRE, he slowly began to eat. Opening a can of water, to wash down his meal, he enjoyed its clean, fresh taste contrary to the rainwater he had been drinking. Finished, he decided to treat himself to canned peaches and drink the heavy syrup.

Steele was suddenly startled awake by the sound of women scream-ing, followed by a burst of gunfire. He grabbed his knife and some stars and slid on his belly into the thick brush. He was not sure of the direction the gunfire had come so he waited, his body coiled to strike. He heard the scream of a child, followed by a shotgun blast. Slowly, Steele got to his knees and then to his feet. He knew the direction of the gunfire, and hearing no more screams guessed that innocent people were dead.

Quickly, Steele rationalized the situation, he could do nothing, invoking the law of the jungle, which simply was that the big, the mean and the bad lived and the weak died. However, he believed that law was reserved for animals, not children.

Unsheathing his knife, Steele set out to hunt down the killers. From his vantage point, he could hear the two-legged animals as they laughed and tormented their captive, trying to position the old woman so they could rape her. Cautiously, he traversed the jungle until he came upon the carnage. When he stopped, he was standing directly behind two of the men who were otherwise occupied with the old woman. Their bare assess gleamed in the sun, as they worked up a sweat. The old woman was trying in vain to defend her honor, but was failing. Steele glanced over to the water's edge, just to his left. There, two more of Mendoza's security guards were enjoying eviscerating a young female who obviously had been pregnant. Now she was dead and the older of the two men was bashing the dead mother's infant against a nearby tree.

Steele knew that killing these pieces of shit could give away his element of stealth. However, the jungle was full of man-haters, and it would be days before they would be missed, if they were missed at all. Lining up his body, Steele took careful aim at the two men, now laughing at the dead baby. "Phew! Phew!" Went two stars, both finding their mark and lodging in each man's throat, tearing out their windpipes and severing their carotid arteries. The other two men were oblivious to the deaths of their comrades, and neither man heard his own death, as Steele's knife sliced their throats from ear to ear.

Steele stuck his knife into the ground then slowly wiped the blade with his fingers as the blood mingled with the dirt on his fingers. Then with a flick of his finger, all vestiges of blood were wiped clean. Then Steele allowed himself to look around at the carnage. He watched as the old woman, bruised, battered and badly shaken, crawled out from underneath one of the dead men. Her tears stained her cheeks as they ran down her face; her eyes were wide with fear. Steele held up his hand gesturing to the old woman, telling her, "It's all right."

Steele sheathed his knife then turned towards the water's edge. He walked stealthily, not knowing if his aim had been deadly. As he approached, he could see that his aim had been on target. Both men lay dead at his feet. He had to work to remove the stars, as they had embedded themselves into the cortex of each man's spinal cord. Upon retrieving the stars, he rinsed them off in the clear water, dispassionately watching the men's blood disappear in the slow current that flowed towards his destination. Glancing over at the body of the once pregnant girl, Steele saw she could not have been more than thirteen. He felt nothing; not anger, not pity, not even contempt. Like the men, he had just killed; Steele knew he was nothing more than an animal living and surviving by the laws of the jungle.

6

ЖЖЖ

THOUGH STEELE DID NOT SEE OR even hear them, he was aware, however, that he was being watched as he saw multi-colored reflections in the water. Something told him to move slowly and show no fear. Why he knew this, he could not say perhaps it was the basic instinct of self-survival? Nevertheless, he knew that if the multi-colored shapes had wanted him dead, he would be dead. Slowly, Steele turned to face his fate.

They were naked except for a scant cloth that protected their privates. Their entire bodies were painted in various colors probably obtained from some sort of vegetable dye. Some of the men carried spears tipped with stone, honed to a razor edge while others welded war clubs, similar in shape to those used by the Crow and Black Feet Indians in the United States. Most carried blowguns, their darts probably dipped in curare poison.

Steele stood to his full, six-foot-four height, his deep-blue eyes looking for an escape route if the need arose. Right now though, all that was happening was that Steele and the warriors were eying one another, perhaps out of curiosity, coupled with mutual respect, as the warriors had seen him kill.

In awe, Steele watched a dozen or so young men, with bows and arrows climb down from the surrounding trees. He had been correct. There were more warriors than he had originally thought. One sudden move and he would have felt the stings of the arrows, as they pierced his flesh. Steele smiled, figuring that a warm smile might put them at ease. He was wrong. Like the monkeys in the trees, they chattered a dialect that had not been heard by a white man for three centuries or perhaps longer. Who could say for sure?

He was not sure, but he believed that he was looking at one of the lost tribes. He was positive that if his hunch was right these little people were fierce warriors. Steele guessed that they were cannibalistic, as well. He seemed to remember the professor saying that many tribes in South America turned their backs on the oppressive Jesuits who ridiculed their gods in favor of one god who lived in a stone hut. The natives believed that their gods were all nature gods. Eventually disgusted and incapable to communicate with them, the Jesuits simply sold them into slavery when they were powerless to convert them to one god. In response, the natives revolted and fled deeper into the jungle, as bows, arrows and blowguns were no match for gunpowder and steel cutlasses.

A small female child, about five or six, came up behind Steele, grabbed his finger and began leading him away. The warriors gave way and fell in behind Steele and his little barefoot guide. She pulled Steele towards a narrow path that led him deeper into the jungle. With each step, Steele's fears intensified.

Steele could feel the bile churning in his stomach, as his fear became claustrophobic. He wanted to escape, but knew he would never make it. In addition, he needed to take a piss and badly. His sweat burned his eyes, but still he walked down a small path towards his unknown fate, not showing the fear he felt. Just before entering the small village that lay ahead of him, he stopped. Holding up his finger to ask for a moment, he stepped into the brush to urinate. Some of the older warriors followed and watched, as he unzipped his fly and pulled out his manhood and relieved himself. Looking over to his left side, he noticed that the old men were looking at him and pointing. They began laughing and chattering, making him feel self-conscious. One old boy held up both hands and eyed him, measuring his member. Steele swallowed hard, knowing that sometime tonight his male member might be boiling in this old boy's crock-pot.

As they walked into the village, Steele was struck by its simplicity. The huts were all open structures, roofed with banana leaves. In each hut were hammocks for sleeping; the furniture simple enough—just reed mats. Multi-colored earthen pots, with intricate designs, adorned every hut. In the back of each hut, fishing nets were hanging out to dry. Dugout canoes, much like the one he was using, sat on the riverbank.

Steele was startled back to reality when a young warrior began blowing an earthenware trumpet, probably signaling to his tribe that dinner would soon be served. Suddenly, the women of the tribe appeared, carrying various sizes of hollow logs. They placed some logs flat on the ground; others were inclined and rested on the inside of their thighs and still others they rose up off the ground and positioned on large rocks. The women began beating on the hollowed out logs. Each log produced a different sound when struck with what looked like the large bones of dead animals, or perhaps men. He had often heard this slow, rhythmic, melodious sound during the evening

hours when he was camped out in the forest, but had not known what it was. Now he knew! They were calling to the other members of their tribe. In the distance, he could hear other drums responding.

Witnessing this first hand, Steele reasoned that the chief, or perhaps the tribal elders, purposely divided the tribe not putting all their eggs in one basket so to speak assuring their mutual protection and tribal survival. In this way, when Mendoza's security forces raided up and down the river, they would simply sound the drums, notifying each commune that danger was coming and to take shelter.

What had happened this morning must have been some sort of fluke, or perhaps they were simply sacrificing the old woman and young pregnant girl for the bigger kill? However, he stole their kill. Steele could not help visualizing his seldom-used cock floating in the old man's pot—just boiling away.

Then he felt a tug on his pants. Looking down, he saw the same little girl who had taken his hand, now handing him a very large bowl of something. He looked at it and sloshed it around, looking for human remains—perhaps expecting a finger or toe would come floating to the top; he was not exactly sure. Then he smelled it. It smelled like bananas. "Chiza" the old man said. Steele closed his eyes, held his breath and drank, afraid that not doing so would offend his hosts or captors. He was not altogether sure what he was—a guest for dinner or the main course for dinner.

7

Ж Ж Ж

JULIO MENDOZA, **LOOKING LIKE A GIANT** lily plant, in a green silk robe over his bright, orange and yellow pajamas, was sitting at his desk eating breakfast while at his elbow, a Cuban cigar sat gently smoking in a diamond and ruby encrusted ashtray. In the background, Mozart could be heard softly playing. His hair, which hung just past his shoulders, was still wet from his shower. As he ate, he read the newspaper. Of course, he was concentrating on what was, to him, the most important section the financial pages. There was a section dedicated only to him that mimicked the financial sections of other newspapers around the world. However, this specific section was special as it contained country codes taken from the phone book. After each code, a plus or minus symbol would appear, representing either an increase or decrease in business orders followed by a percent sign and a number, which corresponded to that particular country's currency, rounded out to the nearest whole dollar.

This section appeared either in the Friday or Monday edition of the newspaper. In this way, Julio could increase or decrease his production schedules based on supply and demand of that particular country. The beauty of his system was that it was out in plain sight for anybody to see. However, no one saw it for what it really was a simple, yet very accurate production schedule.

Another unique thing about Julio was that he hired brokers that dealt with the day-to-day details of supply and demand. Furthermore, he empowered them to make their own deals and to fix the cost. Then each broker was given a percentage of what they sold. Therefore, if Mr. Smith contracted with Mr. Jones for one hundred kilos at $4000 per kilo, Mr. Smith would get a commission of ten percent, or $40,000 for just one contract. Each broker averaged eight to twelve contracts each day. It was understood by all the distributors that it was a first come, first served contract. Cash was paid up front, while delivery was made at another pre-arranged location; thus eliminating double crosses and violence. If by chance one of Julio's brokers was hurt or killed, whoever did it was dead, along with his family no exceptions, no excuses.

The beauty of it all was that it was done the same way all over the world. It was done in such a manner that each stage did not know of the other. For example, the brokers did not know the suppliers; suppliers did not know the production bosses; the production bosses did not know each other, nor did they know where the processing plants were located. Nameless and faceless individuals, looking forward to make some money to feed their families, did all this. The banker would tell the barber, who would then tell the taxi driver, who would tell some prostitute standing on the corner. The system was so efficient that within an hour from the order being given, it was delivered to the responsible party. It gave the DEA agents fits, as they could not infiltrate Julio's organization. Those DEA agents who had tried were now dead.

Mendoza took a sip of coffee and was about to take a bite of toast when Juan Carlos walked into the office. Carlos was the only man Julio allowed to walk in on him. Anyone else would have been reprimanded, or feel Julio's walking stick over his or her head.

"Good morning, Don Julio," Carlos said, as he sat down and stole a piece of toast from Julio's plate.

Julio threw up his hands, rolled his big brown eyes as he turned his head towards his dog. "Rojo, why does this man insult me this way?" Julio asked laughingly.

Rojo had heard his master's lament many times before and just wagged his big red tail to acknowledge his master and little else. Julio poured his best and most trusted friend a cup of coffee and gave him another piece of toast.

"What is it my friend?" Julio asked, in a low, very serious tone of voice.

Before answering, Carlos took a sip of coffee, his baldhead gleaming in the morning light. "Don Julio, four of our men did not return from patrol yesterday. The construction crews heard gunfire and then silence."

"Do you think the men are dead?" Julio asked, in a soft voice showing concern. His concern was not for the men lost, but for the security of his building operations especially the construction of the bridge and road leading up the side of the mountain where his new hacienda was being built. Another project was tunneling into the side of the mountain where he planned to centralize his operations and go high tech. He was forced to do this in order to keep up with the demand for his "product."

Personally, Carlos thought it was a very costly mistake; maintaining that it would make them bigger targets for their enemies to find and destroy them, especially the DEA.

"Yes, Don Julio, I think the men are dead. I think the tree people got them," Carlos replied as he dunked his toast.

"Hmm, have we not told our men to stay away from that part of the river?"

"Yes, Don Julio we have," Carlos replied.

"So by now they have been eaten and are resting on the jungle floor as shit," Julio said as he sat back and took a puff on his cigar.

Carlos laughed at his boss's assessment. Then Julio began to laugh at his own joke, paying the four dead men little regard.

"What's next?" Don Julio asked, taking another puff of his cigar.

8

⚹ ⚹ ⚹

SHIRLEY LAMB SAT AT HER DESK in the Command Information Center, frustrated because the darkness of the room made her job more difficult. Located in the basement of the State Department's building, the CIC was the nerve center of the world's events. Normally, the senior staff and the Secretary of State used it in order to monitor hot spots around the world. However, right now, Shirley was using it as her own little hideaway. With her glasses pushed up on her head, a magnifying glass in one hand, a cup of coffee in the other and a grease pencil between her teeth, she persevered. In front of her were aerial reconnaissance photos taken yesterday.

Two weeks ago, she had been working for NOAA. Now she was working for the State Department in intelligence, with a top-secret security clearance, playing a very instrumental part in detecting and directing the destruction of illicit drug production in various foreign countries. Her new boss, Rossi, empowered her to pick up the phone, dial a four-digit code and then another four-digit number. Answering on the other end was a very sexy masculine voice that would only say, "Delta Force Cadence." Shirley would give grid coordinates, and hang up.

Rossi had explained that when she called and reported the coordinates, she was calling General Seth Hatfield's command center. The coordinates were reviewed, and a strike force dispatched. The results were often heartbreaking as the Delta Team often found young, naked children, malnourished and hooked on cocaine, freely offering their young bodies to the soldiers for a sniff of the white powder. The troops were aware that without support, food or skills, the children would die. The soldiers simply turned their backs on the children, leaving them alone and allowing time and the jungle to claim them.

"So, Shirley, remember this: Every time you find a processing site, think of the children you are saving and think of your own son Randy and the thousands of sons and daughters around this country and the world. And you, Shirley, have the power to wipe the sons-of-bitches off the face of the planet," Rossi had told her.

Slowly, methodically Shirley ran her glass over each photo. She did not see what she had expected. She saw, in one photo, a man standing in a clearing, surrounded by children. In the foreground were two dark forms that resembled bodies. The photo lying just to her left showed what appeared to be men working on some sort of structure that resembled a bridge. However, it was hard to be sure, as it also could have been an island in the middle of the river. Thinking it was possible, the figures were monkeys playing in the treetops; Shirley ignored the photo and moved on to the next one. This photo showed a wide path, or maybe the beginning of a road bulldozed through the jungle, but not where it led as the large trees provided perfect camouflage.

Ж Ж Ж

Rossi was sitting in Under Secretary of StateDon McGee's office, a cup of hot coffee in one hand and a note pad in the other. Both were listening intently as General Hatfield gave his monthly report. Since the under secretary was going deaf, but refused to accept the fact the volume on the speakerphone was louder than normal. Fortunately, the office door was shut and Ethel, the ever vigilant; knows-everything-but-says-nothing secretary would keep prying eyes and big ears away while the briefing was being conducted.

The general was very graphic and detailed, as he described what his intelligence operatives had told his staff. Evidently, Mendoza had begun a campaign of terror, torture and intimidation; starting first in the smaller towns and villages. His security forces had staged simultaneous attacks against two police stations in Cali and Barranquilla; seven police officers were killed. Both attacks were orchestrated to happen exactly at noon. Witnesses reported heavily armed men throwing satchel charges into the police barracks in Cali, killing five. The men never had a chance.

"General what in your opinion has prompted these attacks"? Rossi asked.

"It appears these attacks are reprisals, against those citizens we had bribed, it has been reported that in the smaller villages, informants have been forced to watch as nameless, faceless men lined the children or young women up against the nearest wall and cut them in half with shotguns. As far as the federal police are concerned, Mendoza has started an intensive and effective counter-offensive by having key police officials assassinated in their own driveways, as they left for work in the morning thus signaling that no one was safe from his reach.

It's been reported and verified, that Mendoza's right-hand man, Juan Carlos, loves going into the larger villages and kidnapping the mayor, police chief, or maybe even an army officer and hanging them in front of the town folk. Other times, when Carlos is really pissed off, he ties the hands and feet of someone and drags them behind a pickup truck through the city or village streets so all can see what happens if you talked to the Americans or police.

"General, do you feel our intelligence operations have been compromised?" Don McGee asked.

"Not at this time, sir," the general replied.

"General, this is Rossi again. Do you have any ideas, or have you heard about any of our operatives since the kidnapping and murder of Colonel Smith?"

"No, Rossi, we have heard nothing about any of the operatives. I still have one captain not accounted for. If I do not hear anything from him soon, I am going to declare him missing and presumed dead. I suggest you do the same with your people." The general's voice showed an almost complete indifference to their questions.

"General Hatfield, if we send more operatives into the country, what should be their top priority?" Mc Gee asked in a matter-of-fact tone of voice.

"Sir, I would kill Mendoza and his right-hand man, Juan Carlos. When you cut off the head of the snake, the body will die and so will Mendoza's empire of evil," the General vehemently responded.

"So you're advocating assassination in lieu of the law?" Rossi asked.

"Rossi, why give a man the benefit of the law when the man is lawless and corrupt? Why show a man compassion when he is without compassion? No, Rossi, the law and its benefits are too good for this animal. Kill him!"

Putnam rolled his eyes and shook his head. He had understood from day one why the military was not in charge of Operation Cadence. It was because men like the general had little regard for international law and treaties, unless they could use them to press a military advantage. However, the general's assessment of Julio Mendoza was accurate and Mendoza would be reckoned with when the time was right.

The call ended with nothing definite being decided, except that all had agreed Mendoza had to be stopped—the how was the only difference? He advocated cold-blooded murder, Don McGee and Rossi wanted to take down all the cartels, at the same time, on the same day, in the same month and in the same year, eradicating all illicit drug production in South and Central Americas. Stupid dreamers, Hatfield muttered to no one, in particular.

That was still the prime directive and goal established by the State Department and the International Drug Enforcement Committee. Only a majority vote of the Organization of American States could change the prime directive, and that was not going to happen anytime soon. Therefore, the State Department pretended to care and play good guys/ bad guys and people suffered and died because the production, sale and distribution of cocaine helped support the economies of the member nations of the OAS.

Rossi took a sip of lukewarm coffee, all the while looking at her boss's face. The furrows in Don McGee's forehead were deep. Experience and wisdom taught Rossi to remain silent. Therefore, with practiced aplomb, Rossi got up from the over-stuffed leather chair and turned to leave.

"Sit down, Rossi! Where the hell do you think you're going?" Don McGee demanded.

Rossi sat down as instructed, knowing from experience that whatever was going to happen, would happen quickly.

"I want you to fly to Bogotá, Rossi. Meet with McBride to discuss the option of pulling out of Columbia and moving to Central America—somewhere like Guatemala or Honduras.

"Operation Cadence has been compromised, or soon will be. I figure that Smith talked. Mendoza probably pumped cocaine and heroin into him, turning him into an addict. More than likely, Smith told them everything, and then they killed him. So, I'm sending you to assess the entire situation and discuss scuttling our operations in Columbia."

Rossi did not reply. A nod of the head was all that was required.

9

ж ж ж

ZACK STEELE FELT THE OLD FAMILIAR biological urge—he had to take a piss. His mouth was dry and tasted like shoe leather. Trying to stand, his legs wobbled, forcing him back to his knees. Slowly, he crawled on his hands and knees towards the river's edge where he found a sturdy tree and managed to pull himself upright. Leaning his back against the tree in a vain attempt to steady himself, out of habit he reached for his zipper. Shock…there was none. He was naked! Looking down at himself, he realized not only was he naked, but he was painted orange and red and his male member was purple with a blue and yellow smiley face!

Shaking his head to try and clear it, he vaguely remembered the Chiza and some kind of pagan ritual. He had a hazy memory of a woman—perhaps goddess would have been a better description. Steele could feel the nausea churning in his gut. He felt the burning sensation traveling upwards, then the explosion. Slowly, he released his tenuous grip on the tree and tried to stand long enough to pee. He felt his feet slide out from under him in the soft mud, while his body slowly began sliding down the riverbank. Frantically, Steele grabbed at sticks and grass, trying to stop his descent. The cold, clear water chilled him and causing him to pee. Steele was now wide-awake. Feeling something on his chest, he looked down realizing that someone had placed a stone medallion around his neck. Where it had come from and how it had gotten there, he could not say.

Taking the medallion from his neck, Zack examined it, trying to remember. He felt its weight in his hand and looked at what could be described as a phallic symbol on one side. Turning it over, he saw on the other side was a rough carving of a woman. The woman held a spear in one hand and a severed head in the other. Steele replaced the medallion around his neck, choosing to wear it. After all, in his line of work he needed all the help he could possibly get, no matter what the source.

Steel scrubbed at the paint until it was almost completely gone. He needed to be pushing on. Although Steele could not speak the language of his hosts, and he was ignorant of their customs, he liked his new friends. In fact, he vowed to say nothing about them to anybody since history has declared them extinct, why correct it?

After walking upstream a few yards, Steele decided it was easier to walk out of the water than to climb. Looking around, he took a deep breath and realized he felt refreshed and his skin tingled in the coolness of the jungle breeze. Somewhere, in the deepest recesses of his mind, he kept seeing glimpses of a woman standing over him. She had been taller than the other women in the village. He visualized her breasts as being larger and firmer than the other women; appearing sculpted, giving them a gently, sloping, downward look, with two very small, but distinctive nipples surrounded by ruby-colored areolas. Her cheekbones had been very pronounced; her eyes and hair jet black, and she had a unique, exotic look about her. For the life of him, Steele could not remember if she was real or a character in his self-induced alcoholic dream.

Looking around, Steele soon found his clothes and got dressed. A quick glance found his knife embedded in a tree. Although he did not remember doing it, what appeared to be a human heart was impaled on his knife. The wind had changed direction and with it came the fragrant smell of death causing his stomach to react to the smell of rotting flesh.

Steele walked over to the hut he called "home" and grabbed his boots. What he had learned about his hosts was most interesting and somewhat amusing. A woman did not belong to any one man, but rather she belonged to the tribe and was shared. The children belonged to the women who bore them. He had found this interesting and wondered to himself: *If western civilization adopted this practice, would there be a need for divorce lawyers and alimony?*

The village was starting to stir. Men paid him no mind; they just smiled or gave a wave of the hand. Then each man disappeared behind his hut. Steele heard the splashes of each canoe as it entered the water—the men were going fishing. Some women were tending to the fires; others were breast-feeding their babies, while others swept out their huts, using fronds from nearby palm trees. Smiling at them, Steele waved good-bye as he started up the same small path he had taken only the morning before—at least he thought it was yesterday. He was not sure, how long he had been drunk.

As Steele walked up the narrow path, he became aware of the silence. No birds were squawking, and the incessant screeching of the monkeys, could not be heard. Only the buzzing sound of insects filled the air. Sensing danger, Steele stopped and took a knee his instincts kicking in. He pulled out his knife and crouch-walked to a clump of bushes that afforded him a minimal amount of cover. His hope was that whoever it was would not be expecting him, giving him the element of surprise. Steele's muscles tensed as he crouched lower, coiling his muscles for a quick and sudden strike. His breath, rancid from poor hygiene, became shallow he was ready to kill.

Seconds seemed like hours as he watched and waited for his prey. Then, he heard a cry of pain, followed by a chuckle; the sound came from upriver. Whoever it or they were; they stood in his way. Steele wondered if they had found his canoe and poncho, but remembered he had pulled the canoe out of the river and concealed it. He was sure it was well hidden. However, if whoever it was had a security dog, his ass was in deep trouble. Reaching around, he unsnapped the canvas pouch; he used to store his stars. Quickly, he examined them for damage, as a damaged tip would throw the star's trajectory off course, making him miss. A miss could cost him his life, and he would not like that.

He smelled smoke—somebody was smoking a cigarette—and heard the yelp of a dog. Since he was crouching upwind of the dog, it would be difficult for the dog to catch his scent. So far, Steele's luck was holding. In his mind, he reasoned: *If I can just stay concealed, this danger will pass...* it was not to be.

Out of the corner of his eye, Steele saw a small, naked little girl. Obviously, she had followed him as her steps were small and fast, giving the impression, she was running to catch him. Just then, the dog began to bark. Steele glanced and saw that the dog's ears were laid-back, the dogs barking turned to growling. The damn dog began salivating, straining its body against the leash, choking itself. Steele recognized the young security guard, as the same one who had shot and killed the monkeys. "This *boy liked to kill.*" *He thought.*

Steele watched intently as the young boy shouldered his machine pistol and unleashed the dog. He pointed to the little girl and shouted a command. Without question, the dog obeyed, not caring who or what it was about to kill.

Quickly, Steele launched one star, followed by another; both found their mark. In mid-stride, the dog yelped in pain, then stumbled and rolled, falling dead at the little girl's feet. The young security guards face registered shock followed by fear, as he came face to face with Steele. Like two Hollywood gunfighters, both men stared at each, waiting for the inevitable. The young hapless guard reached for his weapon. Steele's aim was deadly, as he flicked his knife with the twist of his wrist the knife finding its mark deep in the boy's heart.

Walking up to the boy he had just killed, Steel placed his boot on the young man's chest and removed his knife, wiping the blood on the boy's shirt. After sheathing his knife, he walked towards the little girl who stood transfixed, staring down at the dead dog. He smiled at his little friend, bending down on one knee he pulled the stars from the dog's body, idly noticing the first star had caught the dog in the throat while the second had hit its heart.

Without a word, Steele picked up the dog and placed its limp, lifeless body onto the little girl's shoulders. Though the weight of the dog bent her small, delicate body, she looked trustingly up at him and smiled, understanding what she had to do. She turned and started walking back towards home and the safety of her village.

Steele smiled. *She will be a hero this day. H*e thought, watching as her tiny naked body carried food back to her people.

Once she was out of sight, Steel picked up the boy's weapon and stripped his body of the extra ammo clips, even taking the boy's cigarettes and lighter. He lit up a cigarette and took a deep drag, filling his lungs with smoke. Then he suddenly began to cough. The tobacco was black and very strong; he was not used to it. Turning his back to the boy, Zack proceeded upriver towards his canoe.

Now that the fear and adrenalin rush from his recent encounter with the dog and boy had passed, Steele's stomach began to grumble telling him he was hungry and thirsty. His canoe was just around the bend, close to the river's edge and hidden behind some scrub brush. His thoughts focused on what he planned once he arrived at his canoe: *First, I will grab some water, brush my teeth, and eat some food. Snake, lizard, boar and crawdads are okay for a while, but they do not come close to Spam with peaches and cookies. Since I now have a lighter, I will build a small fire, boil water, and have some coffee. I will boil the water in the Spam can and then pour the hot water into the peach can with the instant coffee grounds...*

He walked faster, as he was hungry and wanted his peach-flavored coffee.

Ж Ж Ж

Once all his biological needs had been met, except for the need of a woman, Steele paddled his canoe down the river. Now that he knew what to look for, Steele tried spotting his little friends, who stood sentry over the village perched in the trees, keeping close vigil on the jungle below, being alert for food and danger.

Steele was quick to spot them, and though he waved, his friends did not return his good-bye gesture. Instead, they watched him glide slowly down the rivulet, the only sound being that of the water hitting against his canoe.

By the position of the sun, Steele guessed it was about ten in the morning. He used to have a watch, in fact, a very good watch. However, it was gone now. Somewhere in his mind, he seemed to remember arguing for something; then, there was a slap of the hands and the watch was gone. All Steele had to show for his watch was a headache, a sore tooth and bad breath. He began to smile and then a small chuckle escaped past his lips, as he thought, "I've been had by a bunch of half naked, little tree people with whom I've fallen in love."

Steele realized the stream had begun to pick up speed. At the same time, he could hear the sound of rushing water down river. His daydreaming had almost cost him his canoe. Paddling hard, he managed to steer into the river bank. Exiting the canoe he proceeded on foot until the deafening noise of the water falls caused him to pause and gaze at the rocks below. He shuddered at the thought that lapse in judgment almost cost him his life. His death would have ended—suddenly and painlessly in the middle of the Columbian jungle. There would have been no one to mourn or remember him. The army would type a report to some nameless person somewhere in the USA who would read it, file it and forget it. Captain Zachary Steele was missing and presumed dead. There is no next of kin.

Scanning the area, he saw something dark rising up on the horizon. He walked along the top of the river gorge, mindful of the lack of cover. He had walked about a two hundred yards when he heard men talking. He slid forward on his stomach using his elbows and toes to scoot his body over to the edge of the gorge to peer below. The deep banks of the river gorge acted like an echo chamber, amplifying the three men's voices allowing him to hear every word. The man in uniform he recognized as General Pablo Gonzales, head of the Columbian Anti-Drug Force, which worked closely with the DEA and DOD. Next to him was a funny looking, little man with a big stick, dressed like a Victorian dandy, whom he did not recognize, unless it was Don Julio Mendoza himself. Since Steele had left his weapons in the canoe, he only had his knife and his stars with him. Assessing the situation, he realized from this distance and angle, it would be a long shot at best. Steele decided to remain silent and listen.

General Gonzales was talking, gesturing with his hands, the smoke from his cigar writing patterns in the air around him. Then he began making, what could only be described as, sexual gestures as he moved his pelvis back, and forth, making squealing noises? The other two men began laughing uncontrollably at the general's antics.

Then, as if a switch had been thrown, the bald man with the funny ears asked a question. Suddenly the conversation became serious. Steele knew just by the tone of his voice that the general was selling out the DEA, and the DOD. The other two men stood still and listened intently; the laughing and silly antics had given way to serious discussion and obvious negotiations. Steele heard a name mentioned. A Victoria something or other was coming from America. She was coming to move the DEA and DOD out of Columbia to Guatemala and Honduras.

How the fuck did, he know that. Steele thought. *Wishing he had the machine pistol, as he could end it all right now. One burst, one squeeze of the trigger and three key cartel leaders would be dead.*

The bald headed man asked the general a very simple question, "What does this woman look like, and when will she be coming to Columbia?"

"I don't know, but will get you that information," the general replied.

"Surely, Juan, you don't plan on killing her?" the funny little man asked in a very serious tone of voice.

"No, Don Julio, she will not be killed. However, she can be converted and become a very important information source for us," Carlos confidently replied.

"Hmm," Julio muttered. "See to it; I like the idea."

Therefore, the funny little man with the big stick is Mendoza. Now I know what the bastard looks like, Steele thought to himself.

10

ЖЖЖ

JACK MCBRIDE hung up the phone A large order needed to be placed, and he would need space to store it. He would also need a meeting with the customers to discuss finances and transportation costs. Translation: A big wig was coming for a visit, and he was to make suitable arrangements for lodging, set up a meeting with the Columbians to discuss possible withdrawal of U. S. personnel and set up transportation of equipment and labor, to another, yet to be determined, location.

To say that he was miffed was an understatement; he had been assigned to a foolish mission, with no chance of success and following an ill-conceived protocol established by someone in the State Department who had no idea, on how to operate a clandestine mission. Moral coward's is what they were. Doing nothing and accomplishing even less, allowing Mendoza to stay in business, so he could go on with the killing. What he had intended to do was move the operation out of Bogotá to a remote location near an airfield, hence allowing for a quick escape if the need arose, but still maintain a presence in Columbia. It would've allowed covert operation teams to come and go virtually unnoticed, and the same for big wigs. *"Perhaps at the next location" he* thought.

Pushing his chair away from his desk, Ryan stood up, clasped his hands behind his back and looked out his window at the street below. He watched the coming and goings of the workingmen and women of Bogotá. *Except for the language, they are no different from us; he* thought. *These people have their hopes, dreams, and ambitions, just as we do. I wonder if they are aware that some of their political and military leaders are crooks.*

Suddenly, an inspirational idea came to him. He would walk down the street to Hotel Columbia and buy a woman, get something to eat and then get drunk.

Ж Ж Ж

Rossi walked the long hall back to the office and entered through the rear door in order to avoid anyone who might be in the outer office. The wall clock showed that the meeting withDon McGee had taken over an hour. The familiar "You-were-called" slip was resting on the phone. Alice only did this if she felt the call was important. All other calls she kept at the corner of her desk and handed them to her boss. Picking up the phone, Rossi dialed the four digits that would connect her to Shirley in CIC.

"Lamb," the small voice announced to the caller.

Rossi smiled. It had not taken Shirley long to learn the known, but never discussed power plays at the State Department. Those in positions of authority used only last name and never did they use a Mr. or a Ms. proper title. Proper etiquette was fine for the others, but for the power brokers and power players, it was last names only.

"Yes, Lamb, you called?" Rossi asked.

"Yes, I did. I have something on film I think you should see. I'll put these photos in an envelope and be there in twenty minutes."

After Rossi hung up the phone, she paged Alice and asked her to book a flight from Miami to Guatemala and then to Bogotá. The last time the State Department had done this, they booked a cruise to Belize, using the cruise as a cover while covert operations were discussed in plain sight of everyday folks... Five weeks later, Smith had been killed and the other six operatives were missing and presumed dead. For sure, Operation Cadence was not a crowning achievement for the good guys.

It was not a big stretch for Rossi to suspect a mole. Obviously, there was someone well planted by the Mendoza Cartel that passed along secrets for money, sex, or drugs. There was only two individuals who met the criteria. General Pablo Gonzales, who was in charge of the Anti Drug Task Force for the Columbian Government and Julio Mendoza's father. Rossi felt the general was the leak.

Gonzales was an obvious snake-in-the-grass; ruthless to those he could oppress an ass-kisser to those above him, a tyrant to his subordinates and most of all, and a liar to all who knew him. Rossi had asked the Columbian State Department to have him removed for incompetence numerous times. The problem was, nobody else in the Columbian hierarchy wanted or needed him. In truth, he was an ass hole with connections that had money, and he knew who to bribe. In other words, General Gonzales was undermining the entire operation, and nobody seemed to care.

ЖЖЖ

McBride zipped up his pants; the young whore was still lying on the bed, having a hard time moving. She was crying and holding her groin as if she had been kicked. McBride's male member was huge in comparison to the men of Bogotá, a full foot in length with a girth of three inches. When he was angry, depressed, or just horny, Ryan would take out his frustrations on some unsuspecting young whore and rip her apart, oftentimes putting her out of commission for a few weeks. He took delight in doing that. *"Maybe that's why my wife doesn't mind my inclinations"*, he thought. *Better somebody else than her.*

His lust satisfied and his anger modified, McBride walked down the stairs to the hotel restaurant. He was hungry and thirsty after his work-out. She had taken him for one hell of a ride, and she had drained him completely. His legs were still weak and he had trouble walking, but he was definitely a very mellow fellow.

Ryan took a seat and ordered a beer. The waiter brought him a menu, and he ordered the special. As he sat quietly nursing his beer, his thoughts turned to Operation Cadence. *Something is definitely wrong and smells of incompetence and disloyalty. However, by which side the Columbians or some dirty diplomat at the American embassy.*

Since he was not sure who exactly he would trust neither side. He had told General Hatfield his feelings. The general told him to go with his gut instincts. So not knowing, he decided to stand-alone and develop a wait-and-see attitude. Something had to break, and soon.

Taking another sip of his beer, Ryan watched a very large man, with a ponderous stomach, come into the restaurant. He was cursing in Spanish and broken English, holding a straight razor and looking directly at him. Obviously, he was the whore's pimp, and he was pissed off. As Ryan stood up and braced for the inevitable attack, he looked around for an escape route, but there was none. Knowing that a life or death altercation was about to begin, Ryan thought, "*God have mercy on this pimp.*"

It was over almost before it began. Ryan heard the razor make a hissing sound, as the pimp swiped at his throat. Though the fat man was quick, two, hard punches found their mark. One well-placed chop went into the man's larynx, the other to his solar plexus. The fat man fell to the floor, holding his throat gasping for air. Nonchalantly, Ryan bent down and picked up the man's razor, flipped the blade closed and stuffed the razor into his pocket. Grabbing the man by the cuffs of his pants, he dragged the pimp out of the restaurant and into the hotel lobby.

As people looked on, Ryan grabbed his throat, making the universal choking symbol and pointed to the man, who was turning blue and purple. The hotel patrons and staff gathered around and looked down at the prostrate fat man who was choking; then walked away. *So much for life in Bogotá,* Ryan thought, as the man breathed his last. Ryan turned and walked back into the restaurant to finish his beer.

The waiter brought Ryan his order along with another beer. He told Ryan that the beer was free, compliments of the owner, as nobody liked the fat pig, and Ryan had done the owner a favor by removing him from this earth.

11

Ж Ж Ж

FROM HIS HIDING PLACE, HIGH UP on the rim, Steele watched as the three men shook hands and walked back to the makeshift road. He had not noticed the road nor had he noticed the swing bridge. The bridge was under construction, camouflaged with netting making it damn near invisible mixed with the natural canopy of the jungle.

Suddenly, the sound of a woman screaming and the men laughing in unison drew Steele's attention across the river to a small clump of trees. Methodically, Steele worked his way down the river embankment and slipped into the river, letting its warm water bathe his body, soothing his tired muscles. Going with the flow, he let the swift current carry him down river, avoiding any security guards who might be lurking about. He wanted to come up behind the voices, keeping the element of surprise to himself. Steele could smell cigar smoke warning him that he was close. Then he heard a man's voice say, "Tie her up in the cabin and feed her the junk until she is compliant; then pass her around to the men".

Just then, Steele heard the sound of several splash's behind him. He turned his head and watched four large black caiman swimming in his direction. Fear being his motivator he climbed the steep embankment praying the four green-eyed crocs would not follow him.

Hiding in the bushes, Steele watched as Julio Mendoza, Juan Carlos and General Gonzales got into a black SUV and drove off, leaving the young woman to her captors.

Creeping closer, keeping to the shade and hiding behind trees and brush, Steel drew his knife listening as the two men dragged the kicking and screaming girl into the cabin. Steele did not need a lesson in jungle law to know what they were going to do. He figured an hour for the two men to finish with her, then a few more minutes of insults and threats while they tied her up. Suddenly, he heard a howl followed by a punch. It sounded as though she was giving an account of herself. Obviously, the two men left in charge of her were having trouble with this particular girl.

Then came a blood-curdling scream, so loud that the giant fox bats screeched. Throwing caution to the wind, Steele ran up to the side of the cabin and moved aside the cloth door that doubled as a curtain.

He could see the men had hog-tied the woman and turned her over on her back so her womanhood would be vulnerable to their repeated assaults. They intended to do this repeatedly, even inviting a few chosen peons to aid them in breaking her down. Then they would clean her up and invite a few women to introduce her to woman-to-woman sex. All the while, they would be pumping her full of cocaine until her will was not her own. After that, they would sell her to a streetwise pimp.

"Fuck Julio," Steele muttered as he calmly stood up and walked around to the front of the cabin. Leaning against the cabin, were two high-powered rifles, complete with scopes. Steele picked one up, removed the safety, and calmly walked inside the cabin.

One of the men had the most pathetic looking erection Steele had ever seen. Not that he made a habit of checking out other men's erections, but living with a bunch of men you did see a lot of strange, nocturnal things poking through the sheets. The other man was holding his small, demure looking manhood in his hand, trying to get an erection. All the while, the girl kept rolling on her side, agitating her captors.

"Hello, boys," Steele said, as he pulled the trigger twice, splattering both men's genitalia all over the room.

Steele calmly bent down and cut the ropes that bound the girl. Then he walked outside to see if anyone had heard the shots. When he turned around, he saw her for the first time. It was her goddess woman from the village—the woman for whom he traded his watch. According to the chief, she now belonged to him.

There was an immediate problem; she had the other rifle pointed at his groin. Steele knew if he walked towards her; she would kill him, of that there was little doubt. So he turned his back and walked across the clearing, leaving this child of the jungle alone with her thoughts, and her anger.

Noticing an old Chevy pickup truck concealed under some trees, Steele walked over and inspected it. He saw that the tires were bald, but still round. When he opened the door, he stole a cigarette from a pack of Camels lying on the seat. Quickly, he checked the interior, hoping to find the keys.

If only I could make her understand my need. How do you explain to somebody who has been beaten and almost raped that all you want is a set of keys? Looking back across the clearing, he saw her still holding the rifle, but at least it was not pointed at him. She was holding it across her crotch in a vain attempt to cover her nudity.

Leaving the rifle in the truck, Steele got out of the cab and walked towards her. As he approached, she raised the rifle and stepped aside, leaving the doorway to the cabin free for him to enter. Steele looked down at one of the men with the blood-soaked Levis. He quickly checked the dead man's pockets. His heart skipped a beat as he felt the keys. Steele took money from both men and their watches figuring he would need them to trade for gas, food, and clothes.

When he stood up to leave, he noticed food, and water, sitting on the table. Quickly, he opened a bottle of water and took a long drink. Her shadow filled the door, still holding the rifle. She was even so there—all five-feet-six of her with those magnificent breasts and piercing black eyes that were boring holes into his soul. Steele felt his manhood begin to stir. He realized he wanted her and according to the tree people chief, she belonged to him. Holding out the water to her, the young woman hesitantly accepted it. Noticing the rifle was not visible, Steele realized he had not won her trust, but had just proven to her that she was not in danger from him. Over the neck of the water bottle, she kept looking at him, studying him, as if trying to remember him from somewhere. Then she saw the medallion around his neck.

"El Jaguar," she said, pointing to him.

Noticing a slight French accent, he asked enthusiastically, "Parle Vous le Français?"

"Oui!" she replied, smiling. Steele smiled and asked her name.

"Renee", she replied as she nonchalantly pushed past him, walked over to the table, and searched for something to eat.

"Renee, why did you call me El Jaguar?" Steele asked, continuing to speak in French. He was admiring Renee's body. Even though she was filthy, she was beautiful.

"Because the tribal chief named you that," you are quick and silent, just like the jaguar. You showed no fear when you faced down the warriors, and you have a very large dinky. Their words, not mine," Renee said, taking a bite of apple.

"Dinky?" They call my most prized possession a dinky?" he asked incredulously.

Renee began to laugh. Zack noticed her nose it crinkled.

"You are also a war chief by virtue of that necklace. You went through the ceremony of manhood. That's why they painted your body. I painted your dinky. Did you like the smiley face?"

Steele began to laugh. Holding out his hand to Renee, he said, as he looked into her eyes and realizing he wanted her, "J'aime appel, Steele".

Ж Ж Ж

Ryan Ryan Mc Bride had just begun eating his lunch when he sensed danger from behind and to his immediate left. Glancing around he realized the restaurant staff was standing still, no one was talking. Before he saw to whom the eyes belonged, he felt the eyes boring into him. They were a pair of eyes that belonged in the head of a viper, not a man—small and widely spaced). Surprisingly, the eyes were golden in color not exactly hazel, but not brown either. The shape of the man's baldhead was conical. His ears were rather large, making him appear elf-like. His face was sunburned and wrinkled from the sun, looking like a man who had grown old before his time.

At once, Ryan recognized the man as Juan Carlos. Behind him stood two very large and threatening men, obviously Juan's body-guards. Glancing around the room, Ryan saw the barman and wait-er standing behind the bar and the cook standing in the doorway, wiping his hands on his apron. The only sound Ryan heard in the room was the ticking of an old wall clock, telling him that death would wait for a little while longer.

"Ok, take the fucking razor. I don't use a straight razor anyway," Ryan said, taking the razor out of his pocket and tossing it to Carlos.

Carlos deftly caught the razor and put it in his pocket. Slowly, he walked towards Ryan , his bodyguards a step behind him. "You're sitting at my table," Carlos announced, his face contorted in anger.

"So? Is your fucking name on it?" Ryan boldly asked.

Unexpectedly, Carlos burst out in laughter. Patting Ryan on the back, he pulled out a chair and invited himself to lunch. Ryan held up one finger to the barman and ordered a beer for his guest.

"McBride," Ryan said, offering his hand to his guest.

"Juan Carlos," came the soft reply. Ryan made a mental note of Juan's limp handshake.

"So, McBride, you killed that man out there?" Carlos asked, pointing with his baldhead as he took a sip of McBride's beer.

Ryan was about to correct him about his name, but decided there was no sense in aggravating Carlos, especially when he knew he could kill this dumb bastard anytime he wanted. Before his bodyguards could even react, Carlos would be lying dead on the floor with the rest of the filth. *"But decided to find out what he wanted,"* Ryan thought.

"Let's just say that he left me no way out. He attacked me with a straight razor," Ryan replied, handing Carlos the beer the barman placed on the table.

"Why did such a man attack you, McBride?" Carlos said, ordering the special.

"I'm not sure exactly, but it might have something to do with one of the whores upstairs," Ryan replied taking a bite of his enchilada.

"I was told you beat her up so bad she cannot work," Carlos said, his voice dropping an octave.

"Bullshit, I have never beaten a woman in my life. Tell you what, Carlos," Ryan said as he threw the key at Juan, "here is the room key. Send one of your men up to the room and let them see the girl and ask her if I beat her up."

The gesture startled Juan. Nobody ever talked to him like that and lived. Not even Don Julio would dare speak to him like that.

Slowly, Carlos picked up the key and called for Miguel. As he handed the key to Miguel, he whispered something. Miguel nodded his head and walked out.

"You know, Juan," Ryan continued conversationally, "the problem with these whores is that they have never been stretched out. You see, all you Columbian men have small chimpos. How do you expect to pleasure a woman when your willies are so damn small? No wonder the women in this damn town never smile. It's because they are never satisfied. No, Juan, what you need are women with bigger twats," Ryan said, taking a large gulp of beer and ordering another.

Dumbfounded, Carlos just sat and looked at the gringo sitting next to him. He thought to himself, *either he is a fool, or he has the biggest balls in all Columbia.* Just then Miguel came into the restaurant, laughing. He walked up to Carlos and whispered in his ear. Soon, Carlos began laughing as well. Ryan realized he was home free. A sense of relief washed over him, as he chugged down his beer.

Carlos called out to the bartender, ordering the next round. He met a man with big, big balls.

12

⋇ ⋇ ⋇

STEELE WAS FIGHTING BOTH THE ELEMENTS and a bad transmission as he and Renee tried to navigate through the torrential rain, as the wind pounded against the windscreen holding the wipers in place making it impossible to see the road. Forced by circumstance he rolled down the window and stuck his head out, as he tried to negotiate the makeshift road. Every now and then, Steele saw a tire track, showing him the way back to civilization. Renee began to laugh at their situation. Her small, delicate laugh was infectious and caused Steele to grimace in pain as he tried to laugh.

Needing time to think, Steele reached down and took a cigarette from the almost empty pack. Fortunately, before leaving in the cabin, he had hiked back to the canoe, leaving Renee alone to guard the two dead men. He gathered his weapons and the poncho, for Renee along with the dead boys lighter and his cigarettes. His fingers were wet, causing the little white tobacco stick to dissolve in his fingers... Renee pulled out another and placed it in his mouth, gently picking up the lighter she lit Steele's cigarette. Her smile was soft and warm and Steele could not help, but feel a long dormant emotion welling up inside of him. As strange as it might seem, he was falling in love with this creature of the jungle.

He had not felt an emotion like this since his senior year in college when he had met and fallen in love with a girl named Esther Colgate. He wanted to marry Esther, and be with her forever. However, she had the good sense to tell him no and walked out on him, leaving him bitter and disillusioned, about women and life in general.

So pissed off at the world, Steele had joined the army after graduation. Becoming an officer after OCS, he tried out for and was accepted into the Green Berets, specializing in intelligence.

One day—it seemed so long ago—he had walked through the door at battalion headquarters, where the major pointed at him telling him to suit up, he was going to South America for a little intelligence gathering, and that he would be briefed upon arrival. Now, almost twenty months later, he was stuck in the jungle in a torrential rainstorm, with a beautiful, half-naked woman, in a stolen truck, looking at a compass that told him the road ran northeast and southwest, but not where it went.

Steele sat silently, listening to the rain pounding rhythmically against the truck roof, orchestrated by the wind. He watched the rain as it fell in white cascading sheets, pounding against the truck glass and blinding him to the world outside. Steele took a drag on his cigarette, inhaling the smoke and slowly letting it blow out of his nose. He decided to sit tight and wait for the rain to pass.

Ж Ж Ж

Rossi was sitting at the boarding area for Miami's gate 31B, waiting to board United flight 4357 to Guatemala City. The total flight time was estimated to be just less than three hours while the time from the airport to the Hotel Quinta Real was another hour. She intended to use the diplomatic passport trick and Dexter Pierpont, the U. S. Consulate in Guatemala City, as her chauffeur. In four hours time, they would be drinking salty dogs in the hotel bar.

Putting down her book Rossi scanned the area. It was something she had learned from a DEA operative in one of the many how-to-stay-alive classes. Her thoughts drifted back: What had he said? *Learn to read the room and see who does not belong.* Of course, it was difficult to read the room when sitting in an airport terminal lobby. However, a young military officer standing near the jet way did catch Rossi's eye. He was in his late twenties or maybe early thirties. What struck Rossi was that he was wearing the uniform of a Columbian army major. Perhaps he was going to Guatemala City to attend the same meeting. Rossi's flare for intrigue was satisfied, for the moment, as the announcement was made to board the aircraft.

The trip was uneventful; Rossi figured the time-line closely. After check-in, a quick shower and change of clothes, Rossi and Pierpont were drinking longnecks, eating tortilla chips and catching up on personal business.

Dexter had been, madly in love with Dee-Dee Rossi's older sister. However, Dee Dee was not one for adventure, nor was she keen on traveling. She married a simple man and moved to Queens where she taught school and he preached. Rossi thought their lives were complete, but dull.

As her gaze swept the room, she looked over to the bar and noticed the army major sitting at the corner of the bar, drinking a beer. Leaning towards Dexter, she pushed the table candle aside, and asked, "Dexter, do you know the major at the end of the bar?"

"Yes," Dexter replied, "he's Antonio Montoya, the nephew of General Pablo Gonzales. Like his uncle, he is a man you cannot trust. Divulge no secret information tomorrow. Just give the 'what' and 'when' part of your briefing, nothing on the 'how' and 'who' part of your mission. I do not like General Gonzales and I like that ass over there even less. You can bet your last dollar; he followed you here, and is watching your every move and reporting to Baby Cakes Pablo. If you disappear, I will know who took you and from where you were taken. That should help somebody."

Rossi was impressed with Dexter's knowledge and his direct manner. Obviously, he was not one to beat around the bush that was for sure. He was also giving her a warning, although perhaps not intending to do so. *If you disappear…* those words rolled around in her mind and put Rossi on guard. The problem was who could she trust?

Ж Ж Ж

Steele was startled awake when he felt Renee shaking his arm. She stood guard, allowing him to sleep. He did not know how long he had slept, as his watch was now on the chief's wrist.

Renee pointed to a man and woman walking by the side of the road. They were carrying their belongings on their stooped backs. Two very small and probably hungry children were following, as best they could.

The rain stopped and the jungle smelled clean. Rushing water could be heard in the arroyos below. Steele got out of the truck and walked over to the young family. In his best Spanish, he asked the couple a few questions, and then motioned to them to get in the back of the truck. Now, Steele had even more incentives to kill Mendoza. According to the woman, Mendoza's bullyboys raided their village, killing the men, raping the women, and stealing the young girls. The woman explained that she had escaped only because it was washday. She took her boys down to the river to bathe and do laundry. Her husband was hunting, along with his brother. Upon returning, the brother attacked the men in a moment of grief and anger, armed only with a long knife. Mendoza's bullyboys cut him down with their guns in front of his wife and two young daughters.

Steele started the truck and dropped it into low gear, slowly easing his foot off the clutch to allow the transmission to engage. He did what the young woman had told him to do: He turned right and headed towards Bogotá.

By the time, the Chevy truck approached Bogotá it was breathing fumes. It was dark in the east as house lights dotting the countryside silhouetting the mountains. To the west, the sanctuary of Montserrat stood tall and proud silhouetted against the burnt-orange sky.

When Steele first arrived in Bogotá, he spent an entire afternoon lost in city, discovering the street system. After a week or two, he had discovered it was easier just to divide the city into four, separate areas or zones. The northern zone was mostly residential, commercial, and modern. Starting at Calle Number One, the southern zone was the most densely populated and poorest section of the city. The western zone was the industrial section of the city, with various parks where the working person could take his family on a Sunday stroll. In addition, that is where the sports complexes and airport were located. The central zone or downtown section, housed the international center and the colonial neighborhood of La Candelana, it was also the area where the Federal Government offices could be found.

Steele had become knowledgeable about the city of Bogotá and was now approaching from the west. The gravel road had given way to blacktop, which allowed Steele to drive faster. If he did not run out of gas, he reasoned he was about fifteen minutes from home. Off in the distance he could see airplanes taking off, which brought up another concern. How did he get Renee a passport?

Pulling into a filling station, Steele pulled out the money he had "borrowed" from the two dead men. He counted about thirty-five hundred pesos. That was a lot of money for two such men to have, unless they were high up in the cartel.

Steele put twenty liters of gas in the truck's tank and then motioned for the woman in the back to come with him. He paid for the gas and handed the remaining money to the woman, telling her to pick out food and drink for her family. When he walked back to the truck, he could feel the eyes of the children watching him.

Getting back into the truck cab, he lit another cigarette. Renee looked at him and smiled, but said nothing. With gas in the tank, Steele's stress level lessened. He had given the woman all the money he had left. He figured she would be able to find lodging and pay for food and clothing for over a year on what he had given her.

Steele had not been to his apartment for three months and was looking forward to a bath, shave, and then go see Doctor Lovey, his dentist. Lovey was not his real name, but he did speak good English.

Steele began recognizing various landmarks; when he recognized the Avendia that would lead his passengers to safety; he pulled over to the curb letting his hitchhikers off. Steele instructed the woman to take the bus west to Calle 72 there she and her family could find a place to live and work. In addition, they would find poverty, crime, and death, but at least they would be with other poor people, and she did have money, which made her a rich, poor person.

Slowly, he engaged the clutch of the anti-Christ, as he had begun calling the Chevy. Calle 11 appeared on his left. H proceeded up the street when he came to a row of neatly manicured stucco apartment buildings, all painted white with red clay tile roofs. Steele turned into a driveway, making a hard left and proceeded past two apartment buildings to number fifty-seven. There pulled the truck into the assigned parking spot, turned off the ignition and smiled at Renee. Looking into her eyes, he could feel his manhood begin to stir, as he opened the truck and grabbed his haversack and weapons. He proceeded up the pavement towards the back door Renee timidly following El Jaguar, knowing what he wanted from her and knowing she was more than eager to please him.

"Renee, lift the porch mat and look for the key," Steele asked.

13

ж ж ж

MCBRIDE AND CARLOS WERE drunk again, they had started drinking early Christmas morning and had not stopped. They drank, ate, fucked some whores and truly enjoyed each other immensely. All the while, Carlos was checking on McBride. He had his intelligence operatives scouting for any information about this gringo with the big balls.

McBride was no dummy and was quite aware of Juan's endeavors in checking up on him. Though the questions Carlos asked him were seemingly innocent in nature, they were actually fact-finding questions such as "Where were you before you came to Bogotá?" "What did you do before coming to South America?" "What brought you to South America?"

Without Juan knowing it, McBride had gotten word to General Hatfield about what was going on with Carlos. The General had told him, "…play him, gain his trust, and above all, be careful."

Yeah, as if I'd have to be told that, Ryan thought, after the conversation had concluded. Dealing with Juan Carlos was like sitting on a powder keg.

Danger was an irony of and by itself, but still, the liquor was good and the whores were beautiful. They all had exotic names like Desiree and Carmen. The most beautiful was Antigua. Ryan wanted her, but Juan kept her for himself, the selfish bastard. In fact, Carlos and he had actually come to body blows over her. Miguel had to throw cold water on both men; then he scolded them for fighting over a "puta".

In a huff, Ryan left Carlos. He was royally pissed off at Carlos and called him every dirty name he could think of. Carlos returned Ryan 's insults, even throwing beer glasses at him. Once again, Miguel stepped in and separated the two men, laughing, as were the others. Finally, Miguel gently grabbed Ryan 's arm and escorted him to the door, telling him, "Quiet down and go sleep it off. Things will be better in the morning."

Ж Ж Ж

Major Antonio Montoya, grandnephew to General Pablo Gonzales, who was the Deputy Director of the Columbian Anti-Drug Task Force, was a kiss-ass. He possessed neither backbone nor any real aptitude for his job. By training, he was a classical pianist. However, a major's pay was better than starving pianist. Because of family connections, Antonio was invited to gala events where he could perform for the Columbian elite in hopes of being "discovered." However, for the moment, he was watching a beautiful American woman.

Antonio marveled how the candlelight glistened on her chestnut-colored hair. Her lips were full and inviting. In Miami, he saw her deep-blue eyes. Although she was dressed casually, as most American women dressed, she could not hide her beauty. As he watched her, Antonio became sexually aroused, imagining her cradled in his arms.

He was quite aware that this American beauty would soon be in Uncle Julio's stable. She would become one of his many disposable puta's whom he would use and then discard with no more thought than throwing out the trash. Antonio smirked at his novel thought, for that is what they were now to him, human trash. Human waste that was once viable, but now disposable. As he observed her, he decided he would be the one to take this woman during her indoctrination into her new life. A life of endless service to all mankind.

She would start out at the top of the social elite used by both men and women to satisfy their carnal desires. Later, Julio would escort her to his biggest customers. There she would be introduced using only one name, and there she would be passed around from one erect cock to another. Names and faces would be just a blur as her brain began to crave the white powder. She would wash it down with drink in the hopes of killing the endless pain and humiliation. Eventually when her beauty had started to fade she would be passed down to the lower-grade military officers. Finally, on some cold, rainy Sunday morning, this American beauty would be let loose on streets of Bogotá. Her beauty having faded like winter leaves. In an alley, some morning, she would be found with her throat slit, or a needle stuck in her disease-ravaged and malnourished body. So went the life of Uncle Julio's once prized whores.

He determined to take her while she was still fresh and while she could still feel a man inside her. More than anything, he wanted to hear her moan, and whimper, as he held this beautiful woman in his arms;

to feel her breath on his throat, and taste the salt of her skin before the drugs took her beauty…

※ ※ ※

The security briefing on Tuesday morning went well. Rossi did as Dexter had suggested and did not mention the "how" and "who" parts of the plan in her briefing. When the pertinent questions were asked Rossi gave the standard reply: "The details would be worked out later."

Major Antonio Montoya was livid, as he had been ignored when he pressed for more details. Again, Rossi refused to give him any insight, or even the remotest inkling of how and when the tactical withdrawal, and redeployment of manpower was to be achieved. Antonio knew his uncle, General Gonzales, would not be pleased.

※ ※ ※

"What is it, Lamb?" Don McGee, the Under Secretary asked, looking at the aerial surveillance photos she had just handed him.

"Sir, I wanted to show you what I believe is a combination processing plant and fortress complex being built in the jungle, east of Bogotá, at the base of the mountains. I think Mendoza has made a bad mistake and is going high-tech in the manufacturing of his cocaine. I think the tunneling operation into the mountainside is where he plans on processing his cocaine. These drilling rigs, seen here in photos five and six, are for drilling vent holes allowing the fumes to escape. Notice that photos three and four show a road that stops at the river's edge and then picks up on the other side of the river on the way to the complex. Sir, I think this may be a swing-bridge, camouflaged in a vain attempt to prevent us from seeing it.

"Or…it could just be an island." Don McGee said as he looked at the photo.

"Photos nine through eleven reveal several large, sprawling hacienda-type complexes, which probably are living quarters. Please note photo number thirteen. In it, you can actually see workers chiseling out a bunker of some sort. It is either to be used, as a panic vault in case of attack or perhaps a bank vault. I'm not sure at this time, sir."

"Hmm, good job, Lamb. Let me take these photos to the Secretary. He may want to show them to the President," Don McGee said. Standing up, he walked out of his office to tell Ethel that he was going to see the boss.

Lamb smiled as she watched her boss leave. Shirley felt prideful, knowing that her words and work were to be reviewed by the Secretary of State, and perhaps the President. A feeling of self-satisfaction in knowing that she was doing important work overcame her. She threw her shoulders back and popped out her chest. *Shirley girl, it does not get any better than this.* She thought as she turned and walked out of the office.

Ethel smiled as she walked by and said, "Good job, Lamb!"

"Thank you," Shirley replied.

ЖЖЖ

American Airlines Flight 928 to Bogotá was not crowed. Rossi had deliberately taken the later flight, avoiding Major Antonio Montoya or as Dexter had started calling him, Major Pain-in-the-Ass.

She arrived in Bogotá on time. Rossi went through the formality of customs, as she chose to use her tourist passport this time. Ryan Ryan Mc Bride was to pick her up and escort her to her hotel. As she gathered her luggage at the baggage claims area, a young man carrying a sign that read "ROSSI," walked up to her and pointed to the sign. Smiling, she nodded her head that she was Rossi. The young man bowed and grabbed her bags. Then Rossi followed her young chauffeur out of the airport terminal and into the balmy air of Bogotá.

The chauffeur opened the car door and helped Rossi into the back seat. Then he opened the trunk of the limo and gently deposited both bags. He slammed the trunk lid and got behind the wheel. Skillfully the young man pulled out into the airport traffic, paying particular attention to the police cars. It was obvious to Rossi that the car had been idling, and the air conditioning had been set on high; her thin, cotton dress offered no warmth. Goose bumps began appearing on her flesh, and her nipples had started to react to the cold.

She had not been told which hotel she would be staying so could only assume that McBride made the appropriate accommodations. Idly, she noticed they were heading away from downtown. *Perhaps another elegant retreat, secluded for the rich and famous,* she thought.

Rossi watched as the driver made a left turn off the main road onto a winding gravel road. She noted the name Diablo Avendia, and smiled. *The Devil's Boulevard, how quaint,* she thought. *"A hotel with a theme"* she thought. She had read about them in various travel magazines, but never expected to stay in one.

When the car slowed to a crawl, Rossi watched as the driver hit the remote button on his visor, and turned onto a dirt road, large steel gates were slowly opening allowing just enough room for the limo to creep into the courtyard. Rossi was quick to notice that the building had a grotesque, almost medieval look about it. What really got her attention were two, very young, beautiful, scantily clad girls who came out to greet her. They took her hands and escorted her into the lobby. *"Colonel McBride, you are a genius"*, she mused to herself.

Quickly, Rossi checked out the lobby décor. *"Gothic with a touch of Italian Renaissance,"* she thought. Then off to her right she saw the most beautiful woman she had ever seen. The woman was wearing a red dress with a slit up the side. Her more than ample breasts were spilling over the top. She had emerald-green eyes, blonde hair and her lips were full and inviting. Rossi was intimidated by the woman's beauty, and immediately her hackles began to rise.

"Hello, my name is Antigua, and you must be Victoria Rossi?"

"Yes, I'm Victoria Rossi." It had been a long time since anybody had called her Victoria. Only her mother and grandmother called her Victoria. Her daddy always called her Vic.

"Welcome to Diablo's Hideaway," Antigua said, extending her hand.

Rossi smiled as she accepted Antigua's extended hand. Rossi made a note of how soft, and smooth her hand was and wondered what she used to make her skin so soft.

Antigua took Rossi's arm and began walking her down a hallway. "I have put you in a suite. I hope that's all right!" Antigua said. "You can check in later if that is agreeable with you?"

"That will be fine with me," Rossi replied.

Looking back over her shoulder, she noticed the two young girls following at a respectable distance. Antigua stopped and opened up a door. After Rossi and Antigua entered the room, the two girls entered and nodded their heads as they passed in front of both women. They worked quickly and efficiently, preparing the room for their guest. Each girl knew that this beautiful woman, named Victoria, would never be the same again and the life she knew would be over soon. She would become a *Punta* just like them.

14

ж ж ж

STEELE woke to the smell bacon, and fresh coffee. Turning onto his side, he propped himself up on his elbow and looked at his alarm clock. He collapsed back onto the bed exhausted. Pulling the pillow over his face, he tried to block out the smell of food.

Renee was trying to cook again. Cooking was not her forte that was for sure. However, when it came to making love, she had no equal. Holding her was like holding a bolt of satin in his arms and the feeling of her lips, and soft tongue encircling his was pure ecstasy. Steele loved how her breasts felt as she laid upon his chest, her tiny nipples poking his rib cage. She was devoted to him, and he had to admit it; he was quite taken with her.

He was patient with Renee; never raising his voice, always showing her how to do simple things like making bacon and eggs, or explaining to her that when she went shopping, she had to pay for what she wanted. That was one area where Julio's teaching had failed. Renee had no concept of money.

One important thing Renee did master was programming the coffee pot before they went to bed. It *was like teaching a little child how to do things.* In some ways Renee was like a child uncorrupted by modern civilization.

It had been almost a month since Steele had returned from the jungle. The doctors were aghast at his medical condition, and had wanted to send him stateside for medical treatment. However, General Hatfield overruled them; wanting Steele to remain in Bogotá in the care of the doctors and woman who could not cook, or speak English. Her only qualification was that she was in love with El Jaguar. The doctors placed on medical leave, for three months.

ᛗ ᛗ ᛗ

Recognizing Captain Steele's medical condition, General Hatfield had flown over from the states to meet with his captain and discuss what the young captain had seen and what he had learned from his jungle ordeal. What he needed was an insight, and Captain Steele was the man who could give it to him.

He also wanted to sit down with Colonel McBride and Rossi. However, first he wanted to just be a guy and have a beer with a brave man. They relaxed sitting in comfortable chairs under a giant umbrella, smoking Cuban cigars and drinking longnecks. The General noticed the necklace around Steele's neck and said, "Tell me, Steele, what that necklace represents?"

Over time Steele had become so accustomed to the necklace, he hardly paid it any mind. He smiled. "Well, sir, it's some sort of fertility necklace. It's supposed to keep me horny and allow my sorry excuse for a cock to grow hard," Steele said, laughing and taking a swig of beer.

Hatfield chuckled and then asked, "Where can I buy one?"

"Well, general, that request surprises me, sir. Everyone knows that general's balls are so big they need wheelbarrows to lug them around, sir!"

Both men broke into laughter. The beer was working well.

"Tell me, Steele, what went wrong? Where did we fail you and the others? Why do you suppose you're alive, and the others are all dead?" the General asked in a very soft voice that echoed anger that could not be ignored.

"Simple general we were betrayed," Steele said, leaning back in his chair and taking a puff on his cigar.

"By who?" the general asked.

"General Pablo Gonzales, that's who," Steele said, anger resonating in his voice. Hatfield's face went blank. Steele watched as General Hatfield's face went crimson his eyes staring off into space. He began puffing hard on his cigar, causing it to billow white-blue smoke, into the warm, Bogotá air mixing with the other smells of the city. Watching the general closely, Steele saw him take a deep drag on his cigar and hold the smoke, letting it burn his lungs for what seemed like an eternity. Slowly, he exhaled the smoke into his beer bottle, as he took a drink, his face now contorted with anger.

"Captain, are you sure of this?" He asked.

"Yes sir. I saw and heard General Gonzales, along with Julio Mendoza and Juan Carlos, talking on a swing bridge in the jungle. That is where I rescued Renee. They were going to rehabilitate her with cocaine, so she would be compliant."

"You saw the bridge?" General Hatfield asked.

"Yes, sir, I saw the bridge. In fact, I drove on the new road Mendoza has had built. I also killed a bunch of Mendoza's security guards. And sir, I want to kill him."

"Easy captain we will get the son-of a- bitch with his evil empire of associates. I promise you that. And captain when the time is right I'll let you kill him, but only when the time is right. I promise you captain." General Hatfield replied, taking the last gulp from his long neck. "Now tell me about this woman you rescued."

Steele smiled. He could not help it; just the thought of Renee made him smile. "Her name is Renee, sir. She has no last name. And sir, she was once Mendoza's girlfriend—that is until another woman named Antigua came into Julio's life. Renee knows Julio's associates from all over the world, plus all the dirty politicians here and abroad," Steele said, taking the last gulp of his beer.

"Where is she?" Hatfield asked.

"Sir, she is safe. In fact, general, she is crossing the street, as we speak," Steele said, nodding his head towards a woman crossing street wearing a white cotton dress with a straw hat and white sandals the afternoon sun shining through her dress, revealing her shapely legs.

The general looked back over his shoulder, his blue-gray eyes finding Renee in the crowd. He was immediately smitten envious of his young captain for possessing such a beautiful treasure thinking the captain irresponsible for not protecting her from Mendoza and his forces.

ж ж ж

Rossi lay on the table like some delectable morsel ready to be served. She was wrapped in a towel and lying on her stomach as the masseuse prepared her hot oils. No words were spoken as the young masseuse did not speak English or Spanish, only Portuguese. Brazil was where she was from, and Portuguese was the national language. Idly, Rossi figured her to be about twenty-five.

As the oils were heating, the young girl struck a match and lit two scented candles. She blew out the match and walked over to the large plate-glass window. Pulling the curtains closed, then proceeded to lower the lights. She turned on the CD player, the soft, gentle music filling the room. Rossi could feel her tired body beginning to relax.

The young masseuse stepped to the side of the table where she slipped her hands into surgical gloves, all the while smiling and looking down at her client. She removed Rossi's towel, unwrapping her like a gift on Christmas morning, exposing her nakedness.

The oil felt warm on Rossi's flesh as the woman's experienced hands spread the hot oil across her back its warmth penetrating her flesh and relaxing her tired muscles while opening her pores. Rossi found her body becoming aroused with each circular motion of the beautiful young masseuse's practiced hands. Then, the beautiful stranger picked up a small bottle labeled "Baby Powder" and sprinkled the soft white powder onto her back kneading her muscles, as she rubbed the powder into her open pores.

Rossi's inattention to detail and her love for creature comforts made her vulnerable. She had failed to ask the limo driver who had sent him. She didn't notice the masseuse donning surgical gloves and did not ask why surgical gloves were being worn for such an intimate procedure.

Furthermore, she had failed to ask why a masseuse would apply baby powder to her body when she was using scented oils.

Rossi passed the ten-question test given during her training class back at the State Department. However, she did not heed the advice so freely given. Because of this, she had failed to "read" the room. Now, Miss Victoria Rossi was to have only one name. Her memories and perceptions would be altered in time, as her craving for the white powder would obliterate all memories of what and who she had been. She would be transformed into a different kind of "public servant." She would be performing humanitarian acts of sex for her new master all for the soft, white powder that was now enveloping her body so succinctly, so insidiously and so completely that she was gone before she knew she was lost.

Victoria Rossi was to become a small footnote on some "Missing, Presumed Dead" report and for all intents, Victoria was dead. Dead to the life, she knew. Victoria would be servicing man and womankind in various erotic positions for, as long as her beauty held up. Then, as those beautiful women who so freely gave their bodies for the euphoric feeling provided by Julio before her had learned she would be retired and sent to one of the many processing camps and given to Julio's workers as a bonus. On the other hand, she could be turned loose on the back streets of some city someplace in the world.

15

✳ ✳ ✳

GENERAL HATFIELD sat in the hotel lobby, waiting for Colonel Ryan Ryan Mc Bride. Since he had never met the colonel before, he realized he could be standing next to him on a street corner and would not know who he was.

Now both had an important task to do. They had to convince Rossi to change her mind about scuttling Operation Cadence. Thanks to Captain Steele, he knew who the security leak was. In the meantime, McBride had somehow breached Mendoza's inner circle by making friends with his most trusted confidant. The ace in the hole was a beautiful woman who wanted revenge. Mendoza did not know it yet, but he was going to be in deep shit very soon.

Some sort of a commotion abruptly broke the general's concentration. Looking over his shoulder, he saw two scantily clad young women hurling insults, along with mops, buckets, beer bottles and bars of soap, at a red-faced man holding his shoes in one hand, and his trousers in the other. As he walked backwards down the staircase, the man cursed at the women.

The general's Spanish was not that good, but he got the gist of the conversation. He chuckled at the man, who still had on his socks and shirt, but little else. Only a moment ago, the hotel foyer was peaceful and serene. Now it came alive with onlookers. Some people laughed while others cursed at the semi-nude man who obviously had not quenched his lust.

Although he was not exactly sure, the general surmised that when the young women had seen the size of the man's equipment, they panicked. Now the man wanted his money back, and they were refusing. *"Poor boy, he did get screwed, but not in the way he expected,"* the general though, laughing to himself.

The general looked at his watch; he had been waiting ten minutes for Colonel McBride. He was about to leave when the red-faced man walked up to him, pulling out a cigar and asked, "You got a light, sir?"

Hatfield looked up at the redheaded man and said, "Colonel McBride; I presume," as he felt for his lighter.

"Is this the way you treat your superiors, colonel?" the general asked, lighting the cigar.

"Yes, sir, it is if we want to stay alive", McBride replied, his voice soft and deadly serious.

"Now what" Hatfield asked, putting his lighter back into his pocket.

"Sir, please follow me into the restaurant. Sit at the middle table with your back towards the window. I will sit across from you. How's your French?" McBride asked, taking a puff on his cigar and blowing the smoke upwards, towards the two whores who were still cursing him.

"My French is somewhat passable. Why do you ask?" the general asked, following his half-naked colonel into the restaurant.

"Sir, every move we make is being watched and reported. These people make their money selling information about the comings and goings of Americans. Be assured sir, that if you stay longer than three days, you will be checked out. If you fail their investigations, you will be dead. Oh, yeah, and if you pass their investigations you still might end up dead. My observations have led me to believe that these people understand Spanish and English, but they do not comprehend French."

As instructed, Hatfield walked to the center table. The restaurant was busy, but not crowded. He did what he was told and sat with his back towards the street. When he looked up, he noted that McBride was not with him.

The waiter brought over two menus and two beers, without being told. *Obviously, McBride does a lot of business in here. He goes upstairs, fucks a whore, comes back down, and eats. Then does whatever he feels like doing for the rest of the day, all on taxpayer's money. Not too bad,* he thought.

The general sat with his arms folded across his chest and his elbows resting on the table. Taking a sip of beer, he casually looked around the room. His eyes stayed on two men sitting at the bar. One man was tall and dark, his body lean and muscular. A scar ran down his cheek, making him look sinister. The other man was smaller. What you noticed first about him was that he was bald. His head was not proportional to his body, and it was misshapen, while his ears were pointy, giving him an elfin appearance. However, it was the man's eyes that made him look like some sort of reptile. He kept staring, which made the general's skin crawl. Suddenly, he realized the room had become silent. No one moved all eyes turned towards him, looking at him with sadness, as if he were going to die. Hatfield ignored them, taking another sip of beer, waiting for whatever was about to happen. It was eerie and he could feel the hair begin to rise on the back of his neck. His breathing became noticeably shallow; despite the beer, his mouth was dry. Taking up the glass, he gulped more of the beer.

Where the fuck is McBride? He thought.

Out of the corner of his eye, he saw the two men from the bar walking slowly towards him. The tall one was at his back; a large caliber hand-gun stuck in his belt, clearly visible, while the bald creature approached from the front. Immediately, the general's self-defense instincts began to engage; I *will kill the bald man first;* he thought. Slowly, the general lowered his hand and unbuckled his belt, withdrawing the stiletto concealed in the fiber of his belt.

Suddenly, as if by divine providence, a deep voice came booming from across the room saying, "What the fuck do you want, asshole?" It was McBride, still puffing on his cigar, fully clothed with his hair combed and his shoes tied. "Well, asshole, what do you want?" McBride asked, walking towards the table and directing the attention of everyone in the room towards himself.

" McBride, McBride, you know this is my table. I was going to ask this Americano to choose another table. That's all."

"Carlos, I asked you this before. Is your fucking name on the table?" McBride smiled and waved to Miguel, who was now laughing at the antics of the two men.

" McBride, I came to apologize for the other day."

"Oh? Should I get down on my knees and say 'Thank you, Carlos?" Thank you for not letting me fuck that beautiful woman while you enjoyed her. Some amigo you are. You're an asshole, Carlos," McBride said, pulling out a chair and sitting down. He took a sip of the other beer.

The room was in hysterics, McBride had diffused the situation. No one was going to die this day.

Uninvited, Carlos sat down at his table and took a sip of McBride's beer.

"Who is this gringo?" Carlos asked, pulling out a panatela.

"I don't know him, Carlos. I expect he is here to discuss buying coffee from me. You know that's what I do for a living," McBride said, pulling his beer back from Carlos. Then as he lit Carlos' cigar, he motioned for the waiter to bring four more beers.

"Oh, by the way, amigo," McBride said to Carlos," those two puta's took my money and never serviced me. They threw bottles at me, and one came at me with a straight razor that looks very similar to the one I gave you."

Carlos and Miguel began laughing, as Carlos reached into his pocket and produced his razor.

"Just checking, Carlos," McBride said, moving back to allow the waiter room to place the beers on to the table.

"Carlos, you got to get women with bigger twats. These girls can only handle little men," McBride said, handing Miguel a beer, sliding one towards Carlos and the other towards the general.

" McBride, these girls can handle any man. They just can't handle a fucking giant like you got," Carlos said, looking first at Miguel and then at the stranger sitting to his right. The three men started laughing, causing McBride's face to turn red.

ЖЖЖ

Steele lagged behind Renee, watching her as she ran ahead of him, picking up seashells, inspecting them, slipping the pretty ones into her pocket, and discarding the others. She laughed freely and marveled at the sea gulls, as they flew around her looking for food. *Renee sure is beautiful, of that there's no doubt,* he thought as the warm, Florida morning sun served to accent her magnificent lines and make her even more gorgeous.

It had been ten days, since the three of them had sat under the big umbrella in Bogotá. Steele and General Hatfield had listened intently to Renee, as she described her experiences while living with Mendoza. The more the general heard and learned, the more he knew that Renee was the key to dismantling Mendoza's empire. The general realized that it would be safer for Renee in the United States. Once in the U. S., the DEA and Customs could debrief her. After that, Steele could take her on a series of vacations to various places in the U. S., all very hush-hush at the taxpayer's expense, making it difficult for Mendoza to find and kill her, as both Steele and the general knew he would do if he found out she was alive, and if he could find her.

Renee was being debriefed in four-hour sessions; her knowledge of Mendoza's cartel, and his associates was mind-boggling. The intelligence agents would hold up a picture of some suspect, and she dished the dirt.

Steele was being treated for acute exhaustion, along with anemia and various other infections that had settled in his body. His jungle exploits cost him fifty pounds. His clothes hung on him like rags flapping in the Florida breeze. Another effect of so much weight loss was his gums. They receded, exposing his teeth to infection. Now Steele fully understood how the jungle had a way of reducing people to their lowest common denominator survive or die. It was that simple.

Ж Ж Ж

Steele got off the hospital elevator and started walking across the lobby, when saw her. He dismissed it at first not believing his eyes. However, the closer he got he knew it was her. She wore a flight suit now, and she had gold oak leafs on her shoulders. He had not seen her in over five years, but she still stirred his blood. He started walking towards her, looking at her, as tears began to form. She saw him approaching, but could not place him. However, her eyes were telling her brain that she should know this man. Smiling, she gave him a faint sign of recognition. Then when she heard his voice, her soft, warm smile gave way to disbelief, as recognition gave way to tears.

"Hello, Esther, it has been a long time."

Esther stood silent, staring into Steele's deep-blue eyes, knowing that if she spoke she would crumble. Until this moment, she had not realized she still loved him. Years ago, she had run away from him telling him she would not marry him. She wanted to live her life on her own terms, and that she had just used him for her own enjoyment. What a bunch of bullshit that was. Tears began streaming down her cheeks, as she gently took him in her arms, and once again pulled him close holding him tightly for fear of letting go and losing him again.

Ж Ж Ж

"How long are you going to be in Bogotá, senor?" Carlos asked, looking at the general from the end of his beer bottle.

"Well, I have plans to leave the day-after tomorrow," Hatfield, replied taking another sip of beer.

"What is it that you do back in the states?" Carlos asked, putting both his hands around the longneck bottle, caressing it picking at the label with his thumbnail.

"Jesus Christ, Carlos, this guy is a fucking potential customer of mine! It's none of your fucking business what he does or doesn't do back in the states," McBride vehemently declared. "And you, sir, let's go back to my office, so we can discuss business. Do not worry about the tab. Carlos is buying'— and do not forget. I want my money back from those two little Chiquita's. Next time get me a whore with a bigger twat; someone I can really get it on with," McBride said, standing up and nodding his head to Miguel.

The two men walked outside, into the street and started walking west.

"Forget that remark about treating superiors with respect, McBride. I now have seen what it is like. I can only guess that was Juan Carlos," General Hatfield said, stopping to light his cigar.

"Yes, sir, that was Carlos up close and personal," McBride responded, turning his back momentarily to shield his body from the wind while he lit his cigar.

"What an evil, arrogant, son-of-a-bitch he is. That man actually made my flesh crawl. What a creep he is. You know, I was actually scared back there. Moreover, you face that every day "God McBride" you're either the bravest man I have ever met, or the craziest," the general said taking a puff on his cigar. Then he turned and faced his colonel. " McBride, Rossi is wrong. That bitch is dead wrong. We now have a decided advantage and we must capitalize on it. For the first time since Operation Cadence was initiated we now have two advantages. I really think McBride we can take Mendoza's cartel down. He is diabolical

McBride, but not infallible Mendoza's success is built on intimidation, blackmail, and murder, while his empire was built on information, now we will start a campaign of misinformation. We will give him so many lies he will not know what to do. When that happens, he is ours."

16

⚹ ⚹ ⚹

utnam slammed down the phone receiver. His cool demean-
or vanished, replaced with raw anger. He was exasperated,
and exhausted because Rossi was officially missing. She
had just simply vanished. The authorities knew for sure that she
got on the plane in Guatemala City. After that, nothing was known.
Conflicting reports added to the confusion. Don McGee's worst fear
was that Mendoza had stolen her. If that fear was true, then Rossi
was dead.

General Hatfield had requested that he be allowed to continue with
Operation Cadence as he had a new plan; something about spreading
lies and creating mistrust within Mendoza's empire. He had in his
possession somebody who once was close to Mendoza, and now Hatfield
knew Mendoza's entire inner circle of associates. Colonel McBride had
managed to infiltrate Mendoza's cartel through one of Mendoza's trusted lieutenants. However, all this meant nothing toDon McGee without
Rossi. Therefore, he did what any politician would do. He deferred to

Lamb. Though she was new to the State Department, she had proven herself in the short time she had been there. Moreover, if there were any repercussions or political fallout, she was expendable.

Lamb felt the men in the field needed support, not indecision or political intrigue. If General Hatfield said he had a new plan, then the State Department and DEA should be supportive of the General Hatfield and his men. She recommended thatDon McGee go with the general's idea.

Ж Ж Ж

It was Easter Sunday, and McBride was sitting in his apartment at the combination desk, dressing, and dining table. His head rested in his hands, his eyes were downcast, as he read an article in an old USA Today newspaper. It seems an American diplomat disappeared. There was no picture, not even a name. It was hardly worth reading, except that he knew the story was a plant by the general's staff. Every Friday, stories would appear in the people section, or financial section, telling all the field operatives what had happened, or what was currently happening. Sometimes codes would be used to tell a certain person to do something, or move somewhere else.

McBride took a sip of coffee, noting that there was no news for him other than the story about the diplomat. He had heard that Rossi was missing, but did not think he could do anything. Just as he was about to pour himself another cup of coffee, he heard a knock at his door. Grabbing his gun, he put it behind his back and walked to the door. Since the door had no peephole, McBride calmly and respectfully asked, "Who is it?"

"It is Miguel, McBride. Carlos wants you to come to his hacienda for lunch. He has a new, hardly used. American puta for you. She is very beautiful."

Opening the door, McBride allowed Miguel into his apartment, if you could call it an apartment. In one corner, it had a bed; there was a small bathroom and a living-kitchen area. A black-and-white television sat on a nightstand at the foot of the bed. Miguel crinkled his nose, showing his disdain for McBride's apartment. He felt McBride deserved much better than this.

ЖЖЖ

As the Mercedes sped through the deserted streets of the city, McBride was amazed by the comfort of the back seat. He had enough legroom to cross his legs. A mini-bar sat on the floor, dividing the back seat. Encased in the armrest was a car phone and hanging from the ceiling was a small television. *Carlos has it all; that's for sure. McBride* thought. *Money, power, and women…*

Ryan observed Miguel's whisper something to Jesus and soon, Jesus slowed the car. Obviously, he had been speeding. Jesus was quiet and the most lethal man McBride had ever known. He was Carlos' actual enforcer—being both perverse, and cruel. He actually loved to kill. It did not matter what he killed—animal, man, whatever suited him. Miguel told him of the time an old man had rebuked Jesus for cursing. Jesus simply slit the old man's throat and walked away, cursing.

Sensing danger, McBride calmly sat up in his seat and scooted forward, closing the distance between him and Miguel. He figured that if Miguel reached for his gun, a well-placed karate blow to his windpipe would kill him. Since Jesus could not kill and drive it was a decided advantage, as it would allow him to reach for the gun, he was wearing on his ankle. He had strapped it on just before they had left when he had gone into the bathroom.

Casually, McBride asked Miguel, "How much further?" as his free hand slipped down to his left ankle and un-holstered his snub-nosed. Though the .38 caliber was not his revolver of choice, it was effective in close quarters.

"Not far," Miguel answered.

Miguel got out first and opened the car door for McBride, motioning with a sweep of his hand to follow him. McBride smiled, as he got out of the car, his eyes surveying the area, looking for an escape route if the need arose, and checking out the domicile of Juan Carlos.

The house's exterior was something out of the dark ages. It resembled a medieval castle, as it actually had ramparts. What really caught his attention were the grotesque figures staring down at him.

"What a great place to hold a Halloween party" McBride commented, as he followed Miguel inside.

"We've done that," Miguel said clapping his hands.

Suddenly, two young women appeared. McBride smiled, as his eyes traversed their bodies. They were clad in white see-through material, which revealed their womanly charms.

McBride continued to follow Miguel, both young women followed at a respectable distance down a long corridor that opened up into a lavish dining room. They continued through a large wooden door and down another smaller hallway until they came to a set of French doors that opened up onto a large veranda. Miguel pulled out a chair for McBride and motioned for the two women to set the table.

"I will inform Carlos that you are here. Please feel free to walk about and enjoy the view," Miguel said, turning and walking towards another door that led back into the hacienda.

Miguel was right; the view was incredible. To the east were the mountains. McBride looked over the railing and looked down at a thousand-foot chasm to a raging river that was always ready to carry anybody, "accidentally or on purpose" away. A waterfall could be seen above him cascading another thousand feet above him charging the river below.

Reaching into his Ryan et pocket, McBride pulled out a cigar, his first one of the day. He snipped the end, and felt for his lighter. As he lit his cigar, he felt something rub up against the back of his legs. Curiosity made him look down. He would have been better off if he had not. McBride found himself alone with a very large cat. He thought it was a cheetah then realized it was a leopard. He turned to walk away; another one appeared at his side. Silently both cats escorted him back to the table. As he took his chair, the two cats sat down next to him, each one staring at him. Not sure what he should do he did what any civilized man who soon may be dead, he lit a cigar and waited for Carlos.

McBride puffed on his cigar, his thoughts turning to his childhood memories. He had been raised on a farm in southern Illinois. Animals had always been a part of his life while he grew from boyhood into manhood. For a fleeting moment, he remembered talking to his mother about a stray dog that had followed him home from school. The dog had been a black lab that someone had dumped off on the county road. He remembered the dog being close to death. His brother chided him about the dog telling him the dog was sick and would be dead soon. Ignoring his brother, he handed his schoolbooks to his brother to carry home while he picked up the stray dog and carried it home. Upon arriving his brother rushed into the house calling for their mom to come and look at what Ryan had done. She took one look at the dog and asked his brother to fetch the rifle. Ryan pleaded for the dog's life, actually begging his mom not to kill the dog. Begrudgingly, his mother relented and Gus had gone on to live ten more healthy and wonderful years.

One night at supper, while he was home from college, his mom had told him that a dog was a good judge of character and that Gus had picked him, as his friend because of his character. It was a startling realization for him to know that he had been judged for his character by a dog.

That thought brought him back to the present, he realized that at this very moment, Carlos and Miguel might be watching him, and that these cats were a test! Evidently, Carlos had contrived all this. McBride knew something big was about to happen. Slowly, McBride reached out and began petting the cats. He actually grabbed one by its cheeks and kissed it while the other cat began rubbing itself against his legs.

From above, Carlos and Miguel watched. "Are we sure that this man is not the El-Jaguar the natives talk about, Miguel?" Carlos whispered.

"No way McBride is the El-Jaguar, Carlos!" Miguel assured him. "See how the cats love McBride? Sheba would not let me kiss her. There, Miguel, look at Simba see how she throws herself at his feet. McBride is our man. You have checked him out?"

"Yes, Carlos, he checks out," Miguel said. Then he walked out of the room and descended the back stairs into the dining room. A few quick steps and he would be with McBride.

The same two women appeared carrying breakfast, as Miguel passed through the dining room. Miguel opened the door and held it against the cool wind that suddenly arose from the valley below.

McBride stood up as the two women began setting the table, deciding to use the bathroom before Carlos appeared.

"Carlos is getting dressed. He will be here momentarily," Miguel said, watching the two women with more than a casual look.

"Miguel, where's the restroom?"

Miguel turned and motioned for McBride to follow him. They proceeded through the same door that Miguel had taken only minutes earlier. A circular staircase was on the left, as McBride entered the foyer. Continuing down a hallway, Miguel abruptly stopped and pointed at a spot in the wall. There was the bathroom, tucked neatly and inconspicuously behind the staircase. It was built in such a way that McBride had difficulty finding the entrance, as it blended so well with the dark mahogany wood trim.

His business completed; McBride returned to the veranda. His two feline companions were there, waiting for him to return and take his seat. Miguel was pouring the coffee as he sat. Noticing only two cups, Ryan figured that Miguel was not to be in attendance "A *very rare honor"*, McBride thought.

"Morning McBride" Carlos said walking out on the veranda through the same door that Miguel used.

"Good morning, Juan," McBride replied. Standing up shaking Carlos's limp hand and wondering what Carlos was going to say, or more importantly, what Carlos was going to ask him to do.

17

Ж Ж Ж

RELAXING IN HER BATHTUB, DOMINIQUE WAS preparing herself for Juan and his friend. Antigua was washing her back, her hands, like the water, were warm, soft and felt good on her body. Juan told her to be ready in an hour to break his friend's nuts and take him without squealing like a stuffed pig. She smiled Juan told her that his friend was well endowed.

It had been three weeks since Miguel had picked her up at the airport and brought her to Juan. She wasn't exactly sure, when she fell in love with Juan. All she knew was that he spoiled her with money, jewels, beautiful clothes and all the cocaine she wanted. In return, all she had to do was satisfy some politician, perhaps a general or a wife of some politician. Then she could have some more cocaine and make love to Antonio, the handsome nephew of General Gonzales.

In the deepest recesses of her mind, Dominique seemed to recall another name. She thought that she had been somebody of importance.

However, now it did not matter, as she was with Juan, and he loved her and that was all that mattered.

Ж Ж Ж

"Tell me, McBride, do you make a lot of money selling coffee and coca?" Carlos asked, as he took a sip of coffee.

"You already know that I don't!" Ryan said, putting down his fork and reaching for the coffee pot.

Carlos began to laugh. "Yes, McBride, I know, your poor. I also know about Mexico and Costa Rico. You are not a good boy, McBride."

"I never said I was, Carlos! What's all this about, Juan? You invite me to your beautiful house. You entice me with two beautiful, young women who are practically naked. You turn two leopards on me trying to scare the hell out of me, and then you tell me that I am broke and that I am not a good boy! Jesus Christ, Carlos, all you had to do was ask me. I would have told you. However, I would have asked you why you wanted to know. And don't ask me why, but I sense a very lucrative business proposition coming my way."

Carlos began slapping the table as he broke out once again in spontaneous laughter. " McBride, you're too fucking much! Yes, I am about to make you wealthy. That is if you want to be wealthy, McBride!"

"Who do you want me to kill? And hell yes, I want to be rich. I want a car-like yours, and I want a woman like Antigua. I want a hacienda like this. Does that answer your questions, Carlos?"

"Yes, McBride, we shall be good friends and business partners, and we will both be very rich," Carlos said, clapping his hands to summon the help to clear the table.

Both men remained silent, as the table was cleared. Ryan reached down and picked up his cigar off the ground. He knocked off the cigar ash and relit it, and blew the smoke upwards, letting the breeze carry the smoke away.

Saying nothing, Carlos watched his new partner light the cigar. It struck Carlos, as odd that McBride was so poor he had to smoke a cigar that someone had thrown to the ground and he did it without hesitation. Miguel *was right about McBride he was a good man. Carlos* thought. *Before he became rich, he too had smoked other people's cigars.*

"McBride, follow me!" Carlos said, standing abruptly and walking back into the house.

Ryan followed his host his two, furry feline companions ambling at his side.

ЖЖЖ

Miguel knocked on Dominique's door. Per Carlos' instructions, he was to check on the new puta and make sure she was getting ready. There was no reply. He turned to leave when he heard a scream coming from the room. Turning back to the door, he slowly pulled out his revolver, as he pressed his ear to the door and listened, recalling the last assassination attempt against Carlos. Slowly, Miguel began pushing down on the door handle, his heart beating wildly against his chest, as his breath came to him in small gasps. He felt the door give way under his body weight. Again, he heard the muffled scream.

Poking his head into the room, he saw Antigua lying across the bed. The new puta, Rossi/Dominique, was kneeling at her crotch. Miguel closed the door, and turned away, holstering his gun as he walked back down the hall. He had important work to do and could not be bothered with two whores who in a year or less would be discarded on some dirty, lonely street, high on drugs, with no money and no name. He had learned his lesson about getting involved with puta's by a young girl Julio had called Renee.

Carlos brought her home one night from Don Julio's. Julio had given Renee to Juan as a gift. Actually, Don Julio wanted Antigua all to himself, so he had given Renee to Carlos to keep peace in the family. Renee was a real heartbreaker. Of all the women in Julio's stable, Renee was special. She was funny, charming and very loving and giving. By all of Julio's business associates, she was the favorite. The one and only time Carlos and Don Julio had ever gotten into a fight, had been over Renee.

Julio gave the order to dispose of Renee. Carlos refused, opting to keep her for himself, saying that Renee would be his exclusive property to be used sparingly. Mendoza replied that she was trouble and knew too much about the cartel.

The argument proceeded from a yelling match to a physical altercation when Julio had grabbed his walking stick and struck Carlos across the chest and shoulders. In response, Carlos pulled his pistol and struck Julio several times across the face and head. He had even pulled back the hammer, cocked the pistol and pointed it at Julio's head.

Though Julio relented, he warned Carlos that the girl was now his responsibility. Carlos said nothing. He just shouldered his weapon and walked out. For three months, neither man spoke to the other; messengers carried out all cartel business between them.

Carlos had become devoted to his young beauty, and for a while, Renee seemed happy with the new arrangement. Then one Sunday morning, Carlos had decided to withhold the cocaine from Renee because he had wanted to get her straight, so she would love him for himself and not for the drugs, he provided. Renee's withdrawal was painful to watch. She begged and pleaded with Carlos for the cocaine. Carlos did nothing for her, except watch, her beg and cry. Miguel watched as the tears streamed down Carlo's cheeks powerless to help the woman he loved. Though Carlos could be cold and heartless, Renee had melted his heart.

Renee was dead now presumably killed by Julio, although Julio denied giving the order. By all accounts, Julio had arranged to have Renee forcibly taken from Carlos's home and deposited deep in the jungle where she was supposedly stripped naked and turned loose. Miguel knew that nobody ever survived the jungle, especially someone like Renee, who was soft and beautiful. She would be able to do nothing for herself, having been taught everything except how to survive in the jungle without weapons, clothes, food or water.

For some reason, Miguel actually believed Don Julio. Instead, he suspected that Antigua had used her position as Don Julio's mistress to have Renee stolen and disposed of, thus eliminating a beautiful rival.

18

ЖЖЖ

STEELE FELT THE URGENT CALL OF nature. He stretched on the king-sized bed, contorting his body until his bones stretched and popped. Looking around the bedroom, he realized it was not his. He could hear a TV in the other room and smell the aroma of freshly brewed coffee. He stood up and stepped into the bathroom to use the toilet. He chuckled to himself; his memory was now restored he was with Esther.

Renee was now under very tight security. Some place in the Washington D.C. area. General Hatfield had told him that Renee was unbelievable. She pointed out dirty politicians at the state and federal levels and other prominent politicians and key law enforcement officers in the United States, Europe, Columbia and Panama. A fount of knowledge he called her, she was giving names, dates, places and in some cases, how the drugs were being delivered into the United States.

When Steele had asked the general how long Renee was going to be gone, Hatfield had simply replied, "When she tells us all she knows, and we are ready to take down Mendoza."

Zack interpreted that response to mean, "How the hell do I know?" In the meantime, Steele had walked the beaches of Ryan sonville and even tried some fishing. Nevertheless, no matter what he did to keep busy, his mind always returned to Renee. He was lonely and horny, a bad combination. He felt that if he called Esther, he was betraying Renee. However, Renee was not here, and in all likelihood would not return for sometime if ever.

General Hatfield was sitting at the bar in the Mayflower Hotel, waiting for a man he had never met and had only spoken to twice— four days ago when they had set up this meeting and once again around 9:00 a.m. this morning when he had called to confirm the time and place.

The general was watching the local news when he sawDon McGee reflected in the mirror over the bar. Immediately, he recognizedDon McGee from his self-description: a small, balding man with silver-gray hair.

A pretty good self-description, the general thought, asDon McGee walked towards the bar. Their eyes met in the mirror, asDon McGee walked up along side of him and asked, "You Hatfield?" Before he could respond,Don McGee called out for a scotch on the rocks.

"I'm Hatfield," the general replied.

"Thought you were"Don McGee replied.

"Oh and how did you guess that?" the general asked.

"Because, asshole, you were the only man in the place. That is, until I walked in."

The general broke out in a belly laugh, his face turning red from too many cigars. Don McGee took the bar stool next to him, as he looked around the room, familiarizing himself with old memories.

"Last time I was in this bar was the night that Tricky Dick abdicated the presidency. What a party that was,"Don McGee said, taking a sip of scotch.

"My God, I was just a kid!" Hatfield said, taking a sip of his beer and smiling.

"In the words of that immortal general what's-his-name, fuck you Hatfield."

Putnam started laughing, as did the general. "I'll have another scotch and bring my friend here a beer. Okay, barkeep?" McKee said, sliding off the barstool and heading towards an open booth.

The general knew their meeting was about to begin. He also knew that no record would be made of their conversation. Moreover, unless it became necessary, this would be the only time he andDon McGee would meet.

Putnam selected the booth that afforded him a view of all the comings and goings of the patrons. The Mayflower Hotel had a reputation for intrigue and adulterous affairs, and he wanted to hide in plain sight as he and the general discussed murder. After all, wasn't that what drug trafficking was murder? Not the bang, bang, shoot 'em up type of murder, although that was a common occurrence, but the slow, insidious and torturous corruption of the human body that consumed a person's essence, eroded the fabric of societies around the world and left cities, towns and villages depleted of that spark called love.

Putnam waited for the bartender to sit down the drinks and a bowl of pretzels before he spoke.

The young, very attractive barkeep took the empty glasses, smiled at both men and walked back to her station. Don McGee watched her as she walked away, smiled and shook his head, turning his gaze back to the general.

"If only I was twenty-five years younger!" Mc Gee said, chuckling to himself.

"She'd kill you," the general responded, taking a swig of beer.

"Okay, sir, explain to me how you plan on taking out Mendoza and how I can help you," Don McGee said as he reached for a pretzel.

Ж Ж Ж

Steele had showered and used Esther's mouthwash before he dressed in the same clothes he had worn yesterday and walked out into the kitchen. Wearing only a tee shirt and panties, Esther was busy at the stove, frying bacon. *How many military men could say that they had made love to a superior officer and watched her make him breakfast in her panties?* Steele thought with a smile, as he walked up behind her and kissed her on her neck. He encircled her in his arms and pulled her close, rubbing her cheek with the stubble of his beard.

"Do you want your eggs sunny side up or scrambled?" she asked, reaching into the refrigerator and exposing her beautiful backside to him.

"Scrambled," Steele, replied, and dropping two pieces of bread into the toaster.

Esther smiled at him, as she shut the refrigerator door, remembering the way; Steele had made her feel while they made love. She still felt that same thing that stirred her blood and left her limp feeling abused and begging for more. No other man ever did that to her. Still wanting him, she intended to take him again after they ate. Once, she had lost him because of her arrogant pride, now she was determined that would never happen again. She loved this man with the cold blue eyes, who could make her body react to his every wish.

19

ЖЖЖ

ALONE IN THE LIVING ROOM OF his townhouse apartment, McBride sat lost deep in thought, thinking of his new life. Now he had a new car, beautiful new clothes and furniture that Dominique had picked out for him. He had over a million dollars in his bank account and had only been in the smuggling business for a month.

Carlos supplied the cocaine, while he devised ingenious new ways to smuggle the cocaine into the United States; pretty simple really, except for the methodology of hiding two or three thousand kilos from the United States Customs, the DEA and the DOD. He had managed to come up with two good ways of concealing the cocaine. His ideas were so simple that when he presented them to Carlos and Julio, they both scoffed at him. That was until he produced two plastic bags; one filled with confectionary sugar and the other with cocaine. He asked them to point to the bag containing the cocaine. The laughter stopped.

"Okay, McBride, explain your idea to me," Don Julio said.

The plan was simple and direct. He would have plastic bags made that contained chambers. The cocaine would be in the middle and the confectionary sugar would be placed on multi-colored pallets and shipped in the open. The cocaine would be manifested, as sugar with the proper weight and quantity. Moreover, if a customs agent happened to asked about the pallets various colors they would be informed that the colors represented the various companies who purchased the sugar. Since by Columbian law he was allowed, to export coffee and sugar both raw and refined, he could have U. S. Customs inspect the product for a fee before it left Columbia. With the manifest stamped by customs, the cocaine would pass through the port without incident.

The other method he came up with was using what he called, "Large coffee bricks." He would make storage containers of light-weight cardboard, soak coffee beans in a light wax and pour a six-inch layer into a wooden box. Then, he would place the storage container into the wooden box. Next, he would stack the cocaine bricks inside the container and pour more of the coffee bean-wax mixture around and over the container. When the wax hardened, a large, six-inch thick coffee brick was formed. The wax acted as a protective coating for the coffee beans and insulated the smell of the cocaine from the drug-sniffing dogs.

As with the sugar shipments, he paid to have the U. S. Customs inspect the boxes prior to shipping. If the customs agent opened a box to inspect the contents, he would see exactly what he was supposed to see: A brick of coffee. If the agent asked about the wax, they would be told that the wax protected the flavor of the coffee beans. He even invited the custom agents to watch the process, except without the cocaine, of course. The large, wooden crates filled with coffee and cocaine was safely shipped to the United States, or any other country, for that matter.

※ ※ ※

With each passing day and every shipment, he was becoming more and more depressed. He was a man in conflict with himself. The conflict was simple: his devotion to his duty and to his country versus the sweet seduction of money. His marriage was a pretense of convenience, nothing more. His chances of making general were remote, as he had disappeared from the ranks and had lost any chance of being promoted.

What bothered him was not the promotion board, or even his marriage. What bothered him was that he had taken an oath to defend his country. Now he was helping to destroy his country. That was his conflict: Duty and an honor versus the envious life-style and creature comforts. He had to be honest with himself. He was leaning towards creature comforts, as duty and honor had become cruel taskmasters.

※ ※ ※

Putnam sat in his office, his head resting in his hands; his eyes closed. He was drunk, and he knew it. So did his secretary, Ethel, but she said nothing? She just held his calls and took messages while waiting for her boss to recover from his temporary illness.

Leaning back in his chair, Don McGee folded his hands across his chest, as he visualized Hatfield's plan. The plan was divided into four, separate and very distinct operations, all were to be completed simultaneously. The first step was to initiate a campaign of misinformation. Second was to exploit Mendoza's paranoia by creating mistrust, between him and his lieutenants, concentrating on Juan Carlos. Step three was to attack Mendoza's production facilities, crippling and interrupting his production and delivery schedules. Last step was to steal his money bankrupting him and his organization creating friction between Mendoza and his business associates. However, this multi-staged plan all hinged upon Colonel McBride, and he had not been heard from for a month.

Ж Ж Ж

McBride had to admit he hated Don Julio Mendoza. He did not care much for Juan either, but could tolerate Carlos, as they had some things in common mainly good cigars and fine looking women. That Sunday afternoon, after they had formed their partnership, they had celebrated with a bottle of good wine and two of the most beautiful whores Ryan had ever seen.

That's how he met Dominique. Carlos presented her as a present to him. He knew that she was an American and somehow there was a familiarity about her. He could not place it, nor did he understand it. The only thing he knew for sure was that when he shoved his engorged manhood inside her, she moaned in pleasure. She did not squeal in pain or beat his chest while trying to escape him. Dominique just threw her long, shapely legs around his back and took him ever deeper.

When she reacted with such uncontrollable passion, she scared him. Her legs would suddenly tighten around his back and in the heat of her passion; she would squeeze him so hard that he could hardly breathe. Her breath would come in gasps, as she threw her arms around his shoulders and pulled her lover tighter against her body. Then she would throw her head back, arching her hips, raising him off the bed. Clenching her teeth, she would climax so violently that she often fainted. The first time he had her, he had thought, *Ryan , boy; you must ride this one again.*

Since that Sunday afternoon, Dominique had been his to do with as he pleased. The only condition Carlos had made was that once a week Dominique had to be back to his hacienda to be tended to. Ryan took that to mean her nails, hair, and of course, her ration of cocaine.

Miguel would call and ask for Dominique. All Ryan heard was, "Yes; I'll be ready," and, "Please don't be late, as I'm almost out of the stuff." Ryan had correctly interpreted that the "stuff" was cocaine.

It was Tuesday morning when Dominique started asking him questions. At first, the questions were innocent enough: "Are you married or divorced?" "Where were you born?" Each question became more intrusive than the one before. In some ways, it reminded him of his wife. She always asked questions like that when she suspected him of wrongdoing.

However, it was not the questions, per'se, but the way Dominique asked them. It was more as though someone of importance, pointed, direct and almost rude, was asking them. Sometimes the questions were asked in such a way that he would be damned if he did and damned if he didn't. Ryan finally tired of her game, asked what it was exactly that she wanted to know. He raised his voice for emphasis, but his ploy did not work, as Dominique did not respond. Instead, she went into her bathroom, shut the door and prepared herself for Miguel.

For a fleeting moment, McBride wondered if Dominique could be Rossi. He had never met her nor talked by phone. Rossi was described, as tall like Dominique. However, Rossi had dark hair where Dominique was blond. Her eyebrows were blonde, and if she had pubic hair, it would be blonde. He decided that there was no way Dominique was Rossi.

As Dominique was getting ready for her weekly spa treatments, it occurred to him that Dominique wasn't his lover, but an informer. She was probably telling Julio and Juan everything he did, where he went, whom he talked with and what they talked about. He decided to do nothing knowing what was going on was information that would be used and exploited when the time was right. Hatfield was right. Mendoza was ripe for the plucking. It was time to start the war.

20

※ ※ ※

GENERAL HATFIELD SAT IN HIS OFFICE, staring at the ceiling, counting the holes in a water-stained piece of tile. His hands were behind his head, and his fingers were interlocked. This was his traditional thinking pose. He was dubious at best about using Captain Steele and Renee in his plan. Both already had given way to much: Steele his health, Renee her body. However, when Mendoza learned that Renee was still alive, he would go nuts. Renee was the bait the general knew Mendoza would take. For Steele, it all boiled down to a promise. Steele had asked him for the right to kill Mendoza, and he had said, "Okay."

※ ※ ※

Aerial surveillance photos showed no towns or factories, nothing except Mendoza's hacienda under construction. When completed, the hacienda would resemble a medieval fortress. She thought it odd that somebody would build such a structure in the jungle, so far-removed from civilization; it was being built for some nefarious purpose. On Tuesday morning, Shirley's suspicions had been verified. She was looking at the satellite imaging photos under her magnifying glass. The toxic pollutants were indeed emanating from inside the mountain. Clearly, the satellite photos showed a small dam built in such a way that it changed the course of the river. Since the river had been manually diverted, it disappeared into the mountain, only to reappear somewhere else.

So now, she knew for sure: Somebody was manufacturing cocaine and by the depth and scope of the color imagery photos, it was a very large-scale operation. Another thing that caught Shirley's eye was a dark line that appeared across the river. Upon closer inspection, she decided it definitely was a swing bridge, something akin to a moat bridge.

Taking a swig of water, Lamb set the bottle down, reached for her plotter and calculated the coordinates the general's staff would need. She re-checked her figures, making sure that the information was accurate before she dialed the phone number. A strong, masculine voice announced that she had reached General Hatfield's Headquarters. Per procedure, she gave her code name: "Bo-Peep- 4" followed by a number that was changed daily. It was always the same routine. The sexy male voice would then say, "You are cleared, Bo-Peep-4. What is your message?" She would simply give a brief description or overview of the subject matter, and the coordinates and hang up. That was it! She loved this job!

Ж Ж Ж

Steele was grateful that General Hatfield had sent his plane to NAS Ryan sonville to pick him up. Furthermore, he was appreciative that he was the only passenger. No one else was on the plane except himself and the two pilots.

As the plane lumbered through the blue sky, he sat in the General's chair, facing backwards and watching the Florida coastline pass by. Idly, he wondered if his life was passing him by.   Other men his age had wives and children. They had mortgages and real jobs. In all their conversations not once, had Esther asked him what he did for the army? He debated whether to tell her wondering what her reaction would be. He decided to tell her about being assigned to the embassy in Bogotá, and gathering Intel on drug cartels. He would, also tell her about Renee.

When she began to ask questions, he explained everything to her. He told her about the tree people, and how he had been initiated into the tribe, as a war chief and the stone around his neck signified this. He told her about his body being painted and how Renee painted a smiley face on his penis causing Esther to break out in laughter. He told Ester in detail about Renee and how Mendoza took beautiful, young girls, educated them, and turned them into prostitutes and how he disposed of them when he was done with them.

Now, less than twenty-four hours later, Steele was on an airplane heading to Aruba and Esther's words still ringing in his brain. "Zak I want you to kill the son- of- a bitch" now if everything went right her words were about to become prophetic.

21

ЖЖЖ

RENEE LAY IN HER OVERSIZED BED, her eyes staring blankly at the ceiling as she rested her body, still wet and shiny in the afterglow of passion. Resting in her arms was the female companion Mike had hired to cook and clean for her. However, Renee had another need and that was for someone to satisfy her sexual wants.

She had become lonely and bored, returning to an empty apartment and watching television in a language that she did not understand. When she complained to Mike, who was her handler, that she was bored and lonely, Mike hired a young woman named Allison to keep her company.

Allison was taller than she was. She also had red hair. Renee had never seen a woman with natural red hair before. Nor had she ever seen a woman with green eyes. She found herself drawn to this young naive woman. The more they bonded, the more Renee knew she wanted her, and she proceeded to seduce her. Still, her urges had not been satisfied. What she wanted and needed was a man, preferably the man she called

Steele. He could satisfy her passion and leave her begging for more—
but he was elsewhere.

Ж Ж Ж

During one of her sessions with her psychiatrist, Doctor Steward, he
played back a tape recording of her that he had made while she was in a
deep, hypnotic trance. Doctor Stew, as Renee called him, always taped
his sessions with her, in the event that she revealed something signifi-
cant, he could merely give the tape to Mike, who would listen to it and
decide if the information was relevant.

This particular recording revealed a glimpse of another time
and life. It was apparent that Renee's mother had not kept her
past a secret from her children, and Renee could recall much of
her family's history. Renee was not alone, as she had originally
thought. In fact, she was from Spain. There she had a mother,
father, a younger sister and an older brother as well. Originally,
her family lived in Madrid. Her mother's name was Maria. Her
sister's name had been Mia, her brother's Antonio and her real
name was Angelica Montoya.

Maria Reyes was Andalusian by birth and an aristocrat by status,
which meant she lived in Madrid and had noble blood coursing through
her veins. She had been raised in affluence, and her papa was indulgent
with his only daughter—only the very best for his beloved Maria. When
she had graduated with honors from The Royal Conservatory of Music
in Madrid, her future, as a concert pianist seemed bright. However, life
had other plans for this young and beautiful woman of privilege.

It was on a very warm and sunny Palm Sunday morning that Maria's life changed. While she was walking home from church with her parents, her papa complained that he wasn't feeling well and had to sit down, as he could not breathe. While her mother loosened his tie and fanned him, Maria hailed a cab and ordered the driver to take them to Clinical Fuensantz Hospital.

Less than an hour after paying their respects to Jesus, God's death angel took the soul of Doctor Salvador Reyes. Although the doctors tried valiantly to save him, all their efforts were in vain, as Jesus had claimed the good doctor for his own. The famed heart surgeon and beloved husband of Teresa Reyes, and father of Maria Reyes, died of heart failure in the same hospital where he had gained his fame. Dr. Reyes was only forty-six.

After her father's funeral, bill collectors, who wanted their money, started calling. Teresa was frantic, as she had never paid a bill in her life. Salvador had taken care of everything when it came to money concerns. Maria and her mother decided to take fate into their lily-white hands and walked arm in arm the few blocks to her father's bank.

A young man sat behind the desk with his hands folded. He listened intently to Maria with downcast eyes, so he could stare at her breasts, as she explained their circumstances. He smiled, as he stood up and asked them to wait while he checked the account. In the meantime, Maria held her mother's hand, silently praying that Papa had provided for them. About five, minutes had elapsed when the young man returned, carrying a folder stuffed with papers. Maria noticed that his facial features were tight, and his eyes were downcast. As before, he kept staring at her ample breasts.

"I'm sorry to report, but Doctor Reyes owed us money," the young man said, taking out his calculator and figuring the exact amount.

"How much did my father owe you?" Maria asked, trying to remain calm for her mother's sake.

"The truth?" he asked, his eyes now staring into hers. "There is no money and there will be no insurance, as the doctor used his insurance money to secure his loans."

They soon found out that Papa had mortgaged the house to pay for the schooling so his daughter could receive the best musical education, and Teresa could live the good life and be a woman of leisure. His love for them actually destroyed them. By giving them so much, he took away their inheritance. Now the bank would take the house and all the cars. Both women were at this moment in time destitute.

Maria figured that she could sell her jewels first, then Mama's jewels, which would help for a while. They would have to move out of the house and rent an apartment. Then she could start playing concerts and earn a decent living for her and Mama. However, Maria's hopes and dreams to be a famous concert pianist were not to be. Fate had other plans for the noble Maria Reyes.

A year after her father's death, Maria's once proud and beautiful mother was working as a domestic in a local hotel. Maria worked in various lounges around Madrid, playing tunes that she once considered beneath her. She had tried hard to obtain employment with varied orchestras around Europe, always losing out to women who were inferior musicians. Maria reasoned that they had obtained their jobs immorally by giving blowjobs or by spreading their legs to whoever could help them.

But, she determined to make it on her own terms. However, as the weeks turned to months, and the good jobs disappeared, Maria became increasingly angry and frustrated with those people who did not appreciate her talents. She kept obtaining common jobs, playing substandard music while continuing to go to auditions to display a talent who was becoming eroded by a diminished capacity, invoked by her new friends who lived in small bottles at the bottom of her handbag and in bigger bottles behind the bar. They helped ease the pain that loomed deep within her heart.

Every morning Maria would look at herself in her bathroom mirror and prepare herself to face the day she would rather not face. She would make mental observations of her wrinkles and curse as her beauty faded. The ravages of a poor diet, lack of sleep and the chronic use of pills and alcohol were taking their toll.

Both, she and her mother had taken to selective prostitution, usually around the end of the month, when the bills were due. They had been raised good Catholic girls and knew what they were doing was sinful. However, because of destitution and desperation, they had to forego pride for the sake of survival.

Ж Ж Ж

Colonel Pablo Gonzales was from a very influential family. His grandfather had been the President of Columbia when John F. Kennedy was President of the United States. Before his death, his father had been a senator. His brother Ernesto was Council General of Columbia. At thirty-four, Pablo was the youngest colonel in the Columbian Army. He really did not care what people said about him because he had a job to do and if his subordinates could not handle that, then he would just get rid of them. After all, he had to establish a reputation for something, and it might as well be as a harsh taskmaster.

Presently, there are no wars and the Columbian Army was not large. There were about only twenty thousand men. So, he used his family connections and money to obtain various key positions that would make him look good to his superiors and increase his chances for promotions. At the moment, he was the Military Attaché assigned to the Columbian Ambassador to Spain, an assignment that he truly enjoyed. His wife, Beatrice, was in Bogotá, refusing to come to Madrid with him. Learning of his womanizing in Columbia, she had felt disgraced. In addition, she was pregnant with his child, and she wanted her baby born in Columbia where she was close to her family.

It was at the Navidad Banquette where Pablo first saw Maria. He was standing at the bar, holding a drink in one hand and a dinner plate, piled high with food, in the other, and he was staring at her. Maria made his heart race as she sat there at her piano. He was alone in Madrid, and there this goddess sat, perched upon her throne, waiting for him to make love to her. On this Eve of Navidad, he felt, as if they were alone in the room. The stage lights played upon her hair, causing it to shine, as if she had a divine halo above her. Immediately, he knew he had to meet her, to kiss those beautiful red lips and hold her body tight with his as he took liberties.

While playing the piano and looking around the room, Maria became aware of the handsome officer who was watching her. In his uniform with all his medals, he looked distinguished. She was not sure, but thought he was an officer. Furthermore, he was intently listening to her as she played her various interpretations of holiday music. It had been a long time since anybody had actually listened to her.

During her break, he walked up to her and told her his name was Pablo, and that he was the Military Attaché to the Columbian Ambassador. Then he proceeded to tell her how lovely she was and how well she played the piano. He asked if she were classically trained, when she responded that she had been he asked her to play something classical. She replied that she would love to, but she couldn't because it was a Navidad Banquette."

Since Pablo would not take no for an answer, Maria reluctantly mounted the stage and took her seat. She began by playing Schubert, followed by Gershwin and then Bach. Completely unscripted and unrehearsed, she electrified the audience. Tears begin to well up in her eyes, as the audience began to clap and cheer. As she played, her tears fell, striking the keyboard in time with her music.

Ж Ж Ж

Maria sat on the edge of her bed, combing her hair and thinking about Pablo. Their friendship blossomed into an affair rather quickly. He was handsome, charming, influential and above all, wealthy. Maria and mother needed a rich man, as the end of the month was only a week away.

Pablo called and asked to see her Maria declined; informing him; she had to work to pay her bills. When Pablo inquired how much, she told him an amount that included her mother's bills as well. Pablo laughed, "Is that all?"

"I will give you the money for your debts. Now get ready, we are going to the theater. I will pick you up at eight," Pablo said hanging up before she could respond.

Ж Ж Ж

Pablo was a very considerate man. He would buy gifts and take them places for long weekends. Every month he would make up the difference the two women needed to satisfy their financial needs. She found that she could not control herself when Pablo was with her; he made her giddy with love, like a schoolgirl with a crush on a cute boy.

Maria was sitting at her kitchen table, wrapped in her favorite robe waiting for the teapot to boil. Her wet hair was piled high on her head, wrapped in a towel. While she was painting her fingernails, she felt a burning sensation in her throat. Hoping it would pass, she tried swallowing when she could not she rushed to the kitchen for water however, it was too late.

As she took a drink of water, trying to quell her heaving stomach, it came to her in one terrorizing moment of self-realization. She was pregnant and Pablo was the father. She started to cry, wishing her papa were there so she could tell him that he was going to be a grand papa.

Maria walked into her bedroom, sat on the edge of the bed, crossed her legs and picked up the phone and dialed her husband-to-be. Overcome with joy and excitement, Maria now knew how a new mother to be felt.

While listening to Pablo's home phone ring, she looked at the bedside clock. It read, 7:05 a.m. She knew he would be there, as he had told her, he had to fly back to Columbia for business, and that he would be home in ten days. Today made the eleventh day, so he was there, probably in the shower, or maybe he was sleeping so hard he could not hear the phone.

The voice that answered had a sleepy tone to it. Thinking she had misdialed, Maria was about to say that she was sorry until she heard Pablo's unmistakable voice in the background. She asked, "Who is this?"

"This is Senora Gonzales. Who is this please?"

"Why am I being punished, tormented and humiliated by God? What have I done?" She thought. Curling her body into a tight, human ball. What was to become of her and her baby, as her tears of shame began to soak her pillow?

22

Ж Ж Ж

MIKE ATKINS, TOPEKA, KANSAS SAT AT his desk, listening intently to the tape as Renee described and explained what she had gone through since being sold to Julio Mendoza to cover her mother's cocaine habit. She described in every detail how on her seventh birthday, her mother had dressed her in her finest clothes, without her underwear, and had taken her to see a man with a ponytail who wore big, square-toed shoes with large buckles, clothes that were bright and shiny, and had teeth that were crooked and yellow.

Suddenly, Renee stopped talking. Mike checked the tape recorder, making sure it was still working. In the background, he could hear her sobbing, as she relived that moment when her mother had betrayed her for a little white bag of powder.

Her mother did not even kiss her good bye. The fat ugly man handed her mother a bag of white powder. She had smiled, curtsied and walked out, leaving Renee with this big, strange man who kept staring at her and smiling. Naturally, she wanted to go home and to be with her brother Antonio. But papa was at work and Antonio was away at the military academy. Only she and her little sister, Mia, were at home today with mother and Grandma Teresa.

She only hoped that Mia would not do what she had once done that had made Grandma Teresa beat her with her fist and a belt. Renee had taken some white powder that had been lined up in little piles on the coffee table and applied it to her baby doll's bottom. When her father saw what grandma had done, he became so angry that he had beaten Grandma and Mama and threw them out of the house. Both mama and grandma now lived in a two-room shack at the edge of town. Papa would give them money for food and drink and mama could take them shopping for new clothes on special occasions like birthdays.

ж ж ж

Working in Military Intelligence was at times very tedious, bordering on boring. Mike Atkins had graduated from Kansas State and had taken a Master from George Washington in Psychology. He did not think the army had been prudent when they assigned him to MI, but now he was glad because he could help this beautiful woman, with whom he had fallen in love. He realized it was only a platonic affair, at best. This woman was tougher than any Green Beret and more resourceful. Over time, Mike had learned that if Renee/Angelica ever had the means and opportunity to kill Julio Mendoza, Mendoza would be a dead man.

Colonel Stewart, or "Doc" as everyone called him, had asked Captain Atkins to find her family if he could. He knew from Angelica's recording that her dad had worked for the Spanish Embassy in Bogotá. He also knew he could not just merely pick up the phone and call the Spanish Embassy in Bogotá and say, "Hey, amigo, did you have a dude named Montoya working for you about fifteen, maybe twenty years ago who lost a daughter when his wife sold her into prostitution for a bag of cocaine?"

No. Mike knew this had to be handled through the State Department. Furthermore, he was aware of a man namedDon McGee, who somehow was intimately involved with General Hatfield. Therefore, he reasoned that was the logical place to start. In addition, doing it this way, he would not be taking risks that might compromise Angelica's safety.

Sitting back in his chair, Mike interlocked his fingers across his chest and closed his eyes. He needed a "timeout," as he had to balance his interest, or perhaps desires would be a better word, against the needs of the nation. He was aware of how extremely important Renee/Angelica was. He knew that General Hatfield was going to use her as a mantrap and that is exactly what she was, a mantrap. Mendoza would pay millions to have her killed, and Mike needed the money.

It would be so easy. All he had to do was submit her picture, along with her biographical information, and mail it to the Spanish Embassy here in Washington D.C... They in turn would forward it to the Spanish Embassy in Bogotá. After that, all he had to do was wait for Mendoza.

Mike figured it would take three weeks before he would hear anything. As her handler, it was his prerogative to do whatever he thought best to look out after Angelica/Renee. His argument, if he needed one, would be that once he asked the State Department and the Spanish and Columbian Embassies for help; security concerns could arise, when he thought the time was right, Renee would be whisked away to a yet to be determined locale. He would keep her company all at the taxpayer's expense.

ЖЖЖ

"Hello, this isDon McGee. How may I help you, Captain Atkins?"

Atkins was struck byDon McGee's directness, there was no hello or how are you, just straight and to the point.

"Well, sir, I hope you're the right man to ask. If not, I hope you can direct me to the right person," Mike said, a little intimidated byDon McGee's title of Under Secretary for the State Department. Idly, he wondered how many regulations he was breaking by going outside the chain-of-command.

"Well, sir," Mike's voice was hesitant, as he did not know just how to form his question. "We found this woman in the jungle of Columbia, and we need help trying to find her relatives. She was born in Spain. Her father worked for the Spanish Embassy in Bogotá and her name, sir, is Renee or Angelica Montoya."

"Let me get this correct, captain. You are asking *me* to use my office and influence to ask the Spanish Embassy if they ever had an employee named Montoya, who lost a daughter, and somehow you found her in the jungle? Do I have that correct, so far, captain?"

"Yes, sir, that's correct," Atkins, replied.

"And you want me to ask the Spanish Ambassador to find her relatives, either back in Spain or in Columbia, and you say her last name is Montoya?"

"Yes sir. Her last name is Montoya, and her sister's name is Mia. Her older brother's name is Antonio."

"And this girl's real name is Angelica?"

"Yes, sir, she was called Renee by somebody called Mendoza, who supposedly bought her for a bag of cocaine. I do know that General Hatfield brought her into the country for protective custody and to debrief her," Captain Atkins said, his voice now more assertive, as he felt thatDon McGee knew more than he was letting on.

"Okay, captain, give me your e-mail address, and I will see what I can find out. I make no promises except to say that I will try to help the girl and you,"Don McGee said.

Mike hung up the phone. He was happy, as he had just initiated the first step in becoming a multi- millionaire. The best part was that he would not have to pay taxes on the money.

23

Ж Ж Ж

STEELE WASN'T SURE EXACTLY IN WHAT part of Florida he was. As he deplaned, he was greeted by extreme heat and humidity that only the Floridians could appreciate. As he looked around, all he saw were rows of airplanes. He did not know all the types of airplanes that he saw, except he did recognize the big Starlifter and the ever-faithful Hercules sitting just to the right of him. Those he recognized from Fort Bragg, where he had taken jump school.

He squinted his eyes, trying to block out the noonday sun, as he walked across the tarmac towards a building that had, "Operations" painted on it and just below that he read, "Welcome to Mc Dill AFB" painted in big letters in air force blue and white.

Now, he knew where he was. General Hatfield's headquarters were here somewhere. He was acutely aware that he was not in his element. Green Berets are trained to adapt, persevere and cope with nature and the elements, in other words, to blend in and become invisible. He was not invisible and he was in awe of his surroundings. Never had he seen so many aircraft, representing so much money, in one place in his life

A sergeant who just happened to be walking by grabbed him by the arm pulling him away from a large, fast moving fighter that was taxiing by. As it passed, the aircraft's hot exhaust hit him in the face, burning his eyes and causing his already over-worked sweat glands to produce what he did not need, more sweat.

Ж Ж Ж

General Hatfield was in dire need of sucker play. He had to develop a plan that would divide Mendoza's forces and make him look weak and incompetent to his business associates. Also, he had to get a message to Colonel McBride somehow. He knew McBride was in deep with Mendoza and knew about his involvement with drug smuggling, as did the U .S. Customs and the DEA.

What Mendoza did not know was that McBride had developed a methodology for identifying the palates and the coffee crates containing the cocaine. He simply had brass nails pounded into each corner of the palates and crates, making them easy for the customs agents to find. Then the agents would segregate the containers and the DEA would screw small inconspicuous looking global positioning devices into the crates and palates. The cargo could be sent on its way while, each stop the cargo made was monitored by satellite and the locations cataloged and photographed from space.

McBride is a fucking hero and he can't enjoy the status, Hatfield thought to himself.

24

⋇ ⋇ ⋇

MIKE ATKINS LEANED BACK IN HIS chair. He was feeling pretty smug, as he had just started a chain reaction that hopefully would make him a very wealthy man. By using his chain-of-command, he actually set the wheels in motion to commit murder. Doctor Steward asked him to find Renee's parents. All he had done was ask the Under Secretary of State, a Mr. Don McGee, to check with the Spanish and Columbian Embassies to locate the parents of an Angelica Montoya, or any member of her family. The only starting point was that Angelica's father had worked at the Spanish Embassy about twenty years ago.

He was optimistic that with Mendoza's spy network, Julio would soon be told about Angelica. Mike was positive that General Hatfield would find a way to bait Mendoza. He wasn't sure how the general would have done it. could be as simple as planting a story with her picture or asking the good people of Bogotá for help in identifying this young woman whose only name was Renee. story would ask that anyone who knew anything, to contact either the Spanish or Columbian Embassies. that, the general would simply wait for Mendoza.

In the meantime, Mike already decided to move Renee to Camp Hurlbert, in Florida. Hulbert was next to Egland AFB. The CIA, the Army's Special Force's and the Navy Seals all trained there. Renee would be safe at least.

Ж Ж Ж

As he waited for the pleasure of the general's company, Steele recounted how captivated he and the general were, as they listened to Renee tell her life story that afternoon in Bogotá. She had recounted how her mother had sold her for a bag of cocaine to Mendoza and how he had methodically begun transforming all the children in his service, using whatever it took to obtain the desired results. Renee told of a young and very beautiful girl from Costa Rica, who had refused to have sex with Julio.

One day, Julio called all the children into a large room. He stood on a table announcing that they belonged to him he had bought them. Therefore, he could do what he wanted with them. Then with a nod of his head, two very large and powerful men dragged the Costa Rican girl into the room. With her hands tied behind her back, she was still defiant, as cursed at them calling them names. Spitting on Julio, she called him a, "Pig. A big, fat, ugly pig" Julio stepped down from the table and struck her head with his stick. Then he told the men to hang her. They complied without a moment's hesitation.

The girl dangled from the ceiling rafter. Everyone in the room could hear her gasp, as the rope pulled tighter around her neck, slowly strangling her, as she kicked her feet trying to find something to stand on. She lost control of her bodily functions and urine began to run down her leg and drip off the tip of her shoe onto the hardwood floor below. Julio's demonstration, of absolute control and power worked. From then on, the children did whatever Julio commanded.

General Hatfield heard enough. He had stood up, paid the bill and said, "Come with me." He then put both Steel and Renee on his aircraft and directed his pilots to take them to NAS Ryan sonville.

Now, Captain Zack Steele was back where he started, or soon would be, of that he was sure.

Ж Ж Ж

"Hello," Julio said, annoyed that someone dared to call him so early in the morning, before he had even taken a piss.

"Hello, Julio, it is Pablo. I wanted to tell you that Ernesto called me to say that the Americans have Angelica. Somehow, the Americans have learned that her real name is Angelica Montoya. They are looking for any of her relatives. Wasn't one of Maria's daughters named Angelica? And the youngest daughter was named Mia. If Angelica is Renee what became of Mia?"

In a drunken stupor, Julio's mind began to think. *It is inconceivable that the little puta is still alive! The last time I saw the bitch was that day when I ordered Castro and Raphael to make her compliant. I specifically told them to turn her over to the workers. So, how had she escaped them? What is more important, why wasn't I told that she had escaped? Now the Americans have her. How in the world did they find her?*

Julio knew that this specific little whore could destroy him and his cartel. The Americans were probably holding her somewhere in the states and asking her questions about his operations, and she knew almost everything. He could not tell his clients for then they would want to kill him. She had to be killed, but how, since he did not even know where she was? Hell, he could hardly remember her face. She had looked nothing like her sister, Antigua.

Julio had suspected for a long time that Antigua's father was not Renee's father. He knew Pablo had sired Antonio, but suspected had spread her legs for a tall, good-looking blonde-haired, blue-eyed man who impregnated her and her simple-minded, good-natured, gentle husband was too daft to know that Mia wasn't his. *Hell, I fucked Maria and both her daughters.* Julio thought. *She was so strung out on prescription drugs, alcohol and cocaine, that she sold her daughters, so she and her mother could satisfy their craving for the soft white powder.*

Picking up the phone, Julio called Juan and Pablo. He was not sure about McBride, but he had asked Juan to bring him in the hopes that he could help.

The meeting was to be held at the new hacienda or complex, as Julio referred to it. The complex was not finished yet. However, the processing plant was operational and producing at the rate of a ton a day. He wanted to show his guests the hacienda even though it was not finished and would not be for weeks.

McBride had arrived early as Dominique had already been to the complex several times and knew the way almost blindfolded. She had informed Ryan that she needed some extra "stuff," and also she wanted to visit with Antigua. Translation: Dominique wanted more cocaine.

Ryan just smiled saying nothing. He was growing tired of Dominique and intended to ask Carlos to take her back. Something about her just irked him. She had become nosy and never happy about anything. Once, he had caught her going through his files, looking for anything that would be of interest to Julio or Juan, so she could score more cocaine.

Ж Ж Ж

McBride's military mind kicked in as he made mental notes about the cameras and fortifications. He counted twelve security guards, so he automatically doubled that amount. As he walked towards the large doors built into the side of the mountain, he saw they were made of steel and were at least a foot thick.

He was about to walk into the cave when three large security guards, their machine pistols at the ready, challenged him. Ryan simply waved and turned around.

The meeting was less than cordial, as Julio was in a bad mood. He even went so far as to ban Miguel and Jesus from the meeting for fear of being killed by them.

"Pablo, please explain to us how you came upon this information that Renee is still alive and in the hands of the Americans," Julio asked.

Pablo sensed Julio's anger and decided it was better to tell the facts instead of opening with an amusing story or a dirty joke. "My brother Ernesto called me early this morning to inform me that the Columbian State Department got a request from the American Embassy, asking them to try to locate the parents, or family members of a woman named Angelica Montoya. Since Ernesto knew that my supposed nephew,

Antonio's last name was Montoya, and since Angelica had disappeared while in Columbia, the Spanish Embassy wanted to know if they could help find any living relatives of this poor, unfortunate girl. It seemed a simple, routine request. However, since Angelica's father had been a captain in charge of security for the Spanish Embassy, in Madrid that made it a diplomatic inquiry."

"So, Renee is alive then?" Juan asked, in a soft and caring, almost fatherly tone of voice.

"Yes, Angelica Montoya is alive, and we think she is in the United States," Pablo replied, taking a sip of coffee.

Julio was sitting across the table from Carlos. "You see, Juan, why I wanted this puta killed? If you had listened to me, we would be discussing other businesses, not this."

Carlos said nothing, but anger was clearly visible to all who could see his face. Julio took one look at Juan's eyes and knew that he had said the wrong thing. He knew Juan could kill him without a trace of remorse.

Sensing things were tense, Ryan got up from the table and walked over to the food where he surveyed the offering and selected two plates. He began to pile fruit, ham and roast beef onto each plate. Adding a fork and knife on the side of each plate, he walked to the other end of the table, handing one plate to Carlos, as he sat down. No one spoke they merely watched this gringo get up from the table and make a plate for himself and his friend.

"What about me, McBride, don't I get something to eat?" Julio asked.

"What, are your legs broken? You can't get up and grab your own food? I suppose if I did get up and get you something you'd want me to feed you and burp you!"

Carlos began to laugh. Carlos' laughter caused Julio and Pablo to laugh. Both men deciding to follow the gringo's advice they got up, and walked to the sideboard.

Julio sat his plate down on the table; a funny look appeared on his face. He began to giggle to himself and stamp his feet with glee. He sat down, pulled his chair up to the table, looked at Juan Carlos, and said, "You're a genius, Juan."

"I am?" Carlos asked.

"We have Rossi; they have Angelica. We offer a trade Rossi's life for Angelica's."

"Who is Rossi?" Ryan asked.

"Don't you know, McBride?" Carlos asked, putting down his knife and fork and looking at him. "You have been enjoying her for weeks now."

"So what" Ryan replied. Who is this Rossi person and why would the Americans give up this girl Renee for Rossi?" Ryan asked angrily.

"Once upon a time Rossi, was somebody in the U. S. State Department. She was in command of those that would attempt to destroy us. Now she works for me, and does she not please you, McBride?" Julio said, smiling at him.

"She's a pain in the ass, and I was going to ask Juan to take her back," Ryan replied.

Once again, the room broke out in laughter. Ryan had to laugh at himself. Juan patted his shoulder saying that he would take care of the problem.

After the laughter had died down, Ryan continued with his line of questioning. He was working them, agitating them, making them doubt their decisions, trying to plant seeds of distrust that eventually could lead to internal strife.

"Julio, I think you're wrong! Why would the United States military give up a prized catch for someone from the State Department?"

"And who said, McBride that she is in the hands of the American military?" Julio asked. His wide, toothy smile fading to a lingering sneer; his eyes glaring into McBride's, watching for any slight tell that would unmask him as a traitor.

"Because, asshole who else, but the U. S. Army would be in your jungles knocking off your processing plants and killing your security forces? " McBride retorted, glaring back at the little, pudgy man with contempt.

Julio did not respond to McBride's observations. He was thinking, and he had to admit that McBride might be correct. *Why would the United States military give up Renee for Rossi?* The room remained silent, as all eyes were now watching Julio.

Then McBride got up and asked where the restroom was. Pablo motioned towards the hall and followed him, as did Juan. Julio being left alone with his thoughts while the rest answered the urgent call.

" McBride are you always so direct with people?" Pablo asked.

Juan smiled and looked at McBride, and the two began to laugh.

"Yes, Pablo, he is always like this," Juan said, washing his hands.

"I was thinking, Juan, and perhaps you could answer my question; Pablo asked. What became of Renee's sister, Mia? I asked my nephew, and he said that his mother had sent her back to Spain to live with her father's parents. However, Antonio has tried for years to find them in Malaga. His efforts proved fruitless. I was thinking that if the

Americans want to find Renee's family, then Antonio would be the one, as he is her brother, and he is in the military. He could claim her."

"Pablo, that is a brilliant idea," Juan said.

Ryan said nothing, as he stood beside the two men. Juan was right. Pablo's plan was brilliant. Major Antonio Montoya would simply present himself to the United States Embassy in Bogotá and claim his sister. Then Julio would have her killed. As for Rossi, he had to get the word to the general and tell him that Rossi was alive. He would leave out the part about the sex. Why humiliate her?

When they returned to the conference table, they found Julio petting his dog and cooing like a new parent over a beautiful baby. When they had taken their seats, Julio turned his attention away from the dog, looked at Juan, and said, "Juan, the only person who can find out where Renee is being kept is Rossi. I want you to take her off the cocaine, and then she will be returned to her country."

"Don Julio, how shall we control Rossi if she is not on cocaine?" Juan asked.

"Blackmail and intimidation— Plus, we can always reintroduce her to the stuff in America," Julio said, his eyes looking at each man, seeking their approval.

"Don Julio, why not do it simply?" Juan asked.

"Oh, and what is simple, Juan?"

"Pablo, you tell him!" Juan said.

25

※ ※ ※

Steele was feeling like a prisoner jailed in this five-star chicken coop surrounded by women who paraded their charms around the pool relaxing under a cabana, poolside in downtown Oranjestad. Steele watched the women sunning themselves in the hot Arubian sun... He was feeling sorry for himself wondering if Esther was missing him.

General Hatfield had sent him to Aruba where he was to wait for a Combat Application Group (CAG) a Delta Force. When his unit arrived, they were to rent jeeps and go to the backside of the island where they would pop some beers, while Steele showed his crew the aerial and satellite photos of Julio fortress and explain their mission. If possible, they were to take a woman named Dominique, as hostage and return her to the U. S. In addition, they were to extract a Colonel Ryan Ryan Mc Bride, if possible and return him stateside. Hatfield had not said "how" they were to do it. The only information he gave Steele was the address of McBride's office, along with a phone number.

Steele laughed to himself as he thought *I'd simply rent a car, drive into Bogotá, call Colonel McBride's work number and tell him, "This is Captain Steele. Be out in front of your office in five minutes, you're going home."* He shook his head. *It is just crazy and brazen enough to work. Mendoza certainly would not be expecting that.*

Steele reasoned the woman named Dominique must be the missing VIP from the state department who had gotten herself kidnapped by Mendoza. His reasoning was based on the fact the woman only had one name, and Mendoza liked to give his high-priced hookers one name.

Ж Ж Ж

The Barbarian sat in her small private office, secluded at twenty-nine thousand feet. She could feel the soft, smooth vibrations of the Tom Cat's engines through her seat cushion, as she was propelled effortlessly across the blue sky of the Caribbean Sea at five hundred miles per hour.

Lt. Commander Esther Colgate was not thinking about her upcoming mission, because she had been informed by Air-Ops she would not be briefed until she was onboard the carrier. Esther Colgate, the headstrong and defiant only daughter of Frank and Peggy Colgate, who lived just down the road from the famous DuPont's, was thinking about how it was she had joined the navy. It had been to prove to her socialite mother, and herself that she did not need a man to make it in the world.

Now, in the middle of nowhere, she realized she had been wrong she needed Steele. In fact, it was somewhat of a shock to realize she was madly in love with him. He was a tonic to her otherwise routine and drab existence. Steele made her feel complete. As her thoughts drifted, she realized *I love him so much I'd do anything for him. Hell, I'd even kill for him!*

Ж Ж Ж

Seth Hatfield lay in his king-sized bed; his hands neatly tucked under his head, his eyes closed, lost in his own thoughts. He was waiting for his nurse to finish up in the bathroom, as he needed "servicing" and Kati could service him like his wife used to before she died. The nice part of this relationship was that Kati was happily married to a truck driver, and this relationship was just for mutual, sexual satisfaction. In reality, he liked her. She was witty, enjoyed his story telling, and made him laugh. However, at the present moment he wasn't in the mood for storytelling or laughter.

His mind kept going back toDon McGee's phone calls to the Columbian and Spanish Embassies. Don McGee inadvertently sped up the general's timetable and put Renee at risk...

He knew Mendoza would spend millions to have her killed. The question was how would he come after her? Mendoza was too Machiavellian to try to kill her here in the states besides he did not know where she was. That left him two possibilities first would be to try to swap Rossi for Renee. The State Department, meaningDon McGee, might go for that. However, Rossi was already dead. That is, she was dead to the service, as now her loyalties were to Mendoza, of that there was no doubt. Another ploy Mendoza might try would be to use the soft touch. According to the intelligence report from Captain Atkins, Renee's brother was a Major Antonio Montoya in the Columbian army and he worked for his so-called uncle, General Pablo Gonzales, who took money from Mendoza for information.

"Yep, that's the way Mendoza would do it," the general muttered under his breath.

"Seth, do you want the bathroom light on or off?" Kati asked, wearing only her smile.

"Off, honey," he growled impatiently with a teddy bear grin.

26

Ж Ж Ж

Don McGee WAS SITTING BEHIND HIS desk, waiting for Ethel to return with her steno pad and pencil. He had asked her to get them, as he had some dictation to do. Usually his mind was clear, but this morning it was pre-occupied. The reason he had not slept well, as he kept thinking, he had somehow been set up by Captain whatever-his-name was.

Stretching his short arms out, he interlocked his fingers, bending them backwards and causing his knuckles to emit a loud cracking sound just as Ethel walked into his office. "Jesus H. Christ, Don, quit that! That's disgusting!" Ethel was not a politician.

Ignoring her outburst, Don said calmly, as he folded his hands in front of him, "Ethel put down your pad for a minute. I have to tell you something, as I need your insight."

Holding up her finger, Ethel got up from her chair, walked back to the office door and proceeded to close and lock it. She had learned that when Don McGee asked her, "to sit down, as I have something to tell you," it was usually something secret, and he was concerned about something, or someone.

"All right, Don, what is it? You want to tell me?" Ethel asked, crossing her legs and leaning forward, ready to listen and help where she could.

"Ethel, I think I've been duped. Or…if not duped, I have made a terrible blunder and may have actually disrupted General Hatfield's plan by divulging to this Mendoza character that we have in our care the one person who can destroy him. Mendoza will stop at nothing to destroy her. I also feel that the young captain has an ulterior motive, and that is why he called me—to set into motion his agenda—and inadvertently I have helped him. Technically, I know the captain did not go outside his chain-of-command, as he does work for the general, and the State Department does have both operational and financial oversight of Operation Cadence…"

"Stop right there, Don! What you are saying, or at least what I understand, is that, for some reason, you feel this captain may have an ulterior motive towards this girl who we are holding. And that this Mr. Mendoza wants to kill her. Furthermore, that the captain has duped you into asking the Spanish and Columbian Embassies for help in finding her parents or any relatives. Since this girl's father worked for the Spanish Embassy, that makes it a political concern, as well as a diplomatic concern. Do I have it straight so far, Don?"

Don smiled, and nodded his head. "Yes, Ethel, you have it straight."

"Okay, sir, continue," Ethel said, propping her small fist under her chin, obviously intrigued.

"As I was saying, I think this captain has ulterior motives. Either he has fallen in love with her and is genuinely concerned for her well-being, or he wants to give her to Mendoza for lots of money."

Ethel chimed in, answering Don's question before he could ask it. "Don, where is the girl now?"

"I think she's at Camp Hulbert," Don replied.

"Don, I suggest you bring her here. I think the captain should be reassigned elsewhere and a woman be made her handler. I would also notify General Hatfield of your suspicions. Furthermore, don't forget to tell him you're sorry. Now, let's get to the dictation," Ethel said, opening her steno pad and pulling down her glasses. She was ready.

Ж Ж Ж

"Major Montoya reporting as ordered sir."

General Gonzales looked up from his desk. What he saw was a young officer standing at attention, waiting for his salute to be returned. Returning the major's salute, General Gonzales watched, as he snapped into the "at ease" position with his feet set at shoulder width and his hands folded behind his back. The young major looked good in his uniform; he could be a recruiting poster.

"Major, I have good news for you," the general said as he stood up and walked around to stand closer to his nephew.

"Yes, sir, what is the news?"

"Antonio, your sister, Angelica, is alive and is being treated well. She is recovering from her illnesses. Evidently, the Americans found her living in the jungle. For now, they have her in the United States. You are to report to the Spanish Embassy with proof that she is your sister.

Furthermore, notify your father, please. Since your sister is a Spanish citizen, she will be returned to Spain. However, if she wants to come here and live with you, I'm sure arrangements can be made." Pablo went into a fatherly mode, letting tears well up in his eyes. Sympathetically, he patted his nephew on the back, watching the tears stream down his cheeks.

ЖЖЖ

"Hello, General Hatfield, this is Don McGee. I know we agreed never to talk again, but this is urgent, and I must tell you a couple of things."

"Yes, sir, please do!" General Hatfield said. Even his fatigue could not hide his disdain for the blunderDon McGee had made.

"First of all, general, Don Julio Mendoza has started to make his move just, as you predicted. Furthermore, a Columbian army major is claiming to be Renee's, or should I say Angelica's, brother. He is using the Spanish Embassies in Bogotá to put pressure on us to return his sister. We have received a communiqué from our embassy in Madrid. It seems this Major's dad is still alive and is asking questions."

So it begins, Seth thought. *PerhapsDon McGee's faux pas was not a blunder, but an unintended good fortune. MaybeDon McGee's information request had caught Mendoza flat-footed and unprepared for the news that Renee was still alive.*

"Excuse me, general, are you there?"Don McGee asked.

"Yes, sir, I'm here. I was just lost in deep thought. What else do you have?" the general asked, sitting up in his chair and reaching for a pad and pencil.

"Sir, I first wanted to apologize for the information request regarding the girl. I was merely reacting to Captain Atkins' request to find the girl's parents, which we have done! Her father is alive and lives in

Madrid and, as you already know, her brother lives in Columbia. I have a sick feeling—call it a hunch—Captain Atkins has an ulterior motive regarding to Angelica. Personally, I think he wants to extort money from Mendoza by telling him where she is."

"So you are asking me to do what, exactly?" the general asked, his anger starting to simmer slowly to the surface.

"I want to move her to Camp Aspen in Maryland, not far from Camp David. Furthermore, I want to change her handler to a woman. You can reassign Captain Atkins to wherever you decide."

"Sir are you ordering me to move Renee to Maryland"

"Yes, general, I am,"Don McGee responded in such a way that the general knew he was treading on thin ice.

"Then it will be done!" Hatfield replied.

NowDon McGee, what exactly is Mendoza doing?" the general asked softly.

"As to what"Don McGee asked, puzzled by the general's question...

"You said that Mendoza was starting to make his move, as I had predicted. Exactly, what move is Mendoza making?" the general asked, shaking his head in wonderment atDon McGee's sudden memory loss.

"He's making his move in response to what you have done. You hit Mendoza's European operation very hard when you had Colonel McBride, with the help of the Italian police, seize a record forty-five tons of cocaine, with a net worth of two hundred and twenty-five million euro's. That equates to about three hundred million dollars! I am told you helped the Belgians confiscate one hundred and ten kilos in Antwerp, with an estimated value of five million euro's. Somehow, they managed to arrest almost all of Mendoza's major distributors in Belgium. I do not know how you are doing it but keep doing it.

"Also, here is a juicy tidbit of info: The Italians, French and Spanish have frozen most, if not all, of Mendoza's European bank accounts, thanks in a large part to Angelica. So now Mendoza is trying to recoup his operating losses by robbing banks and kidnapping prominent citizens around the world and extorting vast sums of money to be used for operating capital,"Don McGee concluded.

"Thank you sir, I hope you tell your boss about this. We need to hear a few Atta Boy's it's appreciated, and sir please tell Lamb that she is doing a great job."

Hatfield hung up the phone, his thoughts turning immediately to McBride, and Steele. He needed to talk with McBride. However, that was out of the question, as McBride was in enough danger. He decided to use the newspaper again an implant a code telling him about Steele and to be ready to evacuate. Then, he had to tell Steele to get his CAG unit in place.

27

The reason for Julio's tirade was the upsetting news in regard to his loss of a three hundred million dollar cocaine shipment to the Italians. It seemed the Italian police had found the cocaine, which McBride had hidden in the argon gas cylinders.

What no one could figure out was how the Italians had found the cylinders with the cocaine inside of them? Out of the fifty thousand cylinders aboard that particular freighter, the Italian police and Italian customs agents managed to find every single cylinder containing the cocaine. Particularly, since all the cylinders looked the same and were scattered throughout the ship, yet the police found all of them.

Though that bust had hurt the cartel badly, what Mendoza could not afford to lose were the politicians, judges and police that were on his payroll. Now, the Italian police were arresting all his political and legal allies throughout Italy.

Ж Ж Ж

Silently, Ryan sat and secretly wishing Mendoza, in his anger, would go for his stick. That is all the provocation he would need and Mendoza would be dead before he hit the floor. After that, Carlos would probably slap him on the back and tell him, "Good job," while Pablo would just shit in his pants.

" McBride, what do you think went wrong with the shipment? How did the Italians know how to find our stuff?" Mendoza asked.

"Obviously, we were betrayed!" Ryan replied.

"By who McBride" Carlos asked, venom oozing in his voice.

"Well, I'm not sure, but maybe some Italian is trying to save his neck," Ryan answered, looking directly into Mendoza's eyes and trying to read this crazy son-of-a-bitch's face; looking forward to seeing if there was something he could exploit to make Mendoza more paranoid than he already was.

"Tell me, McBride, why would the traitor have to be someone in Italy, why not you McBride?" Mendoza asked, his voice calm, his eyes studying McBride, looking for the slightest twitch.

"Because, you fat fuck, I lost millions. You are not paid; I am not paid! Ryan said pointing his finger at Julio then himself. That's why, ass hole!"

Carlos burst out laughing. " McBride, you're too much," Carlos said, laughing so hard his face had turned red.

Though Pablo chuckled, his eyes watched his boss. His boss was not laughing.

Ryan 's face was red, but not from laughing. He was angry with Mendoza for the alleged insult. However, he secretly knew he was the one directly responsible for the largest drug bust in history. What Julio said about the cylinders was true; they looked the same. That is, they were all colored green nevertheless; the valve covers on the cylinders containing the cocaine were different. Ryan had the workers wash the cylinders containing the cocaine with warm soapy water, then give them a warm-water rinse, which contained fluorescent metal particles that glowed a bright yellow when placed under a black light, making the cylinders easy to find.

The only other person who knew about the fluorescent particles and using the black light to find the cocaine was Mendoza's most trusted broker and close friend Alberto Monticello, who lived in the port city of Genoa.

When Julio had first heard the news about the drugs being confiscated he had tried to call his friend Alberto. He made repeated calls, but no reply. Eventually, discrete inquires provided the information that Alberto had sat in his big black Mercedes watching the police unload the cocaine-filled cylinders from the freighter. After that, Alberto simply vanished.

Ж Ж Ж

Even though the air conditioner was on full blast, Alberto could feel his sweat, as it ran down his face. Alberto had been betrayed, but by who, he did not know. When he had seen enough, while sitting in his Mercedes, he flicked his cigarette out the window and drove off. He knew what this drug bust was going to cost him and it was not money. He also knew his life was now numbered in days, if not in hours

Ж Ж Ж

28

ЖЖЖ

Steele had his CAG unit in place despite the unexpected set-backs of a shallow river mosquitoes and carnivorous black flies that left bloody welts. The entire trip could be summed up with three words "a learning experience." Steele and his First Sergeant, Dana Edwards, reviewed the aerial photos and terrain map, to determine how best to enter Columbia undetected. Steele opted to go by chopper rather than a boat. He would have the chopper put them down early in the morning twenty miles upriver from the intended target zone. Using the cover of darkness, they would transfer the gear into the three zodiacs.

For a few moments, Steele ruminated about the fact he was now standing in the exact spot from which he had left six months earlier. He stood apart from his men, taking comfort in knowing that each man with him was a specialist and like himself, each man was deadly. *Mendoza laid his egg in hell, and now it is about to hatch.* Translation: Mendoza was in deep shit, but he did not know it yet.

Steele's thoughts shifted back to General Hatfield's briefing. It was short and very exact. He had said, "You will disrupt Mendoza's ability to produce his cocaine. You will kill his men and dispose of the bodies in such a manner that they will not be found. Make it look, as if his men are deserting him" the general did not go into detail. Wisely, he left the details to the professionals.

ЖЖЖ

The sudden jolt of the airplane touching down and the loud, horrific sound of the turbo-props being thrown into reverse caused Angelica's body to be thrown forward, awakening her from her sleep.

Before taking off, Angelica had overheard a conversation. The man with the stripes on his arm had ask the other man, "How long to Andrews?"

"About three hours depending on weather," the man with the pretty face replied.

Angelica was handed two blankets and told to lie down on the long, hard, canvas-covered bench seat the canvas smelt of old sweat and dirt. However, she was too tired to complain and it was still very early in the morning.

Angelica did not understand why she was being moved. Nor did she understand why Captain Mike Atkins left her so suddenly. Additionally, she did not understand why two, big, scary-looking; black men had entered her room, thrown her clothes at her, and told her, "Hurry and get dressed!" After that, she had been driven to an airplane and now she was here at a place called Andrews.

As she struggled to get up, Angelica became intensely aware she had to pee and urgently! Looking around the plane, she did not see any little bathroom in which a woman could pee. *How uncivilized these Americans are to build airplanes with no toilets; she* thought.

Just then, the man who had earlier handed her the blankets walked by and smiled down at her; however, she did not feel like smiling back. She watched, as he continued to the rear of the plane. Then the man with the stripes turned a little red knob and suddenly the back of the airplane began opening, causing a sudden rush of cold air to envelop her causing the urgency to pee to become more acute.

The taxiing airplane made a sudden, hard turn so that the rear of the plane was now facing into the wind, making the cargo area like a wind tunnel. The wind whipped around her body chilling her. Pulling the blanket, she wrapped it tightly around her body, shielding herself from the cold night air. Feeling it around her feet, she managed to find her shoes and slipped into them.

She saw movement at the rear of the plane and heard a woman's voice. Suddenly, out of the darkness, a beautiful woman walked up the tailgate and looked directly at her. The woman was tall, her hair dark and her eyes were deep, blue-green.

Greeting her in French, the beautiful woman informed Angelica that her name was Sarah. Taking Angelica's hand, they deplaned. Sarah wrapped her arms around Angelica to help shield her from the cold November wind. Sara raised her arm motioning to someone in the darkness. Quietly and slowly, a big black car approached and pulled up alongside them. Opening the back door, Sarah let Angelica in first. She grabbed Angelica's blanket, as she got in tossing it to the man who had given it to her.

"Sarah, where are you taking me" Angelica asked, her teeth chattering from the cold.

"I'm taking you to a very beautiful and secluded military reservation not far from Camp David," Sarah replied.

"Sarah, can we stop before we go too far? I must pee."

Sarah chuckled. "Yes, Angelica, we will both pee."

ЖЖЖ

Sarah Henderson was not a typical handler. She was a intelligence operative for the NSA. In this instance, the State Department specifically requested her for this job. For ten years, she worked for the CIA, as a field operative. Then she had gone to work for the National Security Agency where her assignments had been varied. However, each assignment seemed to build upon the one before, widening her scope of experience and making her an invaluable resource for the National Security Agency. She had the particular gift of putting a person at ease and extracting information from them that they did not even know he possessed.

Sarah was a cross between Mata-Hari as she was sophisticated, articulate, could speak four languages fluently with comprehension of three more, and Sheena, Queen of the Jungle. She was graduated from Brown University with a degree in music. Due to family influence—mainly her mother—she learned to play the piano, violin and guitar. However, her true love was her dad. He is the one who had taught her how to survive in the wilds and had paid for her karate classes. When he had announced that Sarah was going to take karate, her mother had been horrified and asked, "What will the neighbors think?"

They'd probably say, "There goes Sarah Henderson, that kick-ass beauty," her dad had replied.

When Sarah could find no meaningful employment as a musician, she worked, for the Veterans Administration, which she quickly learned to hate. Then she decided to apply for a position with the CIA. Perhaps due to luck, or because she was considered beautiful by the higher-ups, she was assigned to field operations. That was where Sarah was trained and groomed for fieldwork. After that, the CIA sent her to George Washington University where she received her Master's in languages.

Once she had her degree, she was sent to Prague, where the young and beautiful Sarah was to learn the difference between education and schooling. Through bribes and threats, she got a seat as the second violin for the Hungarian National Symphony. Because of her beauty, Sarah became an instant hit with the affluent and powerful. Soon, she began dating the political elite, along with the wealthy and famous people of Prague's upper society, not caring if they were married or single. She shared her body with anyone—male or female—who could provide her with the information, she either wanted or needed. At the time, Prague was a hotbed of intrigue and indulgence. Monogamy in the upper class of polite society was just a word found in the dictionary.

After growing tired of Prague, she moved on to Belgium, Berlin and Rome. When alcohol, depression and stress had finally taken their toll on her, she asked to come home.

Her new and latest assignment was to be a high-priced babysitter to this beautiful woman who was helping to destroy the largest illicit drug cartel in history. Don McGee, himself, told her during their meeting: "Angelica's life is in constant danger, and so you need to be constantly on guard for and expect assassination attempts on her life. Furthermore, you may take any precautions you feel are justified. But…under no circumstance is Angelica to be with Captain Mike Atkins! I repeat—no contact!"

Naturally, she asked, "Why?"

Mr. McGee only said, "He isn't trustworthy."

Ж Ж Ж

It would be an understatement to say that Captain Mike Atkins was furious when he returned to Camp Hurlbert and discovered Angelica had been moved. For the past three days, he was in high-level briefings at McDill Base. On the last day of their meetings, and in front of the entire staff, General Hatfield threw him a surprise by announcing that he was being reassigned. As the general put it, "Your charge is no longer your responsibility. She has been turned over to the State Department for safekeeping. Your new assignment will be to track drug shipments and document their drop-off locations in Mexico, Texas and Arizona. You will brief both Customs and the DEA weekly."

Now, as Atkins lay in his bunk, his right forearm covering his eyes, he watched strange wiggly shapes slide across his eyeballs. He was consumed with the need to find Angelica, as he had plans for her. Without her, he couldn't become rich. With the money, he could make from selling her; he could have a hundred whores like her.

I have to find her; that is all there is to it! He told himself. As he lay in his bunk, Atkins realized that Angelica had left the same way she had arrived by airplane. Hurlbert had an airstrip, he would check with air-ops in the morning. The *general told me Angelica had already been turned over to the State Department that meant*

Mr. Don McGee must have smelt something. I must have tipped my hand to Don McGee. Mr. Don McGee told Hatfield something concerning me. The general released Angelica back to Don McGee and had me transferred to another job. Simple, he thought, *and the young captain supposedly would be none wiser of the political intrigue...*

The morning was humid, as Mike Atkins jogged from the Bachelor Officers' Quarter's (BOQ) towards Base Operations. The morning heat and humidity reminded him of his youth back in Kansas. His family was poor. Even though both his parents had worked two jobs, there was barely enough. Rather than ride the school bus, he walked the six miles to school, because poverty hurt and being teased and humiliated about his homemade and hand-me-down clothes hurt even worse. Little did Mike Atkins realize that the twelve-mile daily jogs were preparing him for sports?

Staff Sergeant Taylor looked up from her desk. Standing on the other side of the counter was a tall man who was dripping wet with sweat. Though she did not know either him or his rank, she figured he must be an officer, as an enlisted man would have no need to be at base operations, unless he worked there.

"Can I help you, sir?" Taylor asked.

"Yes, Sergeant Taylor, you may. I want to know the last night when a plane departed here for Washington D.C., or Quantico Virginia."

"Just a minute and I will check the log. That would have been Wednesday morning" the sergeant uttered to herself as she got up from her desk and pulled out the manifest log. "Yes sir. We had a C-130 depart at 01:30 a.m. for Andrews."

"Thank you, Sergeant Taylor. You have helped me tremendously."

"You're welcome, sir!" Taylor replied, placing the log back into it is proper place.

Mike walked out of base ops, put on his sunglasses and began jogging back to the BOQ. With each stride, Captain Mike Atkins worked on formulating his plans. His first plan was to get rich. The next plan was to get even withDon McGee and the general for playing him as stupid.

29

Ж Ж Ж

ARRIVING ABOARD THE ABE, ESTHER WAS greeted by a gusty, "Hello, Colgate, what brings you back to the ABE?" "Well, skipper, I'm not exactly sure yet. I was told by air-ops back at Ryan s that I would be briefed aboard the ABE and until then I was to enjoy my vacation cruise," Esther replied.

"I see you still have your cribbage board," Skipper Nyblade observed, putting his coffee mug down and taking a seat. "Same as before, Ten cents a point," she asked. Dealing the cards.

"Okay with me commander."

The cribbage games between the Skipper of the ABE and Colgate were famous. She would whip him soundly and he would get pissed off and threaten her. In turn, she would laugh, making him all the madder and then he would stand, look at his watch and say, "I'm late for a meeting," and leave.

Everyone knew it was the skipper's way of saying, "I surrender."

Esther's days were filled with playing cribbage, reading novels, and exercising. Her nights were filled with longing. As she lay in her bunk, hands resting on her chest, she wondered what Steele was doing. In her heart, she wondered if he felt the same about her as she did about him. Did he miss her just a little or was he longing for his jungle girl? Being a smart woman, she also felt her being on board the ABE was somehow tied into what Steele was doing. She felt that the special training she had received at China Lake on how to deliver the laser-guided Bunker Buster bomb would somehow connect her to Steele's mission. In the meantime, she killed time by continuing to play cribbage, read, exercise and wait for her orders.

⚖ ⚖ ⚖

Steele called his men to huddle up. As they took a knee in front of him, he pulled out the aerial photos and placed them on the ground so each man could examine them. When the men had finished looking at the photos, he began explaining what each photo was and what "Operation Interdiction" was all about. Plain and simple, Operation Interdiction was nothing more than the assassination of a select few individuals who were threatening the U. S. and her allies. Down and dirty, it was wholesale murder.

In precise detail, Steel told the men how he wanted to proceed, using terror tactics, in much the same way Mendoza had done with the village people. In addition he told the men to steal Mendoza's trucks, thus stopping all shipments going in and out of Mendoza's compound. In addition, he intended to jam Mendoza's cell phone and his computer, making it impossible for him to communicate with his business associates. This would force his staff to come to him at the hacienda.

⚖ ⚖ ⚖

General Seth Hatfield sat at the same table, in the very same restaurant, where he had met his now favorite Colonel named McBride and Carlos four months earlier. Once again, he was posing as a coffee buyer. However, unlike the first time, he was now more knowledgeable of the dangers involved. Glancing at the old clock hanging on the wall, he idly noticed its second hand kept perfect time with each click of the pendulum. He ordered two beers—one for himself and the other for Ryan ... If Ryan did not show up, he would drink that one, too.

Stalling for time, the general pulled a panatela from his shirt pocket and unwrapped it. Casually, he looked around for an ashtray and spotted one at another table. Just as he stood up from his chair to retrieve the used ashtray, he noticed his waiter bringing him a clean one. He smiled and nodded his head, the universal "thank you" sign. The waiter smiled and returned the head nod.

After the general took a sip of his beer, he held his cigar between his thumb and index finger, rolling it back and forth, choosing not to light it. Sitting there, he was lost in thought, trying to figure out the exact moment when he would authorize Operation Interdiction—the wholesale murder of Julio Mendoza and his entire staff. Though he had decided to kill Mendoza, in part to make an example of him to others, the real reason was that Mendoza deserved to be killed. On the scale of life, Don Julio Mendoza ranked lower than whale shit, and that was at the bottom of the ocean. Seth looked again at the wall clock, deciding to give Ryan fifteen more minutes. With that crazy son-of-a-bitch you had to flexible, as there was no telling with what he might be involved?

Ж Ж Ж

As McBride pulled up in front of the hotel, he glanced in and saw the general sitting at the same table, as the last time he was here. *How long ago was that four, maybe five months ago? Boy, have a lot of things happened since then!* Ryan thought.

Ryan got out of Mercedes S-530, walked around, and opened the passenger door of the extending his hand and helping his female companion to her feet. He watched as she carefully adjusted her dress. Dominique was definitely a looker and her dress did little to cover her charms. McBride took her arm, acting every bit the gentleman and led her into the hotel restaurant.

Hearing a commotion coming from his immediate left, Seth slowly turned his head and saw the woman who was creating the excitement. It seemed that the room suddenly became still and the men's eyes followed her as she passed by them. You could hear her high heels as they tapped against the tile floor in rhythm to her swaying hips. Although she was wearing dark sunglasses, Seth somehow knew she was looking at him.

As she approached the table, Seth stood and acknowledged her with a smile. The beautiful and mysterious woman returned his smile. It was only then that he saw McBride. Because the woman's beauty had so captivated him, she had momentarily blocked out everything and everyone.

"Hmmm" the sound came from McBride.

Seth smiled at his favorite colonel's woman, and shook his head at Ryan's good fortune.

"Hello, Ryan, I'm so glad to see you again," the general began.

"Nice to see you again, Seth. I take it you want to buy more coffee?" Ryan asked as he shook the general's hand.

"Sure do!" Seth said, pulling out a chair for the lady. "Please take a seat, and here's a beer for you. I did not know we were going to have company, Ryan . Is this your wife?" the general asked, looking at the beauty sitting across from him.

Ryan began to laugh then said, "No, Seth, this is my girlfriend, Dominique."

"Hello, Dominique," Seth said, shaking her hand and looking more closely into her eyes. Then he understood why she had been wearing the sunglasses: Her pupils were dilated. Ryan had subtly given him the warning upon the introduction—only a first name. In other words, she was working for Mendoza.

"So, Ryan , obviously you're doing well," Seth said, looking at Dominique and smiling.

"I cannot complain. Americans love their coffee and their sugar, which is very good for me," Ryan said, smiling and taking a sip of his beer.

The general was just about to speak when a man walked up behind Dominique and placed a glass of red wine in front of her. Since the wine had not yet been ordered, it was obviously given gratis by the owner to the woman who graced his establishment with her beauty. Dominique smiled, stood and kissed the owner on both cheeks. He was blushing, as he walked away from the table.

Looking at Ryan , Seth smiled and asked, "Does she have this affect on all men?"

Ryan leaned forward, forcing Seth to turn his ear as he whispered, "She does and also on women. You know her as Rossi!"

In shock, Seth leaned back in his chair, looking at Ryan while the color drained from his face as he became ashen. Though he wanted to speak, he was afraid to, as his voice would obviously betray his emotions.

Smiling at Seth, Ryan calmly leaned back in his chair and interlocked his fingers across his stomach. A bemused look had formed on his face, as if asking his general, "What the fuck do we do now?"

30

※ ※ ※

MAJOR ANTONIO MONTOYA HAD BEEN PATIENT. In fact, he had been more than patient with the Americans. According to his Uncle Ernesto Gonzales, who was the Council General of Columbia, the Americans had admitted they had Angelica. They had even sent a photograph of her along with a copy of her complete medical report.

As Ernesto read the file, he noticed that Angelica's medical exam had been performed at the famous Walter Reed Hospital. He knew that was in Washington DC.

"Antonio, I have read your sister's medical report. Of course, this could be nothing more than a fabrication by the Americans, but I think it is true. Evidently, your sister is very sick. We must be patient. I will ask the Columbian Ambassador to arrange a trip and give you diplomatic status so that you can fly to Washington DC, spend time with Angelica and get to know her again."

"Thank you, uncle. That will be nice. Maybe the Americans can find my other sister, Mia?" the young Major asked, standing and offering his hand to his uncle.

Ernesto watched as his nephew left his office. He was happy he had been able to help Antonio, who had suffered so much in his life. There had been the loss of his sisters, the murder of his mother, the loss of his grandmother to an accidental overdose of barbiturates and finally, his father's mental collapse. *If Antonio only knew the truth*, he thought. Then picking up his desk phone, Ernesto dialed the Columbian Embassy. The Ambassador did not know it, but he was going to be instrumental in the death of a puta.

Ж Ж Ж

While dressed in his royal purple pajamas, Julio was taking his morning coffee as he puffed on his cigar, sending the pungent blue smoke upwards into the ceiling fan. At the same time, he was reading his financial section of the newspaper and did not like what saw. Looking at the increases in demand of his product, he knew he could not deliver his goods until whomever was selling him out was killed. There was little doubt in his mind that someone was betraying him. Already he knew about Angelica. Her sister, Antigua, knew nothing, as she had never traveled out of the country.

Julio's survival instincts told him it had to be McBride. He continued, lost in thought: *But Juan and Miguel had checked him out. Even the puta, Rossi, could not find anything on him. Moreover, he stood up to me at the meeting, daring me to use my stick!* Juan had told him about

McBride's skill with his hands. Though he might act crazy, he was not that crazy. He continued with his cogitation: *And McBride had been correct when he had said he wasn't paid unless I got paid. Could it be Juan Carlos, maybe? Not likely, as he has no head for business. Perhaps Pablo is taking bribes from the Americans; buying his loyalty. Pablo certainly knows the organization well enough. However, how would Pablo know the shipping and delivery schedules when I didn't even know them and neither did Carlos? Somehow, it all comes back to McBride!*

The ring of his cell phone interrupted Julio's obsessive thoughts of betrayal. A quick glance at the caller ID window showed that Carlos was calling him.

"Good morning, Juan, what can I do for you this morning?" Julio asked, clenching his teeth hard on his cigar and trying to curb his anger.

"Morning, Julio. I have some good news and some bad news. So what do you want to hear first?" Carlos asked, slowing stroking the head of Antigua as she serviced his manhood in the backseat of the Mercedes.

"Ah, well, Carlos, this morning is a bad news morning so tell me the bad news first!" Julio replied, taking the cigar out of his mouth and taking a sip of coffee.

"Julio, the Federal Police in Mexico City have seized two hundred and six million dollars of our money. Plus, they have arrested most of our key people in Mexico, including the politicians and even the wife and son of the vice president. The police also seized our weapons and even most of our trucks. Julio they have hurt us and badly."

Mendoza did not respond to Carlos' bad news. He calmly asked his trusted friend, "What is the good news, Carlos?"

"We have found Renee!" Juan hissed between clenched teeth as he climaxed into Antigua's hand.

Julio jumped to his feet and literally shouted with glee into the phone. "Where is she, Juan? Tell me, please!"

"She's in Washington DC, Julio, and Ernesto has asked the Columbian Ambassador to give Major Montoya diplomatic status to go visit his sister. I was thinking of sending Jesus along with the major in order to kill her."

"No, Carlos, not Jesus," Julio replied softly.

"Then who, Julio? Not Miguel or me and certainly not you," Carlos said.

"I'll tell you who. The major, that's who," Julio said.

"The Major?" Carlos asked, shocked at the mere suggestion of a brother killing his sister.

"Yes, Carlos, and this is the way we will do it. Major Montoya will have a beautiful box of chocolates and a bottle of white wine laced with a slow acting poison. Renee will be killed by the very man who loves her the most and in the process, he will also die. The beauty of it is that Renee will die in the custody of the Americans. When we begin publishing the story in our newspaper, the whole country will turn against the Americans!"

Laughing, Carlos said, "Truly, you are amazing, my friend! That is true greatness."

Carlos hung up on his boss and proceeded to put his pathetic little pecker back in his pants.

ж ж ж

Sergeant Edwards sat perfectly still, his binoculars grasped firmly in his hands. He intently was watching the hacienda. Since

Sergeant Deal had informed him the GPS transmitter was operational, he knew HQ was aware they were now on location and functioning. Also, Deal had informed him the electronic jamming device, which was about the size of a standard briefcase, was operational but not in use. The major problem with the damn thing, according to Deal, was that two, nickel cadmium batteries operated it and he had no way of recharging the batteries. However, Deal had said he was going to, "...try something revolutionary." *Whatever that means,* Edwards thought.

The other CAG members were slowly taking up their positions. Two snipers were climbing the backside of the mountain, intending to traverse around the mountain and, if possible, create two killing zones.

Four others had taken the explosives and blasting caps down by the river to the bridge. They were rigging the bridge for demolition. After that, they were to proceed up the road and place themselves in any positions they deemed satisfactory to surprise and kill Mendoza's security forces and his drivers. The trucks were not to be destroyed, but hidden along with the bodies. In that way, if needed, the trucks could be used be to help in their escape.

At present, Captain Steele was off post. He had called Edwards over and informed him he was "...going to visit some friends." Now, being a first sergeant often meant being flexible, especially when it came to officers. He knew Captain Steele only by reputation and about his last patrol. But to visit friends in the middle of the fucking jungle was a bit much, especially when the good captain had stripped down to his skivvies. He had watched his captain strap his knife to his leg, just above his boot, sling two ammo belts over his shoulder, counted his stars. He picked up his rifle and nonchalantly began walking back down the mountain. Turning, he had informed Edwards: I'll be back tomorrow night. In the meantime, Edwards, stay alert and watch Sergeant Deal be inventive and imaginative.

"*Fuck you, Captain Steele!*" Edwards thought, peering into his binoculars and counting the guards.

31

Ж Ж Ж

TO SAY DON MCGEE WAS UNHAPPY was an understatement. Sitting at his desk, he was reading letters from the Spanish and Columbian Ambassadors, plus a message from Eddie Johnson, the American Ambassador in Columbia. *I see a showdown looming on the horizon and it could get tense. In fact, it could get downright ugly,* he thought.

In the first letter, the Columbian Ambassador stated he was sending the brother of Angelica Montoya to visit his long-lost sister. The next letter, from the Spanish Ambassador, basically backed up the first by requesting that Angelica's brother be allowed to visit his sister. Eddie's message read like a telegram of old—terse, but an extremely accurate summation of his situation "Being pressured by the Spaniards and Columbians. Not sure, but suspect Mendoza's influence. Strongly suspect treachery. Be on guard."

Putnam knew from experience that the word "treachery," used in diplomatic correspondence, was synonymous with deceit and closely aligned with betrayal. He sat there pondering the situation from different angles: *Was Angelica's brother being sent to kill his sister? Or, was Angelica's brother merely the Judas goat sent to pacify his sister, reassure her and then lead her to the slaughter?* Don suspected Mendoza was not above killing them both in order to gain her silence.

Ж Ж Ж

"Come in, major, please come in. We have been waiting on you," the tall, silver-haired man said, motioning with his hand and standing back to allow Antonio Montoya to enter the office. Standing beside the distinguished gentleman was his Uncle Pablo, dressed in a business suit, which Antonio thought was not only peculiar but totally out of the ordinary.

"Antonio, please let me introduce the Columbian Ambassador, his Excellency Señor Hugo Blanco," Pablo said, sweeping his hand in one continuous motion towards the Ambassador.

Snapping to attention, Antonio bowed his head in respect as he said, "Sir, Antonio Montoya at your service, your Excellency!"

The Ambassador extended his hand to the young major and grasped his arm. "Very nice to meet you, Antonio. Your uncle has told me a great deal about you and all good and that is high praise coming from the general."

"Thank you, Excellency," Antonio replied, smiling at his uncle with great pride.

"I hope you don't mind too much, major, but I have taken the liberty of issuing you a diplomatic passport. You are to be my military attaché and courier. Your uncle has given me a bottle of white wine and a box of chocolates for your sister, also some pastries. These will be put into a diplomatic pouch and you will deliver them, unopened, to your sister, where you both will enjoy the hospitality of your uncle and the Columbian people.

"Thank you, your Excellency. Thank you, uncle," the major said, bowing to them.

Ж Ж Ж

General Seth Hatfield was slowly recovering from his shock at McBride's news. For some minutes, he sat silently, lost in his own thoughts. Then his train of thought was interrupted by the soft and delicate touch of a woman caressing his face as she said in his ear, "Seth, perhaps it would be better if I went shopping so you and Ryan can talk business. I'll be back soon."

With those words, Rossi/Dominique turned and walked from the restaurant. Once again the restaurant became silent as the men stopped to watch her pass; smiling at her, trying to gain her attention either by relying on their good looks or by offering to buy her a drink. But Dominique could not be bothered as she had something more urgent to do.

Seth's smile turned to a burning glare as he turned his attention to his colonel, who was watching Dominique, unaware of the general's anger. "Are you fucking that, Ryan?" Seth asked through gritted teeth, his anger starting to break through his professional facade.

"Yes, sir, I am!" Ryan replied, still watching her walk away.

"Tell me, sir, when you started fucking her, did you know who she was?" Seth asked, taking a slow drag on his panatela then sending blue smoke into the air to mix with the smell of fried fish.

"No,sir. Although I did suspect it at first, I then dismissed the idea because she did not match the given description. It was not until the other day, when I had complained about her being a bitch and asked Carlos to take her back that Carlos told me who she really was. When he complained that her twat was the size of the Grand Canyon and he felt nothing, I just told him his pecker was too small. That's why she was given to me.

"However, she *is* spying on me and reporting every week to Carlos and Mendoza when she goes to get her weekly supply of cocaine. General, though I am not positive, I suspect they have her on some other type of drug as well as the cocaine; something that has blocked out her memories of the past."

Upon hearing Ryan's last comment, Seth's anger began to dissipate. Now he understood how and why Ryan had come to "possess" Rossi. His concern now was as to how he could extract them from Columbia without getting them both killed.

Taking a sip of his beer, the general casually asked, "Tell me, Ryan, did Rossi scream and howl when you stuck it in her?"

Ryan took a sip of his beer then reached for the cigar that was residing in his pocket before he replied with a chuckle and smile, "No, sir, she moaned and purred like a kitten."

"That's good to hear, Ryan. At least she's not a complainer," Seth mused, knocking the ash off his cigar. Then he straightened in his chair, looked Ryan in the eyes and said, "Ryan, we must talk."

"Yes, sir, I have a lot to tell you." Ryan said lighting his Cuban.

Ж Ж Ж

Staff Sergeant Ernest T. Williams, aka The Black Knight, whispered into his microphone, informing Deal that he was in position. A quick "copy that" came the reply.

"Ed, the Black Knight is in position," Deal announced, looking through his binoculars and trying to find his buddy Ernest T, knowing he would probably be unable to see him.

"Deal, has Hawk reported?"

"Not yet!" Deal replied, sweeping the left side of the mountain with his field glasses for Staff Sergeant Henry Hawkins.

"I have counted only nine security guards walking the perimeter," Ed whispered back. "So far, I have seen only four people go into the cave. I have a stinking hunch the guards work in shifts. As far as the guys in the cave, I have no idea. When Hawk gets in position, ask him to verify my count and see how many guys walk the perimeter at midnight. We might just decide to pay them a visit, Deal. Are you up to it?"

Deal looked at his First Sergeant and grinned. "I could do with a walk in the park." So saying, he unrolled his ghillie sack then slipped off his boots and belts.

Pulling his Browning out of its holster he placed it close to him. As he rested on his knees, he looked at the western sky and watched as the fingers of twilight surrendered themselves to the setting sun, then he prayed.

Ж Ж Ж

Steele let the river's current carry him along, only paddling the Zodiac to correct its course. One thing he noticed right away was that the sounds of the jungle were completely different at night. Even though it was totally dark, he could make out the various shapes of animals as they drank at the water's edge. He heard the cry of something, and then a splash as a crocodile claimed its dinner. What Zack was looking for, in the early morning hours on an unnamed river, was a specific clump of bushes along the river's edge. The spot where six months before he had pulled his canoe out of the water to rest and then had come to the aid of a child and an old woman who were being raped. The attackers would not attack anymore, he had seen to that, and in the process, he had been made a war chief named El Jaguar. It was imperative he find the exact spot; as from there, he could find his way to the village. He had remembered to bring his "trumpet," figuring if he got close he could just blow on it and maybe his friends would answer him.

Also in the Zodiac were two metal suitcases filled with gifts for his friends. He had brought three boxes of cigars and long-necked matches with which to light them. Renee had told him it hadn't been the *Chiza* that had made him drunk but the peyote, on that night six months ago. There were also some meat cleavers and candy, along with his favorite bubble gum in the suitcases, along with a half dozen small fishing nets for his small, multi-colored friends, to aid them in catching food.

His plan was simple, yet deplorable! He was going to ask his drinking buddies for help in destroying their mutual enemy. What he wanted to ask of their chief was to terrorize Mendoza's security forces and help dispose of the bodies. Steele figured that since they were cannibalistic, there shouldn't be a problem. After showing the men how to use the meat cleavers, he assumed their natural abilities for dissecting and eviscerating the human body would take it from there.

Normally Steele would have had his men just dump the bodies into the river and let the crocodiles and piranha have their fill; he might still do that in some instances. However, the thought of being killed and eaten by cannibals had to be a psychological distraction to Mendoza's bullyboys as was also knowing that the "tree warriors," as Renee had once called them, were very efficient, silent and deadly killers.

However, none of his plan could be implemented if he couldn't find the spot for which he was looking.

32

⚭ ⚭ ⚭

THE HAWKEYE CAME TO A SCREECHING halt as the airplane's tail hook caught the arresting cable, causing Shirley Lamb to leak a shot of pee into her panties. She had not been prepared for the jolt even though she was strapped in and was wearing her helmet. Even though the crewman had told her what to expect, still, going from 120 mph to zero in one second could definitely cause one to pee. She had never seen an aircraft carrier before and now she was walking the fight deck of the ABE. Hell, Lamb had never seen a Hawkeye before, until she boarded at NSA, Corpus Christi. It was all so exciting, but the hard part was she couldn't tell anyone about it.

Don McGee, had briefed her the day before she left. She was to drive to Andrews AFB and report to base operations. There she was to board a small two-engine jet airplane, which would fly her to NSA, Corpus Christi. Another plane would then take her to her final destination. Don McGee hadn't said her final destination was an aircraft carrier.

A young and very handsome junior officer ran across the flight deck, grabbed her hand and led her to an exit door. As she stepped through the door, sailors coming up the steps greeted Lamb's presence with whistles and catcalls.

"Knock it off, assholes," the officer bellowed, his face turning red from embarrassment at the men's behavior.

The whole situation caused Shirley to begin to laugh uncontrollably. *Here I stand, before a naval officer on a top-secret mission, inside the tower of the ABE with pee-soaked panties, wearing a flight suit that was made for a man twice my size, wearing a white helmet that makes me look like a bubble-headed doll, and I have just been whistled at by a bunch of young sailors. What is next?* Shirley Bo-Peep Lamb asked herself, as she climbed down the steep stairs into the inner workings of the ABE, an aircraft carrier whose duty was to carry out the policies and wishes of the president. Shirley Lamb had been sent by the Under-Secretary of State at the behest of the President to brief a navy pilot; some guy called "Barbarian." Bo-Peep could hardly wait!

Ж Ж Ж

Major Antonio Montoya was awestruck as he looked out the window of the chauffeur-driven limo provided by the Colombian Embassy. He had seen pictures of the Washington Monument and Lincoln Memorial in magazines and on television, but never had he thought that he would be assigned to his nation's Embassy in the Capitol of the United States.

Although it was raining, he had the driver stop the limo to take pictures of the various monuments, reaffirming his arrival in the national capital of the Untied States of America.

He wanted to visit the world famous Smithsonian Museum and the National Art Gallery. Walking Monument Trail and smell the cherry blossoms. However, those desires would have to wait, as he needed some sleep. Excited about this trip, he had been up for too many hours and his body was telling him to rest.

ЖЖЖ

"Ethel!" Don shouted, "Please get me Sarah Henderson ASAP!"

Ethel did not hesitate or question Don's demand. She already knew what was about to happen, as she had read the letters from the Ambassadors of Spain and Columbia. Like her boss, she knew that if possible, the young girl would be taken from them and given to the Spanish. After that, the Spanish would undoubtedly let her brother visit her on Spanish Embassy soil. From there she would be sent to Spain where Mendoza would have her killed.

"Henderson is on line two, sir," Ethel announced over the intercom.

"Hello, Sarah, this is Don. We need to talk!"

Sarah carefully scooted to the side of the bed, not wanting to disturb Angelica, who was sleeping soundly.

"Yes, Don, I'm listening," Sarah softly replied.

"Sarah, I have been officially asked by both the Spanish and Columbian Ambassadors to deliver Angelica Montoya for repatriation. I know that Angelica will be murdered upon delivery or soon after-wards. We cannot let this happen as we owe it to the girl and to General Hatfield."

For a moment, Sarah did not respond to Don's news. She knew a political squeeze play when she saw one, and this one was being orchestrated by a person with power and money. It was not hard to guess who and why.

"Don, is Angelica Columbian or Spanish?" Sarah asked.

"Spanish by birth. Why do you ask?"

"Well, don't we have some military bases in Spain?" Sarah asked.

"Yes, we have Rota Naval Base, an air force base just above Madrid, I think."

"Well, then, send her home to her father in Madrid. That would preclude the Columbians from killing her, and if she does get killed, it will be on Spanish soil, not ours. Then the Columbians couldn't make it a media circus to be used against us. In other words, we would be able to negate Mendoza's influence."

"Good idea, Sarah. I will make the arrangements, but you will go with her, and you will stay with her until Mendoza is destroyed. If I'm correct, it shouldn't be much longer a month, maybe two," Don said, his voice turning back to normal and his breathing less shallow now that his fear was gone.

"Hmm, Spain in the spring, living with Angelica and her father… Don, I must admit you're my kind of boss." Sarah heard a click as Don hung up.

"Who was that?" Angelica's sleepy voice asked as she pulled Sarah down, firmly grasping and pulling her close.

"You're going home, Angelica. We have found your father," Sarah replied, stroking Angelica's hair and staring up at the ceiling, wondering when and how Mendoza would try to kill them.

Ж Ж Ж

"Ethel, would you please get me Hank in Madrid," Don said respectfully, trying to atone for his earlier lack of decorum with her.

Henry (Hank) Williams was one of Don's closest friends. There wasn't anything either man wouldn't do for the other one.

Ethel smiled to herself. She knew Don was about to do something. She wasn't quite sure what, but knew it would be subtle. If Hank "Cowboy" Williams from Montana, who wore his buckskin Ryan jacket, cowboy hat, silver-toed cowboy boots and his bolo tie to embassy functions, was going to be involved, then Ethel knew fireworks were in the offing and it wasn't even the Fourth of July.

Ж Ж Ж

Hugo Blanco was sitting at his desk with his hands clasped as if in prayer. He really wasn't doing anything important, just thinking—*why did I listen to General Gonzales and appoint the general's nephew, Major Antonio Montoya, as my military attaché. Then there is this business about some girl. "Supposedly" she is Antonio's sister. Well, if she truly is his sister, then why is she Spanish and the major Columbian?*

Another thing that bothered him was w*hy was the bottle of wine and box of candy placed in a diplomatic pouch? Unless, of course, it was to avoid U. S. Customs...but Montoya was traveling with a diplomatic passport, so he wouldn't be searched.*

Something was not right and Hugo felt someone had used him, and he didn't like being thought of as a fool. He just didn't know why and by whom. Hugo knew that Pablo was a puta, selling himself and his position to the highest bidder. There had been rumors that Pablo was in bed with Don Julio Mendoza. However, he knew that could not be as Pablo was head of the Columbian anti-drug task force working with the

Organization of American States (OAS) and the United States to try to eradicate the drug lords, a position that required great courage.

Ж Ж Ж

McGee had just hung up from talking with Hank when he heard Ethel buzzing him. Yes, Ethel?" Don said.

"The Secretary is on line one," Ethel said.

Picking up his phone again, Don cleared his throat and said, "Yes, sir!"

"Hello Don," the deep, unmistakable voice of his boss said.

"Hello, sir."

"Don, we have a situation and the President has asked me to investigate. It supposedly involves some young Spanish girl. I'm told we have her in our possession. In fact, I'm told that you personally are holding her against her will, and you refuse to let anybody see her. Is this true, Don?"

"Not entirely true sir. We *are* keeping her in protective custody, and we have been debriefing her. In fact, sir, it is correct to say that she has been responsible for disrupting and even destroying Mendoza's drug operations in Mexico, Belgium and Italy. Sir, Mendoza wants her dead, and I'm not going to give her to him to be killed!" Don emphatically replied.

"Let me get this straight. She is in your protective custody because somebody named Mendoza wants her dead?" the Secretary asked in a questioning if not unsympathetic tone of voice.

"Yes sir!"Don McGee replied. "You've got it right!"

"Don, who authorized you to do this?"

"Mr. Secretary, I was authorized by virtue of my position as the Under Secretary of State and as Chief of Operations for Operation Cadence. This young girl was found in the Columbian jungle by a U. S. army captain. She was sick and only spoke French, and some sort of gibberish that she used when she talked to the tree people

"When the captain asked her name, she told him it was Renee. That's the only name she knew. The captain knew Mendoza gave his prized prostitutes one name, so he was pretty sure she would be of value and he was correct. Renee used to be Mendoza's personal property. So now Mendoza wants her dead because of what she knows."

"Let me see if I understand what you said. A girl was found in the jungle by an army captain and brought to the United States by you for medical treatment and safekeeping. Do I have it correct, Don?"

"How the Columbians got involved, I'm not sure, unless it was the girl's brother who is in the Columbian Army. Evidently, he went to his embassy; they in turn went to the Spanish Embassy, and now both Embassies want us to produce her, which is bull shit!" Don replied acrimoniously.

"Easy, Don, remember who you're talking to," warned his boss.

"Yes, sir, I'm sorry!" Don said before he exploded with a string of vulgarity only reserved for obstinate telemarketers or clumsy and uncaring waiters.

"Now, Don, calm down, you hear me? Calm down!" his boss said, raising his voice trying to get his Under Secretary to regain his composure.

Finally, after repeated attempts to calm Don and disgusted with the abusive obscenities, The Secretary raised his voice saying, "Don, if you can hear me, and you still understand orders, you will produce this jungle girl to the Spanish Embassy tomorrow at 10:00 a.m. You understand me, 10:00 a.m..."

When the line went silent, Don knew he had just killed an innocent, young girl. Taking a deep breath, Don held down the intercom button and said, "Ethel, call Sarah Henderson. Tell her the plans have changed. She is to take the girl to the Spanish Embassy tomorrow at 10:00 a.m. Also, call Hank in Madrid and tell him Operation Rodeo has been terminated."

Don got up from his desk, walked over to the couch, reached behind and pulled out a large pillow. He proceeded to slip off his shoes, loosened his tie and lay down. Suddenly, he was very tired. His jaw hurt, and his left arm began to tingle. H needed to rest.

33

⚹ ⚹ ⚹

SHIRLEY LAMB WAS SITTING IN A very large and spacious room. The sign on the door had said it was the Officer's Lounge. Looking around, it reminded her of a hotel lobby, complete with leather sofas and matching chairs. There were writing desks scattered around the room and a big screen TV on the wall was tuned to CNN. She was waiting for her escort. Per the ship's captain, she was not allowed to roam the ship without one. Which was actually fine with her, as the ABE was so cavernous and everything looked so much, the same she was afraid of getting lost.

She was re-reading her briefing notes when from the corner of her eye she saw a tall, and what could only be described as a beautiful, woman dressed in a flight suit. Shirley turned her head and smiled at this woman, acknowledging her. Instinctively, she knew this was "Barbarian."

"Excuse me, are you Shirley Lamb?" asked the woman.

"Yes, I am and you must be the Barbarian," Shirley said, extending her hand.

"Yes, ma'am, I'm called the Barbarian but my real name is Esther Colgate," Esther explained as she shook Shirley's hand.

Still holding Esther's hand, Shirley set her papers on the side table and stood looking into the woman's eyes. Somehow, she knew her call sign suited her.

"Esther is there a place where we can talk?" Shirley asked, softly.

"Yes, ma'am, we can go to my quarters. They're just down the hall."

"Fine, let me get my papers together," Shirley said, bending over to pick up her papers and stuffing them into her briefcase.

Esther's quarters were sparse: a bed, desk with a chair, a lamp, and a small, stainless steel sink. There was absolutely no telltale sign that this was a woman's room. Shirley wondered if it was Navy policy that all naval personnel rooms be so inhospitable and if so, for what reason?

Pulling out the only chair for Shirley, Ester turned it towards the bunk so both women could face each other. Esther sat cross-legged on her bunk, interlocked her fingers and placed them on her knee.

Shirley smiled as she placed the briefcase on the desk, opened it and removed two manila envelopes that contained both aerial and satellite photos. She set them to the side before closing the lid, then pushing down on the two small brass-colored buttons that held her briefing notes and two folders labeled "Secret." Now ready, Shirley Lamb, aka Bo-peep, sat down in the chair. It was time to discuss Operation Interdiction with a woman she did not know and to ask her to commit murder.

ЖЖЖ

Major Antonio Montoya was getting ready to meet his sister. He stood in front of his bathroom mirror, shaving, wrapped in a towel and singing a Spanish love song as he tried to remember how many years it had been and what Angelica looked like after all these years. True, he had recently seen her picture but in it, she was sitting in a hospital bed, wearing an unflattering hospital gown, with an IV in her arm. The picture of his beloved Angelica was not flattering.

For this special occasion, he had laid out his dress uniform, polished his boots last night and had gotten a haircut yesterday afternoon. He had remembered the chocolates and the Spanish wine given to him by Uncle Pablo and of course, a dozen red roses were provided by the embassy. Once he was ready to meet Angelica, his only concern was that he did not want to cry and make a fool of himself in front of his little sister.

Ж Ж Ж

The sound of the clock's alarm was harsh as it echoed in the sleep-filled recesses of Sarah's brain. Slowly she turned her body towards the annoying sound, reached out and let her fingers crawl across the nightstand in search of the little magic button that would let her sleep a few more minutes. However, it was not to be. She felt Angelica's body begin to crawl over her, reaching, trying to silence the offending device. Sarah tried to move but Angelica's weight had pinned her in place. There was little Sarah could do little as Angelica turned back and kissed her softly on the cheek, cradling her head. Unable to prevent it, Sarah began to cry as she enfolded Angelica in her arms and held her close, knowing that this beautiful child would soon be killed.

She shared Don's paranoia when it came to Angelica's life. What she wanted to do was get dressed and just run away with her. After all, Don had told her she could do that. However, she also knew it would be pointless.

In the semi-conscious state between sleep and reality, Sarah heard the unmistakable ring of her cell phone. Angelica heard it also and handed Sarah her phone. A quick peek at the alarm clock showed that it was almost 7:00 a.m.

"Hello," Sarah said, her voice still filled with sleep.

"Sarah, this is Ethel. Don has suffered a massive heart attack and he is not expected to make it. He told me to contact you and tell you to run. Do you understand what I am saying?"

"Yes Ethel and thank you!" As an afterthought Sarah asked, "Do you have any particular place in mind?"

"General Hatfield! Take her to General Hatfield's headquarters at McDill AFB in Tampa. I'll notify the general of the situation and let him know to expect you."

"Got it!" Sarah said, and hung up.

"Who was that?" Angelica asked, her head resting trustingly on Sarah's chest.

"A gift from God," Sarah replied, her tears now a steady stream flowing down her cheeks.

Ж Ж Ж

It was early when Staff Sergeant Deal was awakened first by the sound of trumpets, then drums. Dawn hadn't broken yet when the jungle suddenly became alive with the sounds of screaming monkeys and the deafening, screeching sound of the macaws. Quickly he sat up and listened, grabbing his weapons for moral support. He couldn't see the first sergeant but knew he was close.

"Ed, what's going on?" Deal whispered loudly.

"I don't know for sure, but I suspect our captain has met up with his friends. He's getting us some help from the locals I think," Ed replied as he cautiously stood, peering all around,and walked towards the path that led down the mountain, in order to take a look.

"Deal, this here is Ernest T, aka the Black Knight, can you hear me?" came a loud whisper over their radio communication system.

"Yeah, I hear you. What's going on?" Deal asked.

"I don't know where that noise is coming from, but it's creating a whole lot of excitement down below," Earnest T replied.

"Hawk, you there?" Deal whispered into his mike.

"Yes, I'm here," Hawk said in a low, monotone.

"What's going on over your side of the mountain?" Deal asked.

Hawk began to chuckle, "ooh, the natives sure are getting worked up over here. They're actually running up the hill. I count eight targets," Hawk replied.

"Roger that!" Deal replied. Deal stood up. Not only did he need too pee, but he was also hungry. As he walked to a nearby bush, he passed Ed. "Did you hear what was going on?" Deal asked while watering the jungle foliage.

"No, I didn't hear," Ed replied as he picked up his binoculars and walked to his observation post. "Tell me."

"Evidently the damn drums and trumpets have Mendoza's security forces spooked. Hawk says eight of them are returning to the hacienda and Ernest T says the others are standing outside acting all excited. I wonder what it all means." Deal asked.

"It means, Captain Steele has found his friends and he and his friends are chasing all the rats into one place. I want you to start jamming Mendoza's communications. Also, I want Hawk to move closer to the cave door and see if he can get inside and start making people disappear. Tell the Black Knight to work himself into a position where he can see inside the hacienda. Tell him if he gets a killing shot on Mendoza to take it."

"Okay, Ed, will do," Deal replied. Then he picked up his radio and passed the first sergeant's orders on to Hawk and the Knight. Then with a flip of a switch, Deal turned on the jamming device. Now Mendoza was not only surrounded but his communications were cut off.

Ж Ж Ж

Yes, indeed, Steele had made contact with his friends. Now the jungle was an amphitheater, as the sounds of trumpets and drums announced his arrival. Steele had forgotten to tell his men about the noise but figured they'd guess and fill in the blanks. It was his intention was that all this hoopla would terrorize Mendoza's security forces, making them desert their posts and run to the hacienda for mutual protection. In that way, all of Mendoza's bullyboys would be in one place, making it easier for him and his little friends to set mantraps.

Steele knew that his first sergeant would have already started jamming Mendoza's communications as they had discussed before he left camp. It was his fervent hope that with the added pressure of his security forces not at their assigned posts to protect him and his operations, and with no way to call for help, Mendoza would feel his world closing in on him as his drug cartel began to collapse.

Ж Ж Ж

192

Major Montoya had been sitting in the Spanish Embassy's reception room for over an hour. The flowers, candy and wine were sitting on the sofa next to him. He could feel his stomach begin to churn, burning deep inside him. Antonio began to fear something was terribly wrong.

His fears were confirmed. He heard an office door open. He could hear the echo of a woman's high heels walking towards him. Protocol and good manners made Antonio stand to receive the news about Angelica.

"Major Montoya, I'm Senora Carmen Vasquez with the Embassy's Cultural Affairs. I'm very sorry to tell you this, but we just received word from the American State Department. Your sister, Angelica, will not be coming this morning. Under Secretary, Senor Don McGee has suffered a massive heart attack. He is in critical condition at George Washington Hospital, and nobody knows where Angelica is or how to reach her. I'm sorry!" And with those words, Major Antonio Montoya was dismissed, as if he were a nobody.

34

ж ж ж

NOW ALONE, Esther laidback in her bunk, holding a diet cola in her left hand while in her right, she held a detailed satellite photo. Though enhanced, the clarity of the images was remarkable. Shirley's briefing had been very detailed, vivid and her explanation of each photo was crystal clear. The coup de grace was when Bo-peep had let the name Mendoza slip out. Until that moment, she had had little interest it was just another job. However, when Mendoza's name was mentioned, she changed her attitude and this mission became "up close and personal." Steele was down in that jungle doing his job. The quicker she blew Mendoza's ass to kingdom come, the quicker her man would be back holding her in his arms.

Esther turned and reached for more photos. Studying each one carefully, she wanted to burn each photo into her memory as she would only have one chance at her target, and it had to be perfect. The plan was for her to "go down the throat." This term was used when describing a particular attack mode. In this case, Esther would come in low and slow from the northeast. Leaving early would put the morning sun at her back, silhouetting her Tom Cat against the sun and making it difficult to be seen.

As she continued memorizing the photos, she viewed the target mountain. It was two thousand feet, give or take a foot or two, with a river at its base. On the left side was a taller mountain of maybe seven thousand feet. A cliff was on its right side with a cascading waterfall. According to the photos, there was one entrance into the mountain. Esther knew that her only chance would be "a toss," meaning she would actually lob the bomb at the entrance and then hope. She would have no room to maneuver; her options were few, unless she could somehow get Steele to use a laser guidance beam. If so, she could then launch the bomb from a safer distance while letting Steele guide the missile to its target. It was a fact that the Bunker Buster bomb could not be accurately delivered. Esther intended to talk with Lamb before she left the ship.

Ж Ж Ж

Hatfield listened intently to Ryan. Every question Seth had asked was met with a terse and adamant response from McBride, followed by a simple, direct plea, "When are we going to kill this fat, arrogant son of a bitch?"

Seth held up his hand and ordered two more beers. From across the room the waiter smiled and held up two fingers, acknowledging the request. The simple request seemed to have a momentary calming effect on Seth's drinking buddy.

Ryan lifted his long neck and gulped down the last of his brew before flicking his lighter and lighting his cigar, extending the flame to his boss. His anger dissipated in a cloud of thick, blue smoke that drifted upwards towards the ceiling and was drawn into the large blades of the ceiling fan and dispersed around the room.

When the waiter placed the two beers on the table, he removed the ashtray and replaced it with a clean one. Picking up the two, empty bottles he then walked away.

Both men sat silent, for the moment, alone with their personal thoughts. After the waiter had returned to the bar, Seth took a draw on his cigar and exhaled. Then, in his perfect and practiced French, asked the question, "Should we kill Rossi or steal her back to the states when we extract you?"

McBride sat silently thinking looking into his general's eyes trying to figure out his motive for asking such a question. He knew Rossi was washed up and that her life expectancy was two years tops. By then Mendoza would turn her loose or give her to his employees for fun. He knew that as a normal, rational, human being; she was already dead. She was merely a human android that was at the disposal of her creators and lived only to serve them. Nevertheless, to kill her in cold blood because she was a security risk was something he had not considered.

"No, sir, we use her! We feed her plausible and sometimes factual information knowing that she will tell Carlos. Undoubtedly, Carlos will tell Julio, and he will make decisions based on that information. Then we counter his move, thus costing him men, material and money. In addition, we create a rift between Pablo and Julio. That's what I recommend, sir," Ryan concluded, puffing on his cigar.

"C'est bon, monsieur," Seth replied. "Now that matter is taken care of, I want you to pay attention to what I need and what I want you to do."

Ryan sat transfixed, as Seth laid out his plan. As he spoke, it became abundantly clear to Ryan that he and Rossi were expendable and would be sacrificed for the glory of the red, white and blue *if* he failed.

Ж Ж Ж

Captain Mike Atkins was sitting in the lobby of the BOQ, drinking his coffee, reading his newspaper. Engrossed in his paper, he paid little attention to the comings and goings of his fellow officers. He was into the sports section when the scent of a familiar fragrance caught his attention. That's when he saw *her* standing at the counter next to a very attractive older woman. Surprised, Mike quickly folded his paper and stood up but was unsure as to what he should do. Did he walk up to her and say "Hello," or should he wave, trying to catch Renee's and hopefully be invited over?

Angelica spotted her friend and hurried over to him, throwing her arms around him and hugging him tightly, her head resting in the middle of his chest. Mike pulled her close, squeezing her gently, as he closed his eyes, kissing the top of her head. He took in her scent, envisioning her in his arms while he kissed her softly. Her body was a tonic to his long repressed male libido. The feel of her in his arms and the seductive smell of her perfume caused his seldom-used penis to stand at attention causing him extreme discomfort.

Mike's delusion of sex with Angelica was short lived. He released Angelica from his grasp and grabbing both her hands stepped back, his cold blue eyes scanning up and down her body, as if measuring her for a casket.

"Hmmm," came an annoying noise to his immediate right. He had been so engrossed in Angelica he had forgotten her companion.

"Hello," the awe-struck captain said.

"I'm sorry, but I don't believe we have met," Sarah said, extending her hand to Angelica's friend.

"No, ma'am, we have not met. My name is Mike Atkins. I am, or was, Angelica's handler. However, General Hatfield reassigned me leaving Angelica's care to you. I believe?"

Sarah's practiced smile hid her fear, as she remembered Don warning her that he believed Captain Atkins had ulterior motives and felt Angelica was in danger from this man. As she shook the captain's hand, she gave him the once-over, noticing the impressive bulge in his pants. He definitely had designs on Angelica and who could blame him?

"Well, sir, Angelica and I are very tired. We have been driving night and day, and tomorrow we will meet with Angelica's friend the general. So we must sleep so we can look our best for him," Sarah said, taking Angelica's arm and steering her towards their suite.

Mike knew he had just been rebuffed by a pro. Silently, he watched as the two women walked towards the locked door that housed the VIP suites, all of which were on the first floor facing the bay. His mind was already planning on how he was going to spend his money. The lost golden egg had been found, all he had to do was call Bogotá.

Good-bye Angelica goodnight Sarah, nice to have met you! Mike thought, as he walked up to the desk. With a smile that hid his evil intent, he asked the clerk for the room number in which Sarah and Angelica were staying.

Ж Ж Ж

Shirley heard the knock on her cabin door. Quickly she folded Ethel's message and put it in her pocket. Her mind did not totally comprehend the impact of Don's sudden departure because of a heart attack. However, per Don via Ethel, she was now completely in charge of Operation Cadence and all the rest of the evil doings.

"Hello, Esther, what can I do for you?" Shirley asked, smiling and offering her visitor a chair.

Esther smiled. "Thank you, ma'am," she said, crossing her legs and leaning forward, resting her hands in her lap. "Well, Shirley, I have studied the photos and have read all the Intel briefs. I cannot possibly use a Bunker Buster."

She waited for Shirley to respond to her news, but Shirley remained silent, knowing that Esther had already come up with an alternate plan that was probably better than the original idea. Deciding Shirley wanted her to carry the ball, Esther's facial features went blank, as she sucked in her cheeks, puckered her lips and then slowly began exhaling, or maybe it was a sigh. Either way, Shirley was sure she was about to receive a crash course in weaponry.

Then, for every weapon Esther named, Shirley gave a dozen reasons why it would not work.

Finally, Shirley just held up her hand and asked, "Commander, which weapon would you select?"

"Oh, that's easy, ma'am, a laser-guided Cruise missile. You see, I can launch that sucker from a couple of hundred miles away. The missile will hug the terrain while flying roughly 600 miles per hour. All the while, its internal guidance is sweeping back and forth across the terrain looking for a little red dot that is emitted from a hand-held laser. Therefore, ma'am, we must get somebody in close, say 1500 yards or maybe closer, to point the laser beam so the missile can lock onto the target and blow the bastards to kingdom come. Hell, Shirley, I could launch two missiles and take out the hacienda, as well."

"My goodness, Esther, you certainly are a barbarian aren't you?" Shirley said, as she began to giggle.

"Yes ma'am, my man, Steele, is down there in that jungle and I want him home so he can tickle my ovaries."

Shirley's giggle became a belly laugh as it now became clear why this beautiful woman would take on such a dangerous mission.

"What must I do to change the weaponry so you can deliver your packages?" Shirley asked.

"Scratch through where it says 'Bunker Buster' in the operational plan and write in 'Cruise missiles.' Specify quantity, sign, initial it, then give it to air ops," Esther said, standing up and extending her hand to her new best friend.

35

Ж Ж Ж

NUDE, STEELE SAT IN A SHALLOW pool of warm water by the bank of the river. He knew his little friends, though he couldn't see many of them, were all around. It had felt good to bathe and he had even managed a shave. In the distance, he had heard the laughter of the women and children as they watched him apply the shaving lather to his face; then he heard the screams of the women as they watched him "skin" himself.

As he relaxed in the warmth of the water, his thoughts turned to Esther. He was remembering a crisp, cold morning, long ago, when they had gone for a walk in the woods near her family's home. They had wrapped themselves in fallen leaves, hiding from nobody in particular, as they kissed their hot breath rising like small, soft, white clouds mingling in the air and then slowly drifting away, carried by the cool, autumn breeze.

Steele's short but delightful trip down memory lane had left him with an erection, a condition that was quickly noticed by the tribal elders.

They looked and pointed, then looked down at each other's maleness and then back at him. Someone would say something and then they would all laugh.

Standing, Steele turned his back to his audience and walked out into the deeper, colder water until his "condition" slowly disappeared. Steele knew it was time for him to return to his base camp. He climbed out of the river, shook himself and dressed. Together, he and his allies had set twenty snare traps along the various paths used by Mendoza's workers and his security patrols. Thanks to his friends, he had also located Sergeants Alphonso Netti and Chadwick Zadgelovich, telling them about the snare traps and informing them to stop any trucks entering or leaving the compound. Cars could enter but they could not leave.

"Like a roach motel," Netti had said, causing Zadgelovich to chuckle.

"Alphonso, your wisdom is beyond your years," Steele had said, shaking both men's hands and reminding them to brief the others when they got back from patrol.

"Sir?" had come Chad's questioning voice.

"Yes, Chad," Steele had said, responding to his sergeant.

"Sir, the other night we heard drums and what sounded like horns of some sort. Do you have any idea what that was?"

With a big grin, Steele had smiled at both men and nodded his head affirmatively saying, "Yes, I do! Those drums and trumpets were the locals acknowledging our presence. They are not to be harmed. In fact, guys, they are our allies and remember, gentlemen, they are cannibalistic." Steele returned their salutes and disappeared back into the jungle.

ж ж ж

Ryan Mc Bride could not sleep because his mind kept turning and churning as ideas came and went in perfect rhythm to Dominique's breathing, her soft breath tickling the hairs on his chest as he tried in vain to come up with a realistic and viable plan of action. The general had told him what had to be done in order to wipe out Mendoza and his cartel forever. What he had failed to tell him was *how* to do it.

To his dismay and chagrin, Ryan now knew his general was not a detail-oriented man. Seth Hatfield thought in global terms and left the details to his staff.

Aware that desperate times called for desperate measures, Ryan knew that Mendoza was getting very desperate. As he lay in his king-size bed with his right arm covering his eyes, he suddenly came up with an idea on how to satisfy his general's orders and just possibly escape with Rossi, although Seth had told him if it came down to Rossi or himself, he was to leave her.

His plan was to create a rift between Pablo and Julio. That would play well to Julio's paranoia. Then he would use Rossi to exasperate Julio's mistrust of Pablo. However, the hard part of his plan was to convince Juan to call a conference and invite all of Julio's business associates from around the world. Ryan knew that if Carlos said no, his plan would fail.

Oh well, tomorrow will be interesting, Ryan thought as he slid down in bed and pulled Rossi closer, gently kissing her head and smelling her hair.

Ж Ж Ж

The general stood behind his desk as the two ladies entered his office. As a rule, generals only stood for higher-ranking officers or political figures. However, Seth was the consummate politician and he admired beauty, especially when it came in two dresses. He walked around his desk and extended his hand to the lady he did not know. However, before he could speak, Angelica interrupted by wrapping her arms around his waist and hugging him.

Chuckling, he momentarily caressed the back of her head before extending his hand once again to her beautiful companion. "Hello, I'm Seth Hatfield."

Sarah smiled, taking the general's hand, "Nice to meet you, sir, and my name is Sarah Henderson!"

"Please, let's sit down before she knocks me down," Seth said, taking Angelica by the hand and leading both women to the leather sofa. Once the ladies were seated, Seth sat down in the matching leather chair that was strategically positioned so he could talk to his guest and still have a view of his office door.

"What can I do for you?" the general asked.

Sarah turned to Angelica and apologized to her, saying she was going to speak to the general in English. Angelica nodded her head and smiled at her friends.

"General, I don't know if you are aware that Under Secretary of State, Don McGee has suffered a heart attack and will be gone for some time. Ethel, his administrative assistant and obviously his trusted friend, called with a message from Don, telling me there was a plot to kill Angelica and to trust no one. Just before his heart attack, the secretary of state had ordered Don to produce her and turn her over to the Spanish Embassy. Since he was the only person other than Ethel and me who knew where she was. For her safety's sake, I was told to bring her to you at your headquarters, here at McDill AFB."

"Hmm, I agree you did the right thing. However, if Mendoza found her in Washington, then he sure as hell will find her here. I'd say a week, maybe two, before he finds you. Other than me does anybody else know she is here?"

"Only Captain Atkins," Sarah replied.

"Atkins you say?" Seth asked, as he began to rub his chin with his knuckles, his eyes now looking up at the ceiling as if he were asking for divine providence.

"Yes, sir," Sarah replied.

"Well, then let's hope we can take care of Mendoza before he hurts Angelica or you. By the way, Sarah, where are you staying?" the general asked.

"I used my NSA credentials and we're staying in the VIP quarters at the BOQ," Sarah said, standing and extending her hand to her host.

The general stood and took her hand. "At least the hallway doors are locked. That's good," he said, shaking her hand and patting it for good luck. "I will see to it you have an assigned security detail. I don't want you to go anywhere without them. Is this understood?"

Seth figured that Captain Atkins wouldn't be so foolish to attempt kidnapping Angelica while she was on the base. However, he would expedite Captain Atkins' reassignment to Mexico.

Angelica stood and looked up, extending her hand to Seth. He took her small hand in his and bent down and kissed her cheek. Somehow, she made him feel fatherly and he enjoyed the feeling.

As soon as Sarah and Angelica were gone, the general picked up the phone. He needed to get Atkins off the base...and soon. *Mexico...* he said to himself as he began to tap in the numbers to set the wheels in motion for Atkins' TDY departure.

Ж Ж Ж

Captain Mike Atkins was a man with a curious nature. His favorite question had always been, "Why?" Why were some people rich and he wasn't? Why were people popular and he wasn't? Now he was asking himself, *Why doesn't the general trust me*? It wasn't so much *what* the general had said to him, but the *way* he had said it and the way he had looked at him when he said it that bothered Mike the most.

He was sitting at his desk with his office door closed, looking through the phone book of Bogotá. There was only one number for which he was looking. Since he knew he couldn't call Julio Mendoza, however, he might be able to call General Pablo Gonzales, only because his telephone number was the only one listed. That is, his office number was listed and that is where Mike planned to begin.

His plan was to simply tell General Gonzales he had heard Don Julio had offered a reward for Renee's location. Though he knew it was a bluff, maybe it would open the door. Anyway, it was a gamble and he knew it. If he got through to the general, he would then tell him that if Julio still wanted the woman killed, it would cost him five million in U. S. dollars to be deposited in an offshore bank account. When the money was paid, Angelica would be disposed of quietly and efficiently.

36

ЖЖЖ

SHIRLEY WAS BACK IN HER CUBBYHOLE at CIC. She was sitting at her desk, drinking hot green tea and eating a bagel. With her granny glasses pushed up on the top of her head, she was thinking how her life had changed in less than a year. How a chance meeting with Rossi had propelled her into a world for which she had not been prepared. Then, when Rossi had been listed as missing and presumed dead, she had been given the reigns of a massive anti-drug task force with the power to kill. What would her husband say if he knew? The hell with him; what would the ladies in her Sunday school class think?

She had just finished her bagel and was wiping her hands and mouth when her phone rang. "Lamb" she said, putting down her teacup and automatically grabbing a pencil and moving the pad of paper closer.

"Shirley, its Ethel, we have to talk."

"I agree. How about the cafeteria?" Shirley suggested.

Ethel was waiting as Shirley walked into the cafeteria. She had selected a table close to the entrance; however, the table was tucked back in the corner behind a pillar that nicely concealed its occupants.

As she approached Ethel, Shirley smiled. Upon closer inspection, she realized that Don's illness had been hard on her, as Ethel was wearing fatigue and stress under her eyes. Shirley also noticed a slight trembling in her hand as she held it out to shake hands.

"Hi, Ethel, how is Don?" Shirley asked, as she pulled out a chair and sat.

"He is recovering, slowly. It was only by the Lord's good luck that I walked into his office when I did and found him. Otherwise he would be dead."

"Thank God you found him!" Shirley said, holding Ethel's hand and reassuring her.

"Ethel, what did you want to discuss with me?" When Shirley looked into Ethel's eyes, she saw the older woman's fear.

"Oh yes! I'm sorry, Shirley. The secretary has appointed Mr. Milo Adams to take over for Don until he returns and according to the doctors that won't be for some time yet.

"Don has asked me to ask you to say nothing whatsoever about what you're doing, nor anything about the people you're doing it with. You're also to tell General Hatfield to stay clear of Milo and you will continue doing business as usual with the general. The appropriations for Operation Cadence are fully funded for three more years so Milo won't know much unless you tell him. Any changes you make to the overall operational plan are yours to make as you see fit."

"Wow," Shirley said, as she began to chuckle. "Will you be ok?"

"I will unless Milo finds out about what we're doing and then it's back to the typing pool," Ethel said with a laugh.

For some inexplicable reason, Shirley confided in Ethel about the Barbarian and her assigned mission. Also, she told Ethel about changing the weaponry and why. "Gee whiz, it sounds like I'm a blood thirsty bitch!" Shirley said, as she hunched her shoulders and laughed.

Ethel sat mesmerized as she listened to Shirley explaining, in detail, what she had done and why. She found herself liking this woman; liked her loyalty and spunk, but most of all she liked her because she took risks and used common sense—a very rare commodity in the U. S. State Department.

Ж Ж Ж

Steele was sitting next to Ed with his binoculars trained on Mendoza's security guards. They were pushing handcart dollies into what appeared to be a vault built right into the mountain. Renee had told him about Mendoza's money room that was supposedly stacked to the ceiling with one hundred dollar bills and euro's. It was Steele's decision not to say anything to Ed or the others about the money. He had no particular reason not to say anything; he just felt that the money would be a distracter to their assigned mission.

Sergeant Deal tapped him on the shoulder and handed his captain a transcribed message. Steele read the message, looked at Deal and nodded his head, acknowledging the message. Deal smiled, knowing that in the not-too-distant future they were going to see some fireworks. No more sitting, watching and waiting. At last, they were going to wipe this Mendoza character off the face of the planet.

Ӝ Ӝ Ӝ

Ryan was lying in bed, watching Dominique as she toweled herself dry. He started getting turned on watching her body. There was no doubt she was beautiful. How long she would remain beautiful he did not know. *Perhaps if I could get her to a hospital in the states and put her in de-tox for a month, then years of counseling, who knows? She might even marry a real nice guy and have kids*, Ryan thought.

But for right now Rossi had two purposes: One, to confuse Mendoza with false information and create mistrust and the second and more immediate purpose, was to satisfy his growing lust. Already he had called Juan Carlos and asked him to lunch. So for now, Dominique was his to use and he needed to use her badly.

Ӝ Ӝ Ӝ

Pablo picked up his phone and dialed Julio's private number again. He put the phone back into its cradle, still not able to get through. He was anxious as he had important news about Renee and he had no one with which to share it. *Perhaps Juan has talked to Julio;* he thought picking up the phone again and re-dialing Juan Carlos' number.

Juan Carlos had calmly listened to Pablo when he told of the strange phone call from America, asking him about a reward for information about Renee's location and that for five million dollars this man would kill Renee for Julio. Then Pablo had asked him a very simple, yet disturbing question. Pablo had asked, "Have you seen or talked to Julio in the last week?"

When Juan replied, "No, I have not heard from the boss," Pablo told of the repeated calls he had made to Julio and how the line was always busy.

Like Pablo, Juan became concerned. He determined to ask McBride at lunch if he knew what was going on and if not; maybe they could drive out together and see for themselves what was going on at the hacienda.

ЖЖЖ

After hanging up his phone, General Hatfield sat back in his chair and ran his hand over his shaved head, not believing his good luck. Shirley Lamb had just briefed him that a Mr. Milo Adams had temporarily replaced Don McGee and under no circumstances was he to tell Mr. Adams anything concerning Angelica or Operation Cadence.

She also informed him of her decision to use the laser-guided Cruise missiles instead of the Bunker Buster bomb and why. And then, ever so politely and succinctly, Ms. Bo-Peep informed him that she was now in operational control of Operation Cadence and that he was in charge of all tactical decisions concerning Operation Cadence.

When he had asked her, "Does that include Operation Interdiction?"

Her response had been, "General, you must do what you must do to destroy this evil. Do I make myself understood, sir?"

"Yes, ma'am!" Seth said, a big shit-eating grin crossing his face.

ЖЖЖ

Lunch was a simple affair: a bowl of soup, tossed salad, roast beef sandwich and a beer. Nothing fancy, as both men had a lot to discuss. Miguel and Jesus sat at another table, each man facing a different direction so they commanded a view of the entire room.

"Tell me, McBride, have you heard from Julio?" Carlos asked, taking a sip of his beer.

"No, not a word," Ryan replied, reaching into his pants pocket for his lighter. "Tell you the truth, I figured he was mad at me."

"No, McBride, Julio is not mad at you! I think you have finally won him over. Pablo told me he has tried calling Julio several times and the line is always busy. Also, his private e-mail address is not working either. I think something is very wrong. Will you drive out to the hacienda with me and we can check things out?"

"Sorry, my friend, I cannot go with you as I have to supervise two, huge, drug shipments—one goes to Miami, the other to Boston. And don't forget, we also have that shipment to Japan. So I will have to beg off," Ryan said, reaching into his Ryan et pocket for a cigar.

"Hum," Carlos mumbled.

"Okay, Juan, what is it now?" Ryan asked as he bit the tip off of his cigar.

"Well, McBride, I did not tell you everything Pablo Gonzales told me," Carlos said, reaching into his Ryan et for a cigar.

"What else did the general have to tell you?" Ryan asked, watching the waiter walking towards them with their lunch.

"Pablo told me that he received a very strange phone call from a man in the states. He told Pablo he knew where Renee was and for five million dollars he would dispose of her."

Ryan waited until the waiter had served them and had walked back to the bar before he spoke. "Let me get this straight: Some guy calls and speaks with General Pablo Gonzales, supposedly from the United States, and tells him he knows where this Renee is hiding and for five million dollars he will kill her. Do I have it correct?"

Carlos did not speak; just nodded his head acknowledging Ryan 's assessment of the situation.

Ryan thought a few moments before he said, "Tell me, my friend, what makes you think the general is telling the truth? Let's say that somehow Pablo *has* learned where she is. And let's say Pablo decides to pay some gringo ten thousand dollars to kill the girl and then he pockets the rest?"

Carlos did not speak, as his mouth was otherwise occupied with his sandwich. However, the look he gave Ryan registered incredulity. Carefully putting down his sandwich on his plate, Carlos took a sip of beer then reached down to his lap, brought up his napkin and wiped his mouth before he said, " McBride, what are you saying to me, you crazy bastard? That Pablo Gonzales is ripping us off for five million dollars? And if so, why?" Carlos, his eyes blazing into McBride's, demanded an explanation.

"Well, Carlos, we both know that in the last three weeks we have lost millions of dollars. How much did the general lose? Not one, stinking peso, that's how much. Pablo has nothing invested in this cartel. All he does is sell information in order to gain favor with Julio. Who's to say the Americans haven't got to him and are telling him what to tell us in order to set us up? I know I did everything right at my end and still we were busted in Italy, Mexico and Belgium one huge bust after the other. I ask you, how did the police know?"

The glare in Carlos's glare softened. Now he was listening intently to Ryan 's rationalization. What scared Juan was that Ryan made perfect sense. Taking another swig of his beer he asked, "What do you think we should do, Ryan ?"

"I would tell General Gonzales that when this gringo calls back— and he will call back—to get all the particulars, especially how he wants to be paid or where he wants the money transferred. Don't ask me why, but I'm betting this guy will want the money sent to an off-shore, numbered account. If so, have Pablo direct him to one of *our* banks. Then deposit half the amount as a good faith gesture. When he calls back, telling us the job is done, pull the money out of the account and leave no trace. By doing it this way, the guy, whoever he is, will have taken care of a problem for us and it hasn't cost us a dime."

Carlos began to laugh, "You're too fucking much, McBride. I will do what you say only because it is a brilliant plan. " Then Carlos picked up his sandwich and took a big, bite to satisfy his hunger.

37

ж ж ж

CAPTAIN MIKE ATKINS WAS ALONE IN his office with the door closed, as per his usual custom. He should have been working on his Intel briefing for General Hatfield; however, he was looking at condos in Brazil and Argentina. Simply put, Mike was spending money he did not have, except in his imagination. There, in the deepest, darkest recesses of his perverted mind, he had millions.

It had been three, long, agonizing days since Atkins had called General Gonzales with his offer to kill Angelica. As time went by, he was becoming more and more antsy, a feeling he personally detested. He sat in his office looking out at the clear blue sky, trying to decide what to do. If he called General Gonzales again, the general might think it was an elaborate scheme concocted by the Americans to trap him, thus discrediting Atkins and destroying his reputation. On the other hand, if he did not call, he would never be rich and the condos, fancy cars and beautiful girls would only be unfilled wishes.

Making his decision, Mike reached into his wallet and pulled out one of the two international calling cards he had purchased. He looked at his watch and automatically subtracted one hour. It was only ten in the morning in downtown Bogotá. The general should be in his office.

Since Mike already had the number written down on his desk pad, he opened his cell phone and dialed. Sweat began to form on his upper lip and his breathing became shallow, he could feel his heart beating against his chest. For some, unexplainable reason, Captain Mike Atkins, of the United States Army was scared. Of course, he had every right to be; he had never murdered before.

Ж Ж Ж

Jesus was driving Carlos' big black Mercedes toward the east. Though he had driven this highway many times, this time he sensed danger. Miguel also sensed that something was terribly wrong with Carlos. Usually when Carlos had lunch with McBride, both men would laugh at each other, tell dirty jokes, have a couple of beers, discuss business and Carlos would be happy. Not this time. Carlos was angry and when Carlos got angry, usually somebody died. Since they were heading towards Mendoza's hacienda, Miguel had a horribly feeling that perhaps Julio was going to die this day.

Sitting in the back of his car, Carlos sat with his arms folded across his chest, his eyes closed and his head bowed. He was lost in thought: *McBride makes a very compelling case against Pablo. The only thing I can't figure out is how Pablo knew the shipping schedules and where the drugs were concealed. I like McBride's idea of inviting all the principal players from around the world to a business conference. Julio and I had even discussed that idea a month earlier. However, the idea was rejected because of security concerns. But now, after three huge and very costly drug busts, Julio and I both know it is time for a conference. It will be risky, but these are desperate times and desperate times require desperate measures.*

Lost in thought, Carlos did not hear the car phone. He had only been vaguely aware the phone had rung when Miguel handed it to him.

"Hello?"

"Is this Carlos?"

"Yes, Pablo," Carlos replied.

"That gringo called me again and I did as you instructed. The two million will be deposited into a numbered account and then upon completion of his task, he'll be paid the balance," Pablo said, starting to laugh into Carlos's ear.

"Very good, Pablo," Carlos said, handing the phone back to Miguel.

"Jesus, turn around and go back to my house," Carlos ordered. Then he began to chuckle out loud. "That McBride is a fucking genius," he uttered softly, still laughing and wishing he could see the expression on the gringo's face when he tried to access his account only to discover that he had no money and that he had murdered an innocent girl for free.

※ ※ ※

Captain Atkins finished typing his very detailed analysis of the Mendoza cartel's Mexican operations for General Hatfield. His analysis concluded: ...that although hurt by the recent drug busts in Mexico, Mendoza is still a very viable and dangerous adversary who has started a systematic campaign of killing police officers in their own homes or at work. Already he has begun killing judges and prosecuting attorneys in the outlining towns and villages. He wants to create anarchy and terror in Mexico for political leverage, by replacing the judges he has killed with judges who are loyal to him. Also, he is having newspaper reporters killed, who have published evil things about him. Julio does not like that and he is letting all Mexico know that he does not like stories published about him that show him in a bad light.

Mike closed down his work computer and turned off the lights to his office. The Captain needed to run. He figured that maybe five miles would do it, as he needed to think and he always thought best when he was running and communing with nature. While walking to the BOQ, the hot afternoon sun warmed his cold and clammy body. It seemed that everyone complained at how cold the building was but nothing was ever done about it. Once, an enterprising solider opened all the doors, allowing the heat into the building. Immediately he was put on report, so now everybody suffered.

As per his custom, Mike opened the door to his room and emptied his pockets, placing their contents on the desk. Then he untied his shoes and slipped them off, putting them side-by-side at the end of the bed. Next, he slipped out of his pants and hung them up, inspecting them for dirt or stains. He decided he could get another day out of them before they needed to be dry-cleaned. Unbuttoning his shirt, he hung it over his pants on the hangar. In the bottom drawer of his dresser, he found his running shoes and gym shorts.

Now, he was ready to beat his feet against the hot asphalt. Before leaving, he took a quick look around the room, just in case he missed something. He had. His room key was lying next to his laptop. *Oh, well, what could it hurt if I checked my e-mail, h*e thought.

He accessed his e-mail and noticed he had two messages. Slowly he moved his cursor over and right-clicked, opening up the title page. One message was from a bank. At first he thought it was an advertisement and was about to delete it when he second-guessed himself and opened it. It was a congratulatory letter, telling him how nice it was to have him as a client and that using the account code listed, he could access his funds and make deposits.

Mike's hand trembled as he copied the numbers down on a sheet of paper. Then he followed the prompts, typed in the numbers and hit enter. With the speed of light, the computer screen flashed his bank balance: $2,500,000.00.

Shaken, he turned off his computer and went for his run. Mike was a creature of habit. He could not feel his feet hit the pavement as he ran one mile, followed by another and yet another. Frantically, his mind tried to figure out how to commit the perfect murder on a military base with his quarry guarded. Knowing there could be no sound that left out a gun. Because of security, he was unable to get into Angelica's suite, thus negating strangulation or stabbing. His options for the perfect murder were just about running out when he saw; in fact, he damn near tripped over, his method. It was quiet and lethal. Now all he needed was the opportunity.

According to the "In case of fire" evacuation plan, Mike knew Angelica's room number was room number 110, the fifth room down on the right. It was an outside room with windows at ground level. Now, he walked around the building, trying to look like he was cooling down after his run, and took a detour alongside the building and counted the windows. It didn't take long to find Angelica's room and what he was hoping for—opportunity. Her window was open. *Thank God for air conditioning,* Mike thought as he walked down the sidewalk, past her window and to the side entrance of the BOQ.

As Mike lay on his bed, the back of his head resting in his hands, he stared up at the ceiling, watching his pet gecko walk across the ceiling, looking for supper. He had already showered and had even shaved after his run. Now he was feeling the rush of excitement as it slowly built inside him. In his mind, he imagined making love to one beautiful girl after another, he felt a stirring deep in his loins. *This time next week, I'll be five million dollars richer and out of the army. Nobody will be the wiser,* was his next thought.

With his plans made, he had only two things to do. He checked his watch. It was 8:00 p.m. He would give her five more hours. That meant he could go to the store and then out to dinner. Feeling an Italian dinner would be appropriate; he knew just the restaurant.

Later, returning from his outing, Mike parked his car in the back and took the long way around to the front door of the BOQ. What he was doing was checking to see if Angelica's window was still open and to his joy, it was! Acting nonchalant, he continued walking, a small smile forming on his face as he opened the door to his room.

Automatically, he put his car keys on the desk and then poured out the contents of his shopping bag onto his bed. There was a pair of extra-large plastic gloves and an eight-inch long universal wrench; that's all he would need to commit his perfect murder. The gloves he would flush down the toilet when he was done while the wrench he would simply throw into his toolbox.

To pass the time, he watched some television but got bored, so he got on-line and played a couple games of chess, not caring if he won or lost. After all, he was just biding his time.

At the time Mike had determined, he walked outside into the warm, humid air of south Florida. He stopped a moment and looked up at the sky, noting there were no stars, just complete and total blackness. The only light was coming from the entrance light around the corner. It gave off just enough light for him to see what he had to do.

As if he knew what he was doing, Mike walked up to a portable welding cart that had been left by the construction crew. A cupola that would house an ATM and vending machines was in the process of being built. He grasped the welding torch in his left hand and with his right, opened up the jaws of his crescent wrench to the right size and turned the nut, then threw the torch to the ground. The oversized tires made the cart easy to handle and Mike began pushing it to his intended destination.

Angelica's room was dark and the window was still open. He couldn't believe his good fortune. Quietly, he unwrapped the hard, rubber hose and stretched it to Angelica's window where he slowly inserted the hose into the room. Mike's only fear was that the air conditioner would be running and if so, the air circulation in the room would probably draw the Argon gas upward.

Argon is a very heavy, inert gas used as a shielding gas for welding. In a confined space, it could replace a room's oxygen, thus causing death by suffocation. Though the principle is simple, the results are fatal. Angelica would be sleeping with the angels very soon. Mike opened the valve all the way, sending the gas into Angelica's room. Mike then walked calmly back to his room and simply went to bed. 0600 hours was fast approaching and he had a plane to catch.

38

⋇ ⋇ ⋇

KATI ROLLED OVER AND ANSWERED THE phone. Glancing at the clock it told her it was 0800 and she had only been asleep for two hours. Seth had been sexually voracious and needed to be fed. Every muscle in her body ached from his sexual antics.

"Hello," she said, waiting for the invisible voice to respond.

"Yes, ma'am, is General Hatfield there?"

"Who should I say is calling?" she asked, leaning on her elbow and sitting up.

"Yes, ma'am. This is Major Strongbow and I'm the base Provost Marshall."

Kati rolled over and handed Seth the phone. As he took the phone, Seth smiled and kissed her shoulder. "General Hatfield!"

"Major Strongbow, sir. I'm calling to report two deaths on base."

Seth quickly sat up. Somehow, he knew. "Yes, major," he said.

"Sir, I believe you knew the victims."

"Victims, major?" Seth asked.

"Sir, the deaths were premeditated; the ladies were murdered," Strongbow replied.

"Where are you right now, major?" Seth asked, turning his body and placing his bare feet on the carpet.

"I'm standing at the front desk of the BOQ. Why?" Strongbow asked.

"Because, major, I'm on my way to see you!"

Major Strongbow hung up the telephone. *Just great! Now I'll have some wild-ass general to contend with,* he thought as he walked outside to see what else his men had found.

Ж Ж Ж

General Seth Hatfield stood in the shower, the hot water massaging his tired muscles and hiding his tears. He was angry; somehow, he felt he had betrayed Angelica and Sarah. Mendoza would pay for this sin in hell and that's where he was going to send Mendoza along with his entire cartel—to hell!

What he had trouble understanding was how Mendoza had found her here in Florida and on this base so soon. Also, how did the person or persons who did this evil deed get on base that late at night, unless they were already cleared to get on base or maybe worked on base? And another thing that pissed him off was how the hell had they found out her room number? *Atkins?* Seth said to himself.

Seth had more questions than he did answers. He turned off the water and reached for a towel but the towel was gone. Kati had done his laundry again. Stepping out of the warm shower stall, dripping wet, he opened the linen cabinet and pulled out a fresh towel. As he approached the sink, he caught a glimpse of himself in the oversized mirror that always showed the truth. He could see that his eyes were still red and he looked exhausted. Reaching over he grabbed his can of shaving cream and proceeded to shave. Seth always seemed to do his best thinking while he shaved.

As he sat in the back seat of his staff car, the general could see the sun creeping slowly upwards, chasing the night away. He was concentrating on his original premise: that whoever had murdered Angelica and Sarah probably worked on base and already had access to the BOQ. So, narrowing the field, Seth made a mental list of who that would be. Security, firemen, BOQ staff and other distinguished guests who were quartered in the VIP wing. Then he expanded his scope a little further. Atkins was billeted in the BOQ. He would ask Strongbow to investigate that theory. Who knew? He might just get lucky.

Ж Ж Ж

General Pablo Gonzales flipped the switch that flooded his office with soft music. He heard that familiar gurgling sound and knew his coffee would be ready in just a few minutes. Hanging up his hat, he slipped off his Ryan et; he was getting ready for work.

Reaching across his desk, he grabbed the out-going correspondence folder. Carefully, he read each letter, paying extra attention to spelling and punctuation. When he was satisfied, he signed each letter for the clerk to mail.

When the gurgling had stopped, Pablo grabbed his favorite coffee cup and poured himself a cup of coffee, adding two lumps of sugar but no cream.

Next, he turned on his personal computer. First, he liked to read the local and world news and then he would read the sports, as he was passionate about soccer and baseball. Looking up, he happened to see he had e-mail. Opening up the message it read: Job completed, send rest of money!

Gonzales leaned back in his chair. He had not expected results so soon. When he looked at his watch, he realized Carlos would not yet be awake. He thought of calling McBride but decided against it. McBride was nothing but an opportunist getting rich off the misfortune of others.

Since Julio Mendoza was still not responding to his phone calls or e-mails, Pablo knew he had a decision to make. Quickly he typed: Prove it!

Just then, his clerk walked in and handed him the morning dispatches and took the correspondence folder. Pablo took a sip of his coffee and smiled as the clerk turned and left his office. It was then that the general realized that if the news was correct, he had just saved Julio $5,000,000 and had also taken care of the puta, Renee.

Ж Ж Ж

Ryan sat in his kitchen drinking his morning coffee and reading his USA Today. He was paying particular attention to the financial section. Finding what he was looking for, he read the message. Ryan knew that Seth had directed the terse, four-line communiqué at him: Suspect treason our end. You are in mortal danger. Strongly suggest you evacuate and bring your package if you can. Mendoza has killed Renee.

Ryan took a sip of his coffee; he needed time to think. He knew that if he jumped ship, Mendoza would escape. If he stayed, he might be killed. Since he hated Mendoza with all his being, he wanted to get all the rats in one place. Once that was done, he could get on an airplane.

General Hatfield had already taken care of Rossi's passport. Ryan did not know how he had done it in such a short time but after all, he was the general. When he had asked, Seth had only smiled and said, "Easy, sir, I just called Little Miss Bo Peep." He had had no idea what the general had meant.

Just then, Dominique broke his concentration as she walked into the kitchen wearing only a bra, panties and high-heeled shoes. Ryan's love-muscle jumped to attention quickly when he saw her. She was holding two dresses, one red, the other a very pretty, dark blue. "Which one do you like?" she asked.

"Why can't you wear what you've got on?" Ryan said, smiling from ear to ear.

Dominique began to laugh and again asked him, "Which one?"

"The blue one," Ryan replied, watching her as she turned and walked back towards the bedroom.

Suddenly, an idea came to him: *The general's message said there was a traitor among us. Why couldn't the traitor be General Pablo Gonzales? If he knew where Renee was all along, how did he know? And how did he know to send Renee's brother to Washington D.C. with wine and candy laced with a slow-acting poison? Julio Mendoza would be very interested in knowing how Pablo could know when not even Carlos had known.*

It was slim chance, Ryan knew, but with the idea he had already implanted in Carlos' mind, it might be just enough to start a fight. He had to get Dominique to ask Julio how Pablo had known about Renee and also plant the idea about the $5,000,000 possibly going to Pablo. That should really get Julio's paranoia going. Poor General Pablo Gonzales, he was such an ass kisser; always trying to be something that he wasn't—smart!

39

ᚖ ᚖ ᚖ

T HE HAWK WAS INSIDE MENDOZA'S SECRET cave, after hours of slow and very tedious movement. He whispered, one quick radio transmission: "The Hawk is in." Then staying in the shadows, he found himself a nice, safe place to hide. He selected stacks of barrels so he could move up and down the aisles and watch. Glancing at his watch, he saw it was 0100 hours and made quick note to himself that the lights were on, but nobody seemed to be home. In the back of the cave he could hear some machines and smelled what he thought was hydrochloride. Off to his left he saw what appeared to be thousands of burlap and plastic bags filled with coca leaves.

It did not take Hawk but a second to figure out what was going on and why. Mendoza had gone high-tech, probably to keep up with the demand and to keep the farmers happy. Because of the warm, humid climate, the coca plants could produce four harvests a year. Though the farmers loved a continuous source of income, the harvesting was labor-intensive and time-consuming. Each coca plant had to be harvested by hand and then the leaves had to be placed out in the sun to dry. Once the leaves were dry and brittle, the farmer would hook up his donkey to a rolling stone, smashing the dried leaves into a powder. Then he took the coca into market to sell. If he were lucky, he would already have a buyer who would pay him in cash.

What Mendoza was doing was buying the leaves still green, transporting them here and then pouring them into large, rolling dryers that dried the leaves and pulverized them into a fine powder. Using conveyer belts, the dried, finely pulverized powder was then sent to large vats where the carbonated salt was added. After that, the powder was sent through a fine, warm water spray that was used to keep down the dust. The coca powder and carbonated salt were then continuously and vigorously stirred while a solvent—usually kerosene—was added, dampening the coca slurry until a paste was formed. When the paste was of the correct color and consistency, the vats were tilted and the contents dumped onto a large, flat table where the paste was smashed and squeezed to get out all the solvent. Now the pressing table was moved into a large, heated room where the paste was dried and cocaine was born. Hawk figured it was simple, fast and economical—an operation that size could easily produce a thousand kilos or more per day.

Hawk snapped several pictures of Mendoza's operation. Also, he snapped pictures of two large pipes that appeared to at least a foot in diameter. What they were for, he did not know. He went over and placed his hand on them. One was cold and actually throbbed under his hand, while the other pipe made no sound.

Suddenly, just as Hawk was about to venture out and cross the floor, he heard voices. Quickly he took a knee, freezing in place and listening as the voices drew closer. The voices belonged to three men; perhaps boys would best describe them. He could see they were unarmed as they walked away from him across the floor. One boy was tall and lean; the other two were shorter and stockier.

Slowly Hawk exhaled and watched as one of the young men turned a large wheel while the other two lifted up a long, blunt-nosed object that resembled a torpedo. Fascinated, Hawk watched as the tallest of the boys opened up the torpedo while the other boys began pouring kilo-sized plastic bags into the torpedo. When it was full, the torpedo door was closed and all three aligned the torpedo and slid it into the pipe, much like a breach-loader on a rifle. Then the large wheel was turned and away went the drugs to who knew where.

A red light flashed. The tallest boy pulled a lever of some kind and the other two boys pulled out an empty torpedo cylinder. They were operating a very large pneumatic tube system in one direction and a hydrostatic pressure system in another. Obviously, the coca leaves were being transported by this method. In this way, no one saw anybody do anything. How ingenious!

This one he had to phone into Deal.

Ж Ж Ж

"Did you copy?" the hushed voice of Sergeant Hawkins asked.

"We copy, Hawk," Sergeant Deal whispered into his microphone.

"Ask Ed what he wants us to do now?" Hawk replied.

"Will do," Deal whispered, looking directly into Steele's eyes.

Steele looked at his watch and figured: It was 0245 hours and if given the order to disengage now, with any luck Hawk and the Knight could easily be there in forty-five minutes, give or take a few minutes.

"Call them all back then notify HQ we're pulling out. Ask for a chopper pick-up at coordinates…" Steele's voice trailed off as he looked at his first sergeant.

Ed was looking at the map. "Baker 8," he whispered.

"Baker 8," Steele repeated. "Then call Zad and tell him to take his men to map reference Baker 8 and wait. We will be there soon. Also, be sure to tell HQ 'No joy.'"

"Yes sir!" Deal replied, notifying Hawk and the Black Knight to return to camp.

Ж Ж Ж

Something is wrong, terribly wrong, Esther thought as she read a fax order from air ops that said Return to Ryan s ASAP. She walked out of the ready room and down the hall to scheduling where she handed the senior chief her order. As he read her order, he looked at the ready board that hung on the wall. Then he looked at the status of her aircraft.

"How about a departure time of 1100 hours?" the senior chief asked.

"That will be fine, chief, and thank you," Esther said, smiling and walking out of the room.

She actually had time to eat, shower and pack. *Life is good,* she thought as she headed towards the officer's mess.

Ж Ж Ж

Julio Mendoza had just finished eating his breakfast when his phone rang. He thought nothing of it as he picked up the receiver. "Good morning, Julio." It was General Gonzales.

"Morning, Pablo," Julio replied, dipping his buttered toast into his coffee.

"I have very good news for you this morning, Don Julio," Pablo said, his voice becoming excited.

"I like good news, Pablo. Please tell me?"

"The puta, Renee, is dead. I had her killed for you."

"Excellent, Pablo. How did you have her killed?"

Julio's simple question was greeted by silence. "Pablo are you there?" Julio asked.

"Yes, Don Julio, I'm here," was the reply.

"So, Pablo, how was she killed?" Julio asked again. This time his voice held a trace of anger.

"Well, Julio, I do not know how she was killed as I hired someone to kill her."

"Then you don't know for sure that Renee is dead, do you?"

"No, Julio, I don't know for sure," Pablo responded, his once exuberant and boisterous voice now a mere whisper.

"Tell me, Pablo, how did you find Renee when Carlos could not?" Julio asked.

"I got a telephone call from some American who said he would tell me where she was for the reward you posted."

"Pablo, I posted no reward!" Julio said through gritted teeth, his voice going an octave higher with each answer Pablo gave.

"How much did Renee's death cost me, Pablo?"

"Actually nothing, Don Julio," Pablo said. "I talked to Carlos and he said to set up the payment account in one of our overseas banks, then make a good-faith deposit of two and a half million, order the killing and when it is done, cancel the account. That way the girl would be dead and it would cost us nothing."

"So the puta is dead and it has cost us nothing, is this correct?" Julio asked, in a surprised voice.

"You are correct. Her death has cost you nothing," Pablo reiterated.

"Very impressive, Pablo, very impressive indeed," Julio said, taking a sip of his butter-flavored, hot coffee. "Pablo, just one more question. How did this person know to contact you and not Carlos?"

Pablo began to stutter, something he always did when he got scared. "I...I...I don't know, Don Julio!"

"You were set up by the Americans. They probably sacrificed the girl to get to you and that means they will connect you to me. You're no good to me now, Pablo. Your usefulness to me is over!" Julio slammed down the phone and smiled as Juan poured him another cup of coffee.

Ж Ж Ж

Slowly Pablo put the phone back into its cradle. He knew by the sound of Julio's voice that he would be killed and his wife and daughter would be put into Mendoza's service. That thought angered him. Julio liked to use intimidation and fear to control people.

Pablo sat back in his chair, placed his hands across his chest and began listening to the music of Verdi as in his mind he began weighing his options. I am a real general with troops. Mendoza is just a bully who uses terror to control. Mendoza did not have a real army or an air force. Leaning forward, Pablo pressed down on his intercom.

"Yes, general?" the young girl's voice asked.

"Call a staff meeting for 10:00 a.m. I want my entire staff!" he barked.

40

Ж Ж Ж

GENERAL HATFIELD SAT IN HIS DARKENED office, looking at aerial reconnaissance and satellite photographs. He was not happy with Steele's decision to pull his men out of the jungle. However, when Steele had asked what he should have done instead, he had been hard pressed to give a decent answer.

On the positive side, Steele and his men had gained valuable intelligence. When told about Renee's murder Steele got an odd look on his face. When told how she had been killed, Steele had replied, "We have a traitor among us, sir!"

Seth wanted to have Mendoza exterminated along with his cartel and the other cartels eradicated off the face of the earth and Steele and McBride were the men who were going to help him.

Ж Ж Ж

Mike Atkins, a captain in the United States Army, drove off the base. As he did so, he raised his middle finger into the air, saluting all who took the time to notice. He turned his Toyota north and followed the signs that said, "Airport".

Mike was now a rich man who did not need the Army anymore. He already had his passport and his airline ticket to Buenos Aires. Looking at his watch, he noted the time. His plane would depart at 9:00 a.m. Thirteen hours later, he would be starting a new life with lots of money. By the time anyone realized he was AWOL he would be in Argentina.

As he pulled into the long term, parking lot things clicked in his mind. He realized that would be a stupid thing to do because eventually the car would be considered abandoned. The police would run the plates and they would discover he was an army man. The Army would then tell the police he had gone AWOL and the hunt would be on. Then BINGO! They would link him to the two murders.

Mike pulled out of the parking lot, deciding instead to ditch the car. He drove it to a scrap yard where he sold his Toyota and had the owner of the scrape yard drive him back to the airport. By this time tomorrow, he figured he would be looking at villas and buying a new car. *Yes, indeed, life was good, even if I had to kill to get the good life!*

Ж Ж Ж

Steele walked up Esther's driveway. It had only been ten days since he had been with her yet it seemed like a thousand years. He needed her and he was going to tell her. He was in love with her and he wanted her to know it. Looking around, he noticed Esther's car was dirty and her lawn needed mowed. Using his key to open the back door, he threw his bag into the kitchen. "Hello?" he bellowed. "Anybody home?"

His call was greeted by silence. Steele picked up his bag and walked to the bedroom where he noticed dust on the nightstand. Tossing his bag onto the bed, he proceeded to unpack. The dirty clothes went into the laundry room and then he changed into gym shorts. Next, he rifled through the mail and brought it inside, placing it on the kitchen counter. Opening the refrigerator, he found the same pizza they had eaten when he left was still there. The lettuce was wilted, the cucumber, and green pepper, were rotten and the milk, was sour.

Steele proceeded to clean out the refrigerator and then decided to wash her car. Once that was done, he would make a quick trip to the store and buy supplies. After that all he had to do was wait.

Ж Ж Ж

Shirley Lamb was sitting at her kitchen table cutting out coupons when her cell phone rang. Glancing at the clock on the stove, she wondered who would be calling her at this hour.

"Hello," Shirley said, continuing to cut out her coupons.

"Hi, Shirley, it's Esther. I'm sorry for calling you at home but this is the only number I had to reach you."

"Oh, yes, Esther, it's nice to hear your voice. Did your mission go well?"

"No, Shirley, that's why I'm calling you. I received orders this morning to return to NAS Ryan sonville so I flew home, disappointed, and a little perplexed, as to why my mission was cancelled. Can you tell me why the mission cancelled?"

"Esther, I have no idea. Give me your cell number and in the morning I will make some inquires and call you back."

"Okay, girlfriend. I will wait for your call and thanks!" Esther said.

"Who was on the phone, honey?" Shirley's husband of eleven years asked, as he opened the refrigerator and pulled out a beer.

"Nothing important, honey, just a friend wanting some information," Shirley replied, cutting out a buy-one-get-one-free ad

Ж Ж Ж

Major Strongbow was waiting outside General Hatfield's office. Per the general's request, he had done a cursory investigation of Captain Atkins. As he dug deeper, the good captain soon became a "person of interest". Requests for warrants were issued for his personal phone records, e-mails, and bank accounts. The result was nothing spectacular except for two credit card calls to Columbia Bogotá to be specific. A trace of the phone number revealed it was a number for the Columbian Government's Anti-Drug Task Force. There was nothing unusual about it except the calls were just prior to the murders. An argument could be made, and rightfully so, that it was just a coincidence. However, when you threw in the e-mail that read, "Job Completed: Send Rest of Money," and the e-mail was sent to a Pablo Gonzales in Bogotá, that definitely was suspicious.

"The general will see you now, major", the second lieutenant said, showing the awe-struck major into the general's office.

Ж Ж Ж

When General Pablo Gonzales walked into the conference room, his attaché had called the room to attention. General Gonzales nodded his head and the young lieutenant pulled out his chair.

"Be seated," the general said, waving his hands in a sweeping motion.

The general superstitiously watched each man take his seat. Out of the seven men that comprised his staff, he knew four were on Mendoza's payroll and this day would be removed and placed under arrest under the charge of conspiracy.

His plan was to bring into his inner circle, officers that were now serving in the field, using their insight and knowledge to help in his planned attack on Mendoza. In addition, he planned to notify the Americans of his initiatives and ask them for help. The orders to his officers would be Take no prisoners. It was his intention to use the same tactics as Mendoza used.

Ж Ж Ж

It was early in the morning when Shirley Lamb picked up her phone and called General Hatfield's office. The invisible, deep, sexy voice asked for her call sign. After she readily gave it, he replied, "Good morning, Bo-Peep. How may I help you?" After she asked to speak with General Hatfield, he said, "Just a moment, ma'am". Then she heard him call, "Bo-Peep line two, sir".

Then she heard the unmistakable voice of the general saying, "Good morning, Bo-peep"

"Morning, sir, this is Shirley. I'll get right to the point. Why was Operation Interdiction cancelled?"

"Shirley, the operation was not cancelled; only postponed. It seems Mendoza has outsmarted us again. We thought we had him surrounded and cutoff, making it difficult for him to produce his cocaine and ship it. Instead, he has built an underground delivery system, using the river to propel his product down river undetected. It appears to be a huge, pneumatic tube system through which he delivers coca leaves."

Taken aback, Shirley thought to herself, *what an ingenious plan! He has held the U. S. prisoner while continuing to produce, ship, and sell his cocaine!*

The general continued, "I also cancelled because I suspect we have a traitor on my end. I won't go into details, Shirley, but Mendoza managed to kill our major source of information and material witness, right here under our noses, while she was on base. If Mendoza can get to someone here on base, there is no telling how much he knows about our operation, especially if Rossi talked.

"Rossi is alive?" Shirley asked in disbelief.

"Yes, Shirley, Rossi is alive and now working for Mendoza."

"In what capacity is Rossi working for that drug lord?" Shirley asked.

"Whore" Seth spat out the word.

At first, Shirley did not respond to Seth's reply. Her anger, which was seldom seen by others, was slowly creeping through her personal and very professional veneer.

"General, I want you to kill this son-of-a-bitch! I do not care how you do it! All I want is a phone message from you saying ROSSI AVENGED. I will know that you and your men were successful and we will go after the next cartel."

General Hatfield smiled. He liked this woman the mens had christened Bo-Peep. *Yeah, Bo- Peep my Aunt Nellie's ass! This woman wants to kick ass and not take names. Maybe they should change her name to "The Bitch!"*

Ж Ж Ж

General Gonzales listened intently to each officer; paying particular attention to the ones who thought what he had proposed was "insane." The irony of it all was that the officers telling him his plan was insane were the officers he was going to have arrested. Just before the conclusion of the meeting, Pablo asked the four men in question to step into his private office.

41

Ж Ж Ж

MIKE ATKINS LOOKED AT HIS WATCH and noted he had been in the air for nine hours. He still had another four hours before he landed in Buenos Aires. Though he did not know one type of airplane from another, he did know this airplane was too damn slow.

Next, he thought about when he landed. His first order of business would be to collect his old B-4 bag then pass through customs. After that, he planned to hail a taxi to the Sheraton Hotel where he would shower, shave and take a nice long nap.

Needing something to occupy his mind, he pulled out his official, black U. S. Government ink pen and grabbed a napkin from the tray of the man sleeping next to him. The currency rate for the Argentina peso was 3.08 to the dollar. Math was never Mike's favorite subject but he could multiply the exchange rate by five and add six zero's.

Upon seeing the figure, Mike began to get excited. He watched the cute attendant, as she walked up and down the aisle taking care of the passengers. Maybe it was the fact that now he could afford the things he had always wanted, but could not have without causing himself financial embarrassment. Whatever the reason for his excitement, Mike had to get up and relieve himself.

Ж Ж Ж

It had been ten days since General Pablo Gonzales had four of his top advisors arrested and placed in prison, out of sight and out of his mind. A trial would come later where they would be found guilty and shot.

Presently, he sat in his conference room with four new, highly respected officers. Each man was a veteran of the drug war who had close liaisons with the Americans and hated Mendoza. Pablo was now going to use and abuse these men in order to destroy Mendoza. He was interested in listening to his staff's ideas, as to how they were going to destroy Mendoza and his cartel of evil.

Knowing Mendoza, Pablo knew he would strike quickly. Therefore, he needed to attack him at his most vulnerable place—his heart. Simply stated, that would be his wife and children. If he could not reach them, he would turn Pablo's brother Ernesto against him for the promises of limitless wealth, and power. Julio was a back stabber and Pablo knew he would never come at him man-to-man. He would give the job to Carlos and Carlos would send his death angel named Jesus.

Ж Ж Ж

General Seth Hatfield stood, alone, with his head bowed and hands folded, as he listened to the young priest describe Angelica's young life:

"Born in innocence, sold into slavery, she reclaimed her soul and was sacrificed for the good of mankind." Those words, *sacrificed for the good of mankind,* stung Seth. He was not expecting them, but in the global and spiritual sense, the priest was right.

Steele and he had gone halves in paying for Angelica's funeral; Steele had given up his pre-arranged burial plot that he had purchased years ago. Supposedly, it was good anytime or anywhere it was needed. The general had personally picked out a very modest casket for his friend and asked the base chaplain for a priest to officiate. Sarah's remains were shipped to her parent's home address per her dad's request.

As Seth listened to the blessing, his mind was recalling this morning's telephone call with Lamb. Milo Adams, the acting under secretary, had gotten a phone call from the U. S. Ambassador in Columbia. Apparently, the Columbian newspapers were telling the Columbians, and anybody else who would listen, how the United States Military had kidnapped a young girl and taken her to the United States under the pretext that she needed medical care. Repeated attempts by the Columbian Ambassador, and even the girl's brother to bring her home had been met with denial. Now they were saying she was dead, supposedly having been tortured and beaten at the hands of the American Military.

The general and Shirley Lamb knew it was Mendoza who had created a public relations nightmare. Seth and Shirley's problem was that they could not fight back without jeopardizing Operation Cadence, thus endangering personnel in sensitive positions. What was needed was a miracle, anything to take the heat away from the USA.

Ж Ж Ж

When Esther rode her Harley into her garage, she immediately recognized that she would not be alone. She noticed the lawn had been mowed and that her car was washed. As she walked into the kitchen, she saw groceries that had not been put away. Walking down the hall, she heard the shower. Next, she saw the dirty clothes and knew her man was home.

Quickly she undid her combat boots, pulled off her socks, unzipped her flight suit, unsnapped her bra, and pulled off her boxers. Opening the bathroom door, she saw Zack in the shower.

"Hey, soldier, you want me in there with you or out here?" she called.

Steele smiled. "In here, woman there's something I want to show you."

As she entered the shower, Steele took her hand and pulled her into his hard, lean body. Running his wet, soapy hand up her back, he grabbed her hair. Holding her head tightly, he kissed her hard and long, his passion becoming a torrent of rage, as he turned her body into the shower spray and mounted her like a wild animal...

Sometime later, Steele held Esther in his arms. Both were naked, wrapped in each other's arms, their lust quenched for the moment. Esther turned into Zack and laid her head down on his chest. She was sleepy. Neither of them paid attention to a news broadcast on CNN. If they had done so, they would have learned of the civil unrest in Bogotá.

The news reporter was telling of a Columbian general named, Pablo Gonzales who was in charge of the Columbian Anti Drug Task Force and that he had mobilized his army and declared unconditional war on a drug lord named Julio Mendoza.

Ж Ж Ж

Ryan held the phone a foot away from his ear and still he could here Julio cursing. Quietly placing the phone down, he continued shaving. All the while, Julio was yelling, never saying anything that made sense. It was something about being betrayed and oh, yeah, the Columbian army had declared war on him. It made Ryan laugh so hard he found it hard to shave. He guessed that Seth had been right in creating paranoia, and isolating Mendoza from the real world and applying pressure. It would create indecision and panic.

When Dominique walked into his bathroom, bringing him his morning coffee, she whispered, "Is Julio done talking about Pablo?"

"What about Pablo?" Ryan asked.

"It's all over the news, Ryan ! Pablo has mobilized his army, has declared martial law, and is going after Mendoza."

"I did not see this coming and I bet neither did Seth," he said under his breath, momentarily forgetting about Dominique.

"What did you say?" she asked.

"I said it's going to be a big-time fight between two assholes and Pablo has the bigger guns."

"You think Pablo can defeat me, McBride?"

Ryan had forgotten about the phone. Julio had heard every word. *Oh well, what's one more in this fight,* McBride told himself.

Picking up the phone, Ryan said, "Yes, Julio, I think Pablo will defeat you!"

"You're a traitor, Ryan , you hear me? You're fucking dead!"

"Calm down, Julio, Pablo can and will defeat you in the city. Your strength is not in the city of Bogotá but in the country. So let Pablo have the Calles and the Carreras. Who cares? His Army is not equipped to fight in the jungle. He has no air force to drop bombs on you, no navy to stop our shipments. Let him run his tanks up and down the Diagonals and Transversals for the news reporters. We will defy Pablo and call a conference of all our major buyers and distributors and we will do it right under his nose. Can you imagine how humiliating that would be for Pablo? Hell, Julio, we will make a joke of him." McBride knew he was pulling out all the stops. It was now or never and it was just arrogant enough to work.

Then Ryan heard music to his ears, as Julio began to chuckle and then laugh. He heard a slapping sound as Julio slapped the table. Obviously, Julio was going to call a conference. Now to notify Seth and let him know when.

42

ЖЖЖ

UPON ARRIVING AT THE AIRPORT, MIKE had plans, or so he thought. He was going to take a taxi to the hotel, then take a long hot shower, shave and then take a nap. Everything was going to be great!

Somehow, he managed to grab his luggage and clear customs and immigration in less than an hour. When he hailed a taxi, he told the driver which hotel. He was handing the hotel clerk his new bankcard a little after 8:00 p.m.

Mike remembered the welcome letter from the bank saying it could take five business days before his card would be active. Nevertheless, he gave it to the young girl anyway, hoping that it would work.

The clerk ran his card, looked at the computer screen, and opened her eyes wide. A message had appeared on the screen telling her that his card was to be "confiscated". The color drained from Mike's face. He was close to being destitute, was in a foreign country, did not speak the language and was wanted for murder in the states. It suddenly occurred to him that Mendoza had screwed him royally and he was helpless to fight back.

Walking back to the desk, he pulled out his MasterCard, figuring the least he could do was take a shower and sleep before he panicked.

⋇ ⋇ ⋇

General Hatfield watched and listened carefully to the CNN reporter describe, in detail, General Pablo Gonzales's plan of taking back his country from the mighty drug cartels. Seth smiled; thinking to himself: *There is a God after all.* He had prayed for a miracle and God had sent him Pablo.

The general knew instinctively that the time was ripe for Mendoza to fall. He figured Mendoza would be too busy watching his ex-friend, Pablo, to pay much attention to what the Americans were doing.

Colonel McBride had sent him a cryptic message, informing him that Mendoza had called an emergency conference of all his buyers and distributors from around the world. The meeting was to take place on Columbia's Independence Day, July 20. *You have to love Mendoza's flare for theatrics,* Seth thought. However, he liked fireworks and Columbia's Independence Day was just as good or maybe even better than another day to kill Mendoza and all his people.

⋇ ⋇ ⋇

The only good thing about the Columbian general going nuts in Bogotá was that Milo Adams had quit asking Ethel questions about Angelica. Milo had even called Don at home in an attempt to find this girl, but Don's wife had astutely told him that her husband was not able to talk. Don had trained his wife well.

The week before, Ethel had informed Mrs.Don McGee that Angelica had been murdered and she in turn had told her husband. Don's only comment about Angelica's death had been, "May God hold her in the palm of His hand and may His angels watch over her".

He then spoke to Ethel and asked, "Does Lamb know?"

His loyal assistant replied, "Yes, she does."

"Ethel, I think by having that young girl killed, Mendoza has invoked the wrath of two very dangerous men. One is a general who hates to lose and by killing Angelica on his base, under his protection, has really pissed him off. The other man is the man who found her in the jungle, saved her and subsequently fell in love with her. Mendoza is a dead man and all I can truly say is, good!"

Ж Ж Ж

"Ryan , honey, does this dress make me look fat?" Dominique asked, walking towards him and wearing a peach-colored, strapless dress that accentuated her charms and then some.

Looking up from his paper, Ryan smiled at her, knowing if he said "yes" she would go into a tirade and if he said "no" then the dress wasn't sexy. Sidestepping the peach dress he said, "Well, I think you're too sexy for that dress; I would wear the red one". Ryan hoped she liked his response.

"I think you're right, honey. I will wear the red one. Carlos likes red," she said as she walked back into the bedroom.

Returning to his newspaper, Ryan found the general's message under "personals". Reading between the lines it told him: Bring his date

(Rossi) to San Miguel's Restaurant. San Miguel's was a small, intimate restaurant near the airport. He and Carlos had eaten there several times after meetings. In other words, Ryan was to make reservations and be there at noon on 20 July.

Ryan wondered why the specified time was noon, as the restaurant did not open up until 4:00 p.m. and since it was a national holiday, it probably would not be open at all. The only thing he remembered about the restaurant—other than knowing where it was located—was that there was a dirt road behind the restaurant that circled the airport. Airport maintenance and security personnel performed routine patrols looking for drug smugglers were the only ones who used this road. To Ryan this idea was ironic, as who would smuggle drugs into a country where the drugs were mass-produced?

He reasoned that Columbian Independence Day would be the day when Seth attacked and killed Mendoza. That left only two weeks for him to get all his money transferred to an offshore account. This was all coming apart in Columbia and he did not intend going home empty handed. His plan was to return home, divorce his wife and then retire to some place where he could play golf and fish.

Ж Ж Ж

Mike Atkins sat on a park bench in Buenos Aires, his feet resting on his B-4 bag and his arms folded across his chest. He was weighing his options, which were few. Mendoza had done to him what he always did with his discarded whores. Now he was alone; a foreigner in a foreign country who did not speak the language and his wallet contained less than a hundred dollars.

Raising his head, he looked at the clear blue sky of Argentina, with big white puffy clouds that floated by, constantly changing shapes. One cloud in particular caught his attention. Its shape resembled an angel. To the angel's immediate left Mike saw Jesus standing on two clouds; His form encased in the colors of orange and gold. His hands outstretched, beckoning Mike to follow Him.

Standing up, Mike grabbed his bag and with tears flowing down his cheeks, he walked towards the large, Catholic Church that sat on the corner across the street from the park. *What's wrong with being a priest?* He thought to himself, as he crossed the street and walked up the steps to begin his new life.

43

⋇ ⋇ ⋇

JUAN AND RYAN WERE SITTING on the veranda of Carlos' hacienda. The cool breeze created by the waterfall was refreshing against the heat and humidity of the Columbian summer. Miguel was hustling the servant girls to bring cool drinks to his boss and friend. Simba and Sheba were curled around Ryan 's feet, softly purring their content.

Both men took the moment to prepare their cigars while they waited for their drinks to arrive. As always, Ryan was meticulous, as he cut the end off his Cuban cigar and licked the tobacco leaf with his tongue, dampening the leaf for a cool, slower burning cigar. Carlos just bit the end off his cigar and spit the shredded leaf out over the balcony where it would eventually fall into the river below.

"Tell me, McBride, why did you talk Julio into having this conference and why have it at Julio's hacienda?" Carlos asked while lighting his cigar.

Ryan waited until the scantily clad, young girl placed their drinks on the table and left before he responded to Carlos. "Juan, as you know I have suspected we have a spy in our organization. I suspected Pablo and I think his recent actions have proved me correct. However, my friend, he did not act alone. After all, the general is not that smart and we both know it. I suspect that one, maybe two of the people who will be at the conference will be our traitor or traitors.

"Another thing, Carlos, I will not attend the opening festivities. I am taking Dominique and we are going to Buenaventura for a three-day vacation. I have not decided if I am going to fly or drive. I will probably fly and rent a car. However, the real reason I am going is to check out the port and surrounding area in case Pablo gets too close or begins interrupting our shipments. I want a back-up plan."

"Good idea, McBride, but you still did not answer my question," Carlos said, taking a deep puff on his cigar.

Ryan chuckled, "Oh, yeah, I forgot the question." He was stalling, trying to figure out what Carlos was thinking.

"McBride, tell me once again— Why did you convince Julio to have the conference at his hacienda? I know what you said about traitors and that may be true, but why ask Julio to have a meeting that will surely draw attention to us?"

"I appealed to Julio's ego. He was having a melt down over Pablo and I told him that Pablo would win and that pissed him off. When he threatened my life, I had to reassure him that Pablo may control a city but Julio controlled the country. So let Pablo play soldier for the cameras and we will conduct business, as usual and discredit Pablo by making a joke out of him. Does that answer your question?"

Juan smiled and then began to laugh. His laughter was cut short as Miguel appeared with lunch. "McBride, you're too much! Your idea makes perfect sense and do not worry about not being there on the first day. However, Julio may want Dominique to be there to entertain some selected guests.

"If he does, tell Julio that Dominique will be there the next day," Ryan said, placing his cigar in the ashtray, opening up his napkin and placing it in his lap.

Carlos laughed then said, "You take one of Julio's prized putas and tell him he can have her when you're through? Julio will be mad, but I suspect he will forgive you."

Ж Ж Ж

Zack rolled over and reached for Esther. Putting his arm around her sleeping body, he pulled her closer to him. He loved the way her body molded itself to his. Softly he kissed the back of her head, inhaling the clean smell of her hair.

"Mmm," she moaned, snuggling her body deeper into Steele's arms. "What time is it?" she asked.

"0530; time for all good soldiers to be getting up," he said, kissing her on her lips. Steele kicked off the covers and proceeded to the bathroom.

Esther reached over, grabbed his pillow, and placed it over her face, drowning out the sound of her stallion peeing. She heard the shower come on and knew she could not hold it any longer. She had to go and go now. When she stood up, she realized she was naked. Walking into the bathroom, she sat on the toilet and smiled. *I guess the honeymoon is over,* she thought. Finished, she stood up and walked into the shower stall. *Isn't this where I came in?* She asked herself with a rueful smile.

Ester and Zack were in the middle of making passionate love when he heard his pager and knew what he must do. It was time to report to the Ryan sonville Naval Air Station Air Operations

Officer. There he would be manifested aboard a very special C-130 flight. He was to make a high-altitude, low-opening parachute jump, or HALO jump as the men called them, from 30,000 feet. Naturally, he would wear his thermals, gloves and his oxygen mask and fall for ten minutes, maybe twenty, and then at around two thousand feet, he would pull his ripcord and steer his chute to a predetermined destination. From there he would recover the gear he and his men had stashed and make his way back to the hideout.

Steele knew instinctively that this was the moment in time he had been waiting for. He would get the opportunity to destroy Mendoza, and avenge Renee. However, for the moment, he was occupied. Both the general and the mission could wait; Esther could not.

44

ЖЖЖ

GENERAL PABLO GONZALES WAS BEING TOUTED as a hero by the press. Everywhere he went news reporters and television cameras surrounded him. He was asked stupid, annoying, and often very personal questions. It finally got so bad he had surrounded himself with a screen of soldiers in order to push the press away so he could do his job.

Pablo sat alone on a straight back, wooden chair in some dirty back alley that the street whores once had used to ply their trade. It was filled with used condoms and different colored shards of glass from broken wine and beer bottles; that almost gave the alley class. His legs were crossed, his elbow resting on his knee and his chin resting in his hand. The smoke of his cigar swirled above his head resembling a halo. He was reading intelligence reports from various parts of the city. People were now actually walking the streets at night. Children were playing under the street lamps, as the drug addicts, pimps, and thugs were now gone. They would not be back; the general had seen to that.

As he read each report from his field officers, the one from his chief of internal security caught his attention. It mentioned men of questionable character arriving at the airport from Italy, Spain, Belgium, Germany, Mexico, and the United States. They were arriving daily and then after passing through customs and immigration were ushered into microbuses and taken away. He wanted permission to follow them.

The general could guess who they were, where they were going, and why—Julio was preparing for an all-out war. Since Julio did not have the weapons or manpower for a sustained battle, he was going to launch a series of terrorist attacks. More than likely, Mendoza had asked for financial support from his "business associates". Of course, Pablo knew he was only speculating.

Turning his head, the general asked his clerk to "Call his Chief of Internal Security and tell him to detain these men for questioning. If they do not cooperate, tell him to throw them in prison." Then he also asked his clerk, "Get me General Leon of the Columbian Air Force. I need to borrow some of Leon's airplanes."

Ж Ж Ж

LCDR Esther Colgate had a glow about her as she walked into the squadron ready room. Her smile came easily, as she said good morning to the other pilots. When she looked at the "ready board", she saw she had a flight at 0800 hours, then her day was clear until 1400 hours when she had another training flight scheduled. However, ready boards were known to be wrong and this morning was no exception.

She was remembering that Zack had asked her to marry him. The way he had asked her hadn't been particularly romantic, unless being impaled by his love-muscle shoved up inside her and hot water cascading down upon her head, making it difficult to breathe could be considered romantic. Between his manly grunts and her moans he had said, "Let's get married". Not exactly, the way a girl dreamed to be asked, but she had said, "Yes".

As she turned to walk into her office, Petty Officer Anderson intercepted her with a message that the commander wanted to see her. She already knew she was overdue on two pilot assessments and was also late on writing her self-evaluation, something she hated to do.

"Morning, sir, you wanted to see me?" she asked.

"Yes, I did. Please shut the door, will you?"

Esther turned, closed the door, and stood at attention. Her experience had taught her the skipper only shut his door when he was about to chew ass. Mentally, she prepared herself for his verbal abuse.

"Colgate, I have a top-secret, encoded fax from the state department via the Navy. You have been selected to join some secret, joint military operation. You are to proceed to some island code name Tiger. I have never heard of it. Anyway, you will go home and pack your bags. You will be gone for as long as it takes. I will call scheduling and get your plane ready."

"Yes, sir" she saluted then opened the door. As she left, she told Petty Officer Anderson to find somebody else to do the two pilot assessments. Then she walked back into the ready room, picked up her discarded coffee cup, poured the cold coffee into the sink, and rinsed out her cup. Five minutes later, she was riding her Harley into the garage.

As Esther walked into the kitchen she saw that Zack was dressed in his BDUs with a knife strapped to his leg at just about boot level. His soft, well-worn Green Beret cap was pulled down to one side. He had just finished packing.

This was the first time she had seen Steele in his uniform. He was awesome-looking even a bit scary.

"Hello, honey," he said, turning towards her and opening up his arms.

She did not need to be coaxed. Immediately she tossed her keys on the kitchen counter and walked into his embrace, enjoying the feeling as his arms enveloped her body and pulled her gently to him. Esther could smell his aftershave; she loved the smell of him. He kissed her tenderly, as if it were a kiss good-bye.

Already emotional, s small tear escaped and ran down Esther's cheek. Although he never said he was returning to the jungle to avenge his jungle girl, she knew that was where he was going. What Steele did not know was that she would be the one above him, looking down and waiting for his word to kill Mendoza.

45

Ж Ж Ж

STEELE SAT IN THE BACK OF the C-130 Hercules; its four, Allison turbo engines lifting the aircraft higher and higher, until the inside cabin temperature caused the aluminum skin of the aircraft to frost over. Zack could see his breath, as he checked his equipment. HALO jumps were not easy to make. If his oxygen regulator valve froze, he would die from asphyxia, or if he lost a glove in his dive, his hand would freeze solid. Many a soldier, sailor or airman could tell you the horror of HALO jumps.

Looking at his watch again, he saw there was another six hours before he jumped. Finding a pile of blankets, he made a bed on the webbed seats and stretched out. *Tomorrow should be a very interesting day,* he thought as the steady drone of the airplane's engines lulled him to sleep.

Ж Ж Ж

Julio was famous for his parties, sparing no expense in entertaining his guests with singers, movie stars and dancing bands. He provided free sex with all his prostitutes, including Antigua and Dominique.

Antigua had planned the party for four hundred guests, not including the hired help. When she had informed Julio how many RSVPs had been received he smiled and asked if that was all. When she replied, "That is all, so far," he asked for the names of the no-responses.

There was little time left, and many details to be done. Julio had less than twenty-four hours before the conference was to begin. McBride was not going to be there on opening day. That annoyed him, though he understood why. Carlos and Miguel had planned the entire agenda, and Julio was going to be the facilitator, answering questions, and deferring to Carlos and McBride.

Julio had already anticipated what question most of his business associates had on their minds and that was "how much is this going to cost us?" Already he had the answer. Another question was going to be about the security of delivery, and McBride would handle that question. The rest of the questions would be answered in the discussion groups.

Surprisingly, Julio felt good. Despite a few setbacks, his cocaine processing plant was now in full production. Sales were rising across the board and he had eliminated the American's main source of information. He was in negotiations to open a new bank where he could launder his illegal monies and turn them into legitimate business dealings.

Ж Ж Ж

LCDR Esther Colgate was cleared for takeoff. Releasing the brakes, she goosed the throttle, steering her Tom Cat onto the active runway.

She decided to forgo the traditional run-up and hit her throttle, taking it around the horn and into after burner on the roll. The two mighty engines kicked in, pushing her back into the seat. Holding the nose down a little longer than normal, she began to roar down the runway. With a slight flick of her small wrist, she pulled back on the stick and the Tom Cat shot straight up into the air. For this maneuver, she had asked the tower for permission. The brass frowned upon it, as it was considered showboating.

Once clear of the flight pattern, she turned to the southwest. "Tiger Island" was a very small atoll stuck in the Caribbean, just off the coast of Columbia and Venezuela. It was more of a desert island than a tropical one and unlike Aruba; Tiger Island was not a tourist destination. Esther was going to refuel in mid-air before landing. A munitions team would arm the plane with two Cruise missiles and cannon shells on the island. Then she would take off again, and be on station at 1500 hours. The Tom Cat would have enough fuel to lurk just off the Columbian coast for about two and a half hours, before she would be forced to return for fuel.

Ж Ж Ж

Somewhere in the zone between sleep and consciousness, Captain Zack Steele became aware of a deep masculine voice, and a hand that was gently shaking him. "Sir, it's time," the voice said.

Steele pulled off his makeshift sleeping bag, and was immediately greeted, by the cold. He staggered to his feet and realized he had to urinate badly. Looking around for a restroom, he remembered that the Hercules was a cargo aircraft, and did not have restrooms. What it had was a chamber pot, which was nothing, but a five-gallon bucket with the caption written in big red letters, "You use it, and you clean it!"

He decided to use the bucket, as he would be gone before anyone realized he had used it. Then he saw the pilot standing in the darkened corner of the cabin, a big, shit-eating grin upon his face as he looked at Steele and said, "All the comforts of home!"

Looking closer, Zack noticed the pilot's penis was stuck in a hole. Above his head an arrow and white lettering said, "Relief Tube". *How appropriate,* Steele thought, as he walked over and tried to put his penis into the hole that was too small.

The young staff sergeant pointed to Steele and motioned to his watch, holding up ten fingers.

Steele nodded his acknowledgment then reached into his pocket and pulled out a stick of gum. Whenever he jumped, chewing gum helped his ears equalize, as he sped through space at 120 mph, give, or take a few miles per hour. He took a sip of water from his canteen and then proceeded to dress for the jump. He carried no weapons except his knife and stars.

There was enough oxygen for one hour. The staff sergeant helped him on with his tank, then his blast mask. A quick check and he was ready to go. The sergeant turned on his oxygen and Steele was set.

The gauges said the outside temperature was a chilly sixty below zero at the airplane's present altitude and speed. A thumb up signal was given and the sergeant pulled a yellow-colored lever then walked back towards the front of the airplane. He climbed a small, four-step ladder and pressed a red button. Suddenly, a gust of cold air swirled about the cargo hold and the giant tailgate began to open. Steele waited for the green light. All jumpers knew the rules of ready, set go. He had passed ready; he was already set, now he needed to go.

Finally, the green light appeared, and Steele stepped off into oblivion. The prop wash hit him hard, causing him to flip backwards. As he looked to his east, he could see the sun starting to peek over the horizon. To his left he could see the darkened sky with stars twinkling in the distance. Below, he could see the Caribbean and off in the distance he could make out the Pacific Ocean. It was too dark to see his regulator, but he assumed it was working, as he was breathing normally.

There was no way he could see any land yet; he was falling through the dense, dark clouds. His only concern was that he might run into an up draft. That was a concern, as up drafts were massive funnels of tubular air that caused turbulence in aircraft, and if he was unlucky enough to get caught up in one, he could be propelled thousands of feet into the air and carried miles away from his intended target zone.

The only sound he heard was his own breathing and the whistling of the wind, as it rushed over his helmet. The oxygen caused his mouth to become dry; his gum was wedged between his jaw and cheek. He had forgotten that with a regulator in your mouth one could not chew. Oh well, it would be there when he landed.

As he broke through the clouds, he could see the sun had risen a few more degrees, casting an orange glow on the waters below him. To his immediate left he could make out his target zone. Glancing at his watch, he had been diving for eleven minutes. As he fell from the sky, Steele could see that at his present speed and direction he would be landing in near darkness, a stupid and dangerous, thing to do. With a nod of his head, Steele managed to maneuver his body into position allowing him to face the light. He watched the large macaws flying below him, and wondered what the birds would do when he dropped in on them from above.

Next, coming into view was the outline of Mendoza's hacienda, and the cave where he made his poison. To his right he could make out the village of his little friends, and to the left was his landing zone. His altimeter told him he was at 6,000 feet. Not until 1,000 feet would he open, then making a series of swooping circles, he would float in, making it easy on himself. He would ditch his chute, grab his equipment, and take the trail his little friends had shown him, when they had set the mantraps.

Back at McDill A.F.B, Steele had studied the aerial photographs provided by General Hatfield. He recalled he had to be above Mendoza's compound, and at the same time be far enough away, to avoid being blown up. The problem was the laser light; had an effective range of 1500 meters. If he climbed one of the nearby mountains that would afford him safety, and a proper view, he would be out of range to guide the missiles to their intended targets. Going back to the old base camp, he would be too close to the targets, thus putting him in imminent danger. Steele made his decision; he did not want to come back here again. He would return to the old base camp, secure a safe place, and orchestrate mass murder then go home.

⚞ ⚞ ⚞

Ryan Mc Bride rolled over and looked at the alarm clock. The little red numbers told him it was early. However, he got up anyway, and walked into the bathroom, turned on the light, and shut the door, so as not to wake Dominique.

He stood in front of the mirror sizing his face up for a shave, he knew that by this time tonight, he would be in the states. Rossi would be placed in a critical care detoxification unit. She probably would never fully recover from her ordeal. Hopefully, the government would give her some sort of pension that would allow her to slip into anonymity. As for himself, he had successfully transferred his millions of dollars into an overseas account. He figured what Seth and the state department did not know would not hurt them.

The details of how he and Rossi, were to escape were still unclear. He knew what he had to do if Rossi put up a fight. He would render her unconscious, tie her up, and gag her. The hard part now was the waiting.

After another glance in the mirror, Ryan decided against the shave, and returned to bed for one more quick roll in the sack with Rossi. A good-bye sort of fuck—and his soon-to-be ex-wife said he was not sentimental!

Ж Ж Ж

Carlos had been up all night. No matter how hard he wanted to sleep, sleep would not come. His mind would not stop working; it kept going back and forth between McBride and Pablo. His mind could not totally accept Pablo as a traitor. *However*, he thought, *Dorgan's arguments are strong and valid. The general is now using his position and his army to destroy Julio. Still, before McBride there had never been any large shipments detected. After McBride showed up and the Americans no longer trusted Pablo, vital information was lost along with big, important shipments and people. How could this be unless McBride was telling someone? But how? His office phone is bugged, his e-mails are being read, and he is always watched.*

Another thing that bothered him about McBride was that he complained about the puta, Rossi, but when he offered to take her back,

McBride said he would keep her. Then there was another thing: The once valuable information Dominique used to give him about McBride's business dealings had dried up. It was almost as if McBride was planting information into his and Julio's minds, poisoning them against Pablo.

Carlos came to a quick decision: After the conference, he would kill McBride, and sell Rossi. He hated losing sleep, especially over two gringos.

Ж Ж Ж

Air Force Captain Thomas Johns, aka TJ, looked at his watch, then the fuel gauges. He had more than enough fuel if he throttled back to sixty percent power. Then he could either fly around the Caribbean for six more hours or fly to Panama. When he radioed Panama City, he asked for a weather report, and then casually asked for clearance to land. Once he received permission, TJ pointed the C-130 in the direction of Panama. Forty-five minutes to the Panama City airport, he figured. Once there, he would change his clothes and find a place to eat. Bogotá was about an hour, maybe an hour and a half away.

Prior to takeoff his squadron commander, informed him he was to make an unauthorized landing around noon at Bogota Airfield. He was to make an assault landing, pick up two VIP's, and take them to McDill AFB. He was to say nothing when he got back.

TJ knew something important was up. First, an Army captain, a Green Beret at that, makes a solitary HALO jump into Columbia, and now the unauthorized landing to pick up two VIP's. And he was to say nothing. *So be it,* he thought.

46

ЖЖЖ

STEELE HELD HIS CHUTE IN A tight, downward spiral. His mask had fogged and his clothes were wet from condensation; however, the jump and his landing were perfect. There was only one minor miscalculation, and that was his friends had seen him. They watched in awe, as he fell from the sky. Zack did not see or hear them, as they approached him. He was too busy catching his chute, and removing his jump suit. When he removed his "skin" and turned around, he heard the name, "El-Jaguar" being whispered in unison. His gaze swept over them, they began dropping to their knees, and chanting over and over, "El-Jaguar!"

This adoration was not something Steele had anticipated. He held out his hands, as if blessing them and smiled at his friends. Suddenly, from somewhere deep in the jungle, the drums and trumpets began to sound. *So much for the element of surprise,* Steele thought, as he walked over to some brush and began throwing it aside, searching for his weapons and equipment that he had stowed previously for this mission.

Ж Ж Ж

Mendoza had not slept well, putting him in a very bad mood. Now those damn tree people were at it again, beating their drums, and blowing those damn trumpets. He wanted to send his security forces into the jungle to shoot the little sons-of-bitches, but his guests would be offended, and his security forces, were already terrified of the little bastards. Especially when one of the older guards had been found ripped in half. The guard should have known better, but had been careless and stepped into a snare trap. This had only heightened the fear of the tree people. No matter, he would concentrate on his business and make more money.

Carlos and Miguel would soon be there, also his lawyers and some representatives from two major pharmaceutical companies. His idea was simple: he could become legitimately licensed by both the Columbian and American Government to be an authorized supplier of cocaine for medicinal purposes, and then he could ship his product under license. After that, he would just pay somebody at the other end to sell the excess. He was p lanning to do the same thing in the Asian and European countries.

Julio looked at his watch, realizing time had been slipping away; he needed to get ready to receive his guests. His plan was to make this holiday a memorable event.

Ж Ж Ж

Esther Colgate sat in what the sailors lovingly called the "flight shack." It was nothing more than a rusted out World War II Quonset hut. It had no real windows, unless you counted the rust holes, and if so, then it had many windows. In the center was a long piece of plywood, supported by two oil drums that served as a table. A Styrofoam container held iced tea, cola and beer.

She had been flying for five hours, and she needed to find the head. Walking outside, she looked around for any building that might have a restroom. She had landed on an emergency landing strip, or what the Navy called a "bingo field"—an expression that dated back to when a pilot had to make an emergency landing. If he spotted a strip of land suitable enough to land he would often say, "Bingo!" How this landing strip got here, she could not say, and right now, she really didn't care. What she needed was a restroom.

Seeing a military truck, she walked over to it. The keys were in the ignition so she opened the door, started the truck, turned it around, and followed the tire tracks back to some place, any place that had a head.

Inside she was surprised to see it had an air-conditioner and turned it on. Already the radio was playing classical music. When she turned the station, all she got was static until in desperation she turned back to the original station, and listened to what she could only refer to as "longhair" music.

Off in the distance she saw a trailer stuck in the middle of nowhere. Esther sped up knowing that it was a race against time before her bladder burst. Pulling up in front, she quickly stopped the truck, jumped out, and ran up the ramp. Upon opening the door, to her amazement the head was right in front of her.

In her haste, Esther failed to notice that the restroom and trailer were not marked, "Government Issue". She became acutely aware of this when she walked out and found a young woman holding a baby, staring at her. She could fell her blood rush to her face turning her face red as she tried to find words.

"Please sit down and stay a while", the young woman said, motioning for Esther to take the lounge chair.

Esther smiled and obliged the young mother by taking her chair.

"My name is Betty," the young mother said, taking a hard-backed chair from the kitchen table.

"Hello, Betty, my name is Stupid."

Betty began to laugh, trying to hide her crooked teeth with her hand. Her laugh was sweet gentle, and allowing Esther to relax.

"Actually, my name is Esther, Betty, and I'm so sorry, but I had to go so badly."

Betty held up her hand, still chuckling. "Well, Esther, I guess this trailer kind of belongs to you, as my husband works for the U. S. Navy here on the island."

"What does your husband do here on this island?" Esther said, crossing her legs.

"Benny takes care of the goats. You see, the Navy bought all our goats a year ago and moved us here onto the island. They gave us this trailer, and a truck like yours. Every other Friday, I am flown over to the mainland, where I do my shopping, and take care of the baby's medical needs, and whatever else we need. The helicopter lands across the way and the sailors help carry my groceries into the house. Occasionally they will stop in, like you, and use the bathroom." Betty began to laugh again.

Esther joined in the laughter, feeling at ease with Betty. She held out her hands, silently asking for the baby.

"Her name is Kara, and she is six months old today," Betty said with a big smile, handing Kara over to Esther.

"Oh, such a big girl," Esther cooed, taking Kara into her arms.

"Betty, why does the Navy need your goats here on the island?" Esther asked out of curiosity.

"I'm told it is because of the birds. The birds make their nests in the tall grass, and when there are too many birds, they can cause an airplane to crash. So the goats eat the grass, keeping it short so the birds nest someplace else, making it safe for airplanes to land here."

As a pilot and victim of two bird strikes, Esther knew what Betty was saying was true.

"Oh? And how many planes land here?" Esther asked, surprised.

"Not a lot; maybe one or two a month, mostly the big planes with many motors," Betty said, getting up to fix Kara's bottle.

Esther figured the big planes were cargo planes dropping off supplies and men to fight Mendoza.

Holding Kara close, Esther stood up as she said, "I must get back to my plane."

"Your plane, you mean you can fly an airplane?" Betty asked, starting to giggle.

Esther began to laugh, realizing that Betty lived in another time and another world. Her world was sweet and simple. Taking care of her babies and her man, that was her only job. The thought of a woman flying an airplane was out of her world.

"Yes, Betty. I tell you what—give me thirty minutes, and then you and Kara, walk outside and watch me take off. I will make a lot of noise just for the two of you."

Betty giggled and clapped her hands, approving of Esther's suggestion. Kissing Kara goodbye, she handed her back to her mother.

Now back in her LCDR Esther Colgate mode, she drove the truck to the flight shack. One glance and she could see her aircraft was armed.

Waiting for her return, the munitions crew sat under the wing, drinking iced tea. She was quick to notice that there was no yellow gear, which meant a battery start.

Going over to her plane, she began her "walk around", looking for cracks, leaks or anything that could cause her problems in flight. Satisfied with her Tom Cat's obvious safety, she waited for her munitions briefing. Although she knew each weapon by heart, she found that being respectful of her crew chief and mechanics got her extra perks; frankly, she liked that. She turned to climb up into the cockpit, when a large hand grabbed her shoulder, and handed her an ice tea. "Take this, ma'am. You might get thirsty."

Smiling, she took the can placing it in the boot pocket of her flight suit. The other boot pocket was reserved for her makeup.

There was no ground crew, or anyone to stand fireguard, as she started each of the engines. All she had was the cockpit light to warn her of a fire. By the time that lit up, the fire was often fully involved, and the pilot often was burned alive.

Although real, Esther's fears were groundless, as both engines performed as expected. Releasing the parking brake, she goosed the throttle, engaged the nose wheel steering, and began to taxi down the ramp towards Betty and Kara. She could see Betty standing on the ramp, baby Kara in her arms.

Esther slowed and turned her Tom Cat into the wind, released her foot brake and pushed the throttle forward engaging the afterburners. The engines roared as the over-loaded Tom Cat sped down the runway. Once again, she broke the rule, as she pulled straight back on the stick, causing the Tom Cat to go vertical. According to her watch, she was on schedule. The plan was for her to fly just off the Columbian coast at 28,000 feet. Then to conserve fuel, she would throttle back to fifty percent power, and wait until she heard the message: "Big Tom, release your kitties." That would be her cue to launch her missiles at thirty-second intervals. When her task was completed, she was to turn, and head for home.

Ж Ж Ж

Ryan was waiting for Dominique to finish applying her makeup. The wall clock over the sofa said that he had an hour before they had to be at the restaurant. In his Ryan jacket pocket, he had two passports and his debit card.

When he had talked with Carlos that morning, Ryan thought Carlos seemed distant and cold, even antagonistic toward him. He had seen this behavior before in Carlos, but never directed at him. The last time he had seen it; Carlos pulled out his gun and shot a man. To this day, Ryan did not know why Carlos had killed the man; but that was Carlos. Now that same animalistic behavior was directed toward him. The only good thing was that in two hours, Ryan would be gone, and he would have Rossi, along with his millions. And if Seth Hatfield, has his way today Carlos and Julio, will be dead by three

47

Ж Ж Ж

CAPTAIN STEEL DROPPED HIS BAGS AND glanced around his old stomping grounds. He looked for a place to hide and watch the upcoming party. Finding one, he laid down. His thoughts turned to Renee. Julio had made this war a personal matter, and today, Renee's murder would be avenged.

The only place that afforded him both an observation platform and a hiding spot, was an old Mahogany tree. Grabbing his equipment, Steele began to climb. The view of the hacienda was excellent, and he could see the entrance to the cave.

According to his watch, he had only twenty minutes before he had to signal for the two kitties, then another twenty minutes for the kitties to arrive as unwanted guests at Mendoza's garden party. By the sound of the band and singer, it was evident the garden party was in full swing. Steele could see a few people dancing, but most were eating, drinking and enjoying themselves.

Opening his spyglass, Steele checked out the cave entrance. No security guards out front, but that did not mean they were not inside the cave. Slowly he moved his spyglass, looking for Julio; he wanted the chance to kill him, man to man, as missiles seemed so impersonal when you wanted a man dead.

※ ※ ※

Ryan checked his watch, as he backed the car out of the garage for the last time. He would miss his fancy car and all his clothes. However, he was not worried; all were replaceable, even Dominique.

The sad part was Dominique had no idea who she really was, or what she had been. Carlos and Julio had seen to that.

According to Miguel, Dominique was being fed, "highballs," which was nothing more than a shot glass filled with cocaine and barbiturates, or benzodiazepine, administered slowly, during sex. Rossi got a double double, which was nothing, but a double dose of cocaine, and a double dose of

barbiturates, which fogged her memory to the point of amnesia. Over a prolonged period of time, this treatment caused dementia and docility, to the point of submissiveness. Ryan checked his speed. He was ten minutes from the airport, and five minutes to the restaurant. With luck, and if the airplane was on time, he and Rossi would be back in the states before dinnertime.

※ ※ ※

Esther Colgate looked at both fuel gauges and her watch. She had enough fuel to fly on station for forty minutes more.. It was possible to stretch the fuel by shutting down one of the engines and throttling back; that would stretch her flight time for another thirty minutes.

Her mind began to drift into thoughts of Zack. Somewhere, down in that jungle, he was waiting for the precise moment in time to radio some nameless and invisible person and ask that person to release the missiles that would wipe out the largest and most powerful drug cartel in the world. She would honor his request, and launch her missiles, and then turn her Tom Cat around and head for home.

In a day or two, Steele would be home, none the wiser that she was the one who had sent the two kitties used to eradicate Mendoza. Sometime, in the afterglow of their lovemaking, she would kiss his cheek and tell him how much she loved him.

Ж Ж Ж

Carlos was sullen. He barely nodded to Miguel, as his trusted lieutenant opened the car door for him. Not only had he not slept well, he had a lot on his mind. Taking his seat in the back of the limo, Miguel closed the door and got in the front next to Jesus. Sensing Carlos's mood, no one spoke. Miguel simply pointed and Jesus pulled into the late morning holiday traffic and headed east towards Julio's hacienda.

In the corner, Carlos sat with his arms folded across his chest, as if hugging himself to ward off the cold. His head was bowed, his chin resting on his chest. His eyes had closed, as if he were sleeping. That was illusory, as his mind could not shut down, and allow sleep to enter his brain and sooth his tormented mind. He had experienced a premonition that was playing in his mind. The vision was so real, that it caused him to cry out in fear. He had actually felt fire upon his flesh, and smelled death. He had seen people lying dead, their bodies blown apart and burning. He remembered that in his vision he had fallen to his knees, as he looked up, he saw a tall gringo soldier carrying a shotgun walking towards him. The last words he remembered uttering were "El Jaguar", and then he had fallen dead. So real were the memories of that vision it actually caused him to shake in fright.

As the limo sped past the airport, Carlos happened to look up and see McBride and Dominique in the opposite direction. McBride had told him he wasn't sure if he would fly to Buenaventura or drive.

Carlos sat straight up; realizing that today was Monday, 20 July. McBride had said he was taking his three-day vacation starting on Friday. Then if McBride had flown to Buenaventura, he would already be there, and if he had driven, why was he going to the airport, when Buenaventura was in the other direction? Something was not adding up. Today he would inform Julio that he was going to kill McBride, and sell the puta bitch, Rossi.

Ж Ж Ж

Ryan knew Carlos had seen him. It was something he had not anticipated. However, it was too late now, because of the freeway design and divided road, Carlos could not turn around and follow him. Ryan knew that he and Rossi were safe in that respect, and in less than twenty minutes, they would be in the air.

Seeing the restaurant up ahead, Ryan turned on his blinker and began to slow down pulling the car into a deeply rutted, dirty and bumpy, parking lot. Ryan did not stop the car; instead, he slowly maneuvered around the ruts, until he was behind the restaurant. Looking around, he saw the exit that opened up onto a gravel road next to the taxiway. He proceeded onto the access road.

Dominique had not spoken since they had left the apartment until now. "Ryan what are you doing?"

"Give me a minute until I get out of this mess we're in and I'll tell you," Ryan said, not looking at her, but concentrating on his driving and praying for the Hercules to come to their rescue.

Ж Ж Ж

The Hercules was on course and on schedule. TJ listened to the Bogotá tower telling him all the needed particulars for landing. He was not supposed to, but he had filed a flight plan in Panama City, claiming humanitarian reasons. This was the only way he could get permission to land in Columbia, since he was flying a foreign military aircraft, without waiting the required forty-eight hours after filing a flight plan.

Twenty miles out, TJ was on his final glide path, touchdown would be in three minutes. Ahead he could see Bogotá and thought how beautiful the city looked from the air, surrounded by the mountains in the background. Bogotá tower had vectored him to land on runway 18, which meant that he would be landing into the wind, and according to his information; his humanitarian pickup would be at the end of runway 18. How lucky could he get?

TJ informed the young, pimply-faced flight engineer what he was to do. "The moment the plane touches down, you are to lower the tailgate. I am going taxi to the last runway exit and turn off. Look for a man and a woman. As soon as you see them, help them on board then close the tailgate. Once our cargo is on board, I will request the Bogotá tower for humanitarian privileges. That will give us head-of-the line privilege. Then we will make a high-speed taxi, a hard left turn onto the active runway and we are gone."

Ж Ж Ж

Ryan slowed the car to a stop, and rolled down his window for a better view. He spotted the plane on its final approach, and felt excitement roll up inside his body. Until he saw the plane, he had not really believed it was almost over.

"What are we doing here and where are we going?" Dominique asked, in a very annoyed tone of voice.

"Didn't I tell you we were taking a holiday, and that we are going to fly?" Ryan answered, his eyes not leaving the dark exhaust trail of the incoming Hercules.

"Yes, Ryan, I remember you telling me, but the airport is over there," Dominique said, pointing to the control tower.

"As usual you are correct, but not if we are to take a private airplane, sweetheart!" Ryan soothed, warily looking around for anything, or anybody, that might hinder their escape.

"Oh, how nice, a private airplane!" She cooed. "Is it a small plane or a big plane?"

For some inexplicable reason Ryan laughed at the question. It was the innocence, in the way she asked the question, like a small child would ask an adult.

"It is a very big plane. I think it has four big engines," he replied in like manner.

"Oh, like this one?" she said, pointing to the Hercules as it passed over them.

"Exactly like that one," Ryan replied, getting out of the car, and walking around to open Dominique's door.

"What about our luggage?" she asked.

Ryan smiled, "Oh yeah, I almost forgot." Opening the trunk, he grabbed both her bags. Looking at his, he debated not taking it, but took it anyway. *Just in case,* he thought.

Being anxious, the wait seemed an eternity to Ryan as the C-130 lumbered down the taxiway, heading for them. Just then, out of the corner of his eye, Ryan saw the airport security car driving towards them, its lights flashing. Ryan watched knowing it was going to be a race against time and distance, and the security car appeared to be winning.

TJ happened to look out the side window and saw the flashing lights. By the cars speed and direction, he knew where the car was headed. He advanced the throttle, picking up speed. TJ heard the loud whine of the hydraulic motor, as the sergeant lowered the tailgate opening up a huge hole for his two VIPs' to enter. TJ could see his passengers, a man, and a woman, standing next to a black car, obviously his "humanitarian" purpose.

Pushing the throttles forward again, the Hercules began to vibrate as he moved over and cut off the security car, the prop blast picking up dust, and small stones, hurling them at the car, forcing the driver to slowdown. Then TJ did the old about-face trick, which was revving up the engines on one side and cutting the engines on the other, forcing the ponderous airplane to turn abruptly. TJ had did the move so proficiently that Ryan and Dominique had only to walk a few feet to the waiting tailgate.

The airplane was moving fast, as the sergeant raised the tailgate, and simultaneously yelled at them to take their seats."

Leaning back in the canvas seat, Ryan began to laugh. He thought to himself, the *get-away has been easy, so far. Now, if the plane can safely get airborne, I will be out of the Army in two weeks, and living in Argentina in a month.*

48

✳ ✳ ✳

GENERAL PABLO GONZALES HAD MADE ARRANGE-
MENTS with General Alano Leon of the Columbian Air Force
to attack Mendoza's stronghold. An attack time of 1500 hours
was reached figuring that all the guests involved with Mendoza's cartel
would be there. Pablo thought that if they got lucky Mendoza, Carlos
and McBride would die.

✳ ✳ ✳

Steele looked at his watch. It was time. Keying his radio, he placed
the microphone to the side of his mouth and whispered, "Big Tom, I
hope you're there and if you are, release your kitties."

Esther heard the voice, and recognized it at once. She pushed the
stick down and kicked the rudder, causing the Tom Cat to turn downward into a gentle dive. She pulled back on the stick, her aircraft now
pointing directly at Columbia. She triggered her microphone "One kitty

lost", she replied, watching the secondhand of the clock that was nestled next to the artificial horizon on the instrument panel. Thirty seconds later, she keyed her microphone again, announcing to Steele, "The other kitty is now lost.

Steele looked at his watch, figuring twenty minutes, maybe less, before the fireworks began. He was wrong. Hearing them before he saw them he thought, *No way could those missiles get here so fast.* Frantically he tried to unhook the laser light from his utility belt, hoping, he had not screwed up the mission. Then he saw them, three jet aircraft, as they raced over him. Steele observed that each plane had two jet engines, and under each wing he could see three large bombs. He watched, as the bombs fell into Mendoza's compound. There was no pattern to the bomb's release, each bomb exploding independently. The shock waves blowing out windows, sending blocks of cement and roofing tile, chards of glass, and fire in all directions. Steele could hear the yelling, and screaming of the injured. The stench of burning flesh began to drift towards him pushed by a gentle wind.

Steele watched in awe at the men and women, being blown apart causing body parts to fly in every direction. Sickened by the carnage, he averted his eyes, and glanced at his watch. It was time to turn on the laser wand, and wait for the light to turn green.

He was waiting for a missile that would be arriving soon. The missile would activate the wand, turning the little red light to green, activating the missile's guidance system. Supposedly, according to the manufacturer's instructions the missile included a Seeker 16 for providing a first signal, indicative of a first-angle epsilon, between a line-of-sight (LOS) 15 from Missile 10 to Target 12, and a longitudinal Axis 9 extending through Missile 10. A Terminal Guidance Subsystem 24 computed acceleration commands from the LOS sigma angle, which used something called Propulsion System 26 that could change the velocity and vector of the missile if needed.

Steele did not have the foggiest idea what all that technical bullshit meant. All he knew was that when the little red light turned green, he was to point the damn laser at the target, and watch.

Peering intently through the clouds of smoke and debris, he noticed the bombs had actually missed the cave, but he was not going to miss. He intended sending the second missile into Julio's new hacienda, finishing what the bombs had missed.

The cries and screams of the wounded were echoing throughout the canyon; the rising black smoke blocked out the afternoon sun, giving the wounded and dead a surreal appearance. Pulling out his spyglass, he surveyed the carnage. The damage to the compound was extensive, but not catastrophic. He spotted the clown prince Julio; yelling and pointing towards a bald headed man. They were tending to the dead and dying.

Caught up in the devastation and activity at the hacienda, Steele almost forgot to watch for the e red light in the guidance wand. When the light turned green, it meant the missile's guidance system had acquired the ground signal. Then he was to point the wand at the intended target, knowing he had only a few seconds to point the guidance wand towards the next target. After that, all he had to do was wait and watch.

Each missile was carrying a conventional explosive package of 600 pounds of very high explosives. Steel decided to point the laser light to the open cave door hoping the missile would fly into the cave, blowing the mountain to bits, destroying Mendoza's drug factory.

The other missile he would aim at Julio's hacienda figuring the high explosives would wipe the hacienda off the face of the earth, removing all traces of Mendoza and his cartel. Then using his trumpet given to him by the tribal chief, he would signal to his little friends, and let them partake of the living.

The light in the wand turned green, Steele aimed the invisible beam at the cave's opening. He could hear the roar of the engine, as he watched the missile pass directly over him, so low he could see the lettering on the side of the missile. He watched the missile disappear into the cave.

Immense was the only word Steele could use to describe the explosion. An orange ball of flame shot out of the cave entrance consuming anything and everything within 300 yards of the cave entrance. He was not sure, but he thought he heard the sound of something resembling the crack of a bull whip. Then the mountain appeared too vibrate for a few seconds then slowly it began to slide into the river below, damming it up, causing the swift, running water to fan out, consuming large areas of the jungle floor.

Steele did not have time to gloat, as the green light in the wand's handle told him another missile was fast approaching. He turned his body, resting his back against the tree trunk, he aimed the wand towards Mendoza's fortress. Steele heard the familiar sound of the pulsating jet engine, as it sped directly over his head and slammed into the remains of the burning hulk of Mendoza's hacienda. This time the explosion was not contained, the massive fireball rose upwards, rolling into itself and forming a devastating fireball.

Steele pulled out his spyglass, surveying the devastation. The destruction was massive and complete. Understandably, he reasoned that nobody could live through that infernal attack.

Climbing down from his observation post, he grabbed his weapons. He was not in any particular hurry to see dead bodies, especially those that were charred to black ash. However, he was looking for one body in particular. Once he had located it, he would send a radio message to HQ: "The Don is dead."

That was it. Then he would call for a chopper to extract him to Costa Rico. He would then catch a commercial flight to Tampa. A quick debrief to General Hatfield, and then a military flight to Ryan sonville—that was the basic plan. However, plans have a way of changing when sudden, unexpected, and dramatic events occur.

Ж Ж Ж

"General Hatfield speaking, how may I help you?"

It was Bo-Peep. In all the excitement and confusion over Generals Gonzales and Leon's celebrated attack on the Mendoza drug cartel, he had forgotten to call her. Then again, he had yet to receive confirmation that Mendoza was dead.

"Hello, General Hatfield, I'm here in the CIC with the Secretary of State, and the acting under secretary. We wanted to know if the reports coming out of Bogotá are true. Did General Gonzales kill Mendoza?"

"I cannot say for sure, but based on the first set of satellite photos I saw, I would have to say no. In fact, the bombing, though terrible, was more of a harassment attack than anything else," the general replied, changing the receiver from his left hand to his right.

"Hmm, so you haven't seen the latest photos?" Shirley asked.

"—did not know there were any more photos. Besides, I have been waiting for confirmation of Mendoza's death before I called you," he replied.

"Well, General Hatfield, I'm looking at the newest satellite photos and where a mountain once stood, there is a pile of rock and where the river flowed, and there is now a lake...probably a very large lake. The hacienda is nothing more than a pile of rubble, and I see many bodies. "Seth," I think perhaps we let the two Columbian generals take credit for this attack, and we slip over to Nicaragua or Panama. What do you think?"

"I think that would be a great idea, and I choose Nicaragua. I want to reorganize and rethink our policy, and our methods. We have learned a lot from Columbia, and we should capitalize on it."

"Ok, Seth. Nicaragua it will be and I will be talking to you when you have your plan prepared." Shirley replied.

If Steele has killed Mendoza, why haven't I heard from him? Seth thought, hanging up the phone. *"Unless Steele is dead, too."*

Ж Ж Ж

It had taken Steele an hour to hike down the mountain trail, grab the zodiac, and head to the swinging bridge. There, by sheer luck, he found a white pickup truck containing two, freshly killed security guards. Counting four darts in each man, he chuckled, as he pulled the dead men from the truck; throwing the bodies to the ground with all the respect, he would give a five-pound bag of potatoes. On the dash of the truck, he found a pack of Marlboros and a lighter. Starting the truck, he lit a cigarette, and dropped the stick shift into first he proceeded up the road towards what used to be a hacienda.

The entire attack had taken less than thirty minutes including the bombing attack. The once-powerful Mendoza cartel lay in ruins. Stopping the truck, Steele opened the door, reaching across the truck seat he grabbed his trumpet, and began calling to his multi- colored little friends. Moments later, there was an answering call of drums and trumpet blasts. Enthusiastically, the Amarekaire warriors began responding to El Jaguar's trumpet call.

Taking one last drag from his cigarette, he flipped it out the window and drove on.

49

ЖЖЖ

ESTHER WALKED INTO HER HOUSE tossing her keys into the small wicker basket she used to hold bread rolls on holidays. She was exhausted normally she would shower, but her back and butt ached, from the ordeal. Stress she thought, walking into the bedroom. She spotted; his underwear and tee shirt balled up, and tossed in the corner. Too tired to pick them up, Ester unzipped her boots, and pulled them off tossing them aside. She slipped out of her flight suit, letting it land on the floor. Dressed only in her shorts, she walked into the bathroom and adjusted the water temperature. She picked up the stereo remote pressing the little red button immersing the room in IL Divo.

Soaking her aching body Esther, could not get Zack out of her mind. She knew she was not scared, as Steele could take care of himself. While aiming her Tom Cat for home, her mind kept thinking about little Kara. Esther came to the realization that her biological clock was ticking faster with each passing month. She decided a husband, and a couple of babies were what she needed. Esther Colgate, aka the "Barbarian", wanted to become domesticated.

Ж Ж Ж

Unable to go any further, Steele pulled the pickup over to the side of the road. The bombs and missiles had made the road impassible turning it into a footpath. When he opened the door of the truck and stepped out, the stench of burning dead was overpowering.

Steele un-shouldered his twelve-gauge and pumped it, putting a shell in the chamber. He pressed the safety button, taking it off safety. He chambered a 9mm round into his handgun, and stuck the Browning into his belt. Since these men were killers he was taking no chances, and if he killed some of them in their hour of need, so what? Who was around to testify against him?

He walked towards the cave, the smell of death and destruction became worse. He pulled off his shirt and reached down unsheathing his knife, and proceeded to cut, and tear his olive green tee shirt into long strips. Then taking his canteen, he poured water over the strips, tying one strip around his head, the other around his nose and mouth. The other two strips, he tied around his biceps.

Steele was on a mission: He needed to find Julio's body. Once found, he would make his call, and walk away for good. He decided that Ester was what he wanted, and if she would have him, he would marry her and have a couple of kids. That would suit him just fine, and he would have no regrets about having been a Green Beret called, El Jaguar...

He counted over thirty bodies in front of the cave entrance. Another dozen, or so lay in various grotesque positions near the retaining wall. The entire back of the mountainside furthest from the hacienda had been blown away. A Mahogany tree, and some flowers that lined the sidewalk between the vault, and hacienda, were untouched by the bomb blasts. Steele watched a honeybee, as it collected nectar, oblivious to its surroundings. Raising the shotgun to his shoulder, he crept around the corner facing the vault. He stopped in his tracks, and took a knee. He did not look up or down, left, or right, as he had been trained. Steele was struck deaf, by greed. Before his eyes, lying on its side and blown open from the bomb blast were the doors to Julio's vault. Somehow, by divine providence, the mountain had spared Julio's riches, leaving them for anyone with the courage to take them. Gold, silver, jewels of every description, and behind the gold, and jewels stood row after row of pallets stacked with money, more money than Steele had ever seen. *"Fuck everyone it's all mine"*. *He thought.*

At that precise moment, while Captain Zachary Steele of the U.S. Army was deaf, and blind, to everything except the fortune in front of him. Julio Mendoza burned and disfigured snuck up on the solider and raised his stick over his head and delivered a crashing blow upon the soldier's head, followed by other vicious strikes to his back, shoulders, and legs. Steele fell forward stunned from Mendoza's attack. Somewhere, in the recesses of his mind, just before unconscious, as Mendoza was kicking him, in the groin, followed up by another blow to his head. Mendoza, in his savage fury, reached for Steele's knife, strapped to his leg. Falling to his knees from exhaustion, Mendoza unsheathed the knife, gripped it with both hands, over his head, to deliver the coup de gras. Mendoza felt a bee sting, followed by another, and still another, as the poisoned darts pierced his body. Mendoza appeared motionless, his only utterances, being grunts in lieu of speech fell to the side dead. Slowly the little multi-colored, semi-nude little warriors, who lived in trees, and asked only to live in peace, assembled looking at Don Julio Mendoza, whom they had just killed to save their war God EL- Jaguar.

50

I T HAD BEEN TEN DAYS SINCE the attack on Mendoza's compound, and still no confirmation of his death. Satellite photos showed the devastation, and the dead bodies. A clearly visible lake now surrounded Mendoza's compound, but little else.

Word around the world was that Mendoza was dead, and that his cartel had been neutralized. The cost of cocaine on the street had risen so high that it was fast losing its popularity. Now, other fun-drugs that had been in the background began to emerge in full force.

General Hatfield was convinced Steele was dead. He dictated a letter to the Pentagon asking that Captain Zachary Steele's name be removed from the active duty roll, with the notation "missing in action, presumed dead".

Ж Ж Ж

Colonel Ryan Ryan Mc Bride put in for retirement from active military duty. He asked his wife, Linda, for a divorce. She did not hesitate to grant it. Ryan gave her the house, plus a cash settlement of $150,000. Upon receiving his discharge papers, Ryan moved to Argentina, bought a nice, secluded estate outside of Buenos Aries.

Victoria Rossi, per Bo Peep's orders was transferred to a hospital in Tampa, for drug addiction. There Rossi received intensive counseling, and psychotherapy, regaining her identity, and most of her memory. She became a consultant to the DEA, and State Department specializing in white slavery trafficking, a subject she knew very well.

Ethel retired from the United States Department of State with over thirty years of credible service. Not once did she divulge Don's, Shirley's or her involvement in one of the largest anti-drug task force operations in American history.

Don McGee retired from the United States Department of State. He and his wife moved to Taos, New Mexico for no particular reason other than it was far away from Washington D.C.

Mike Atkins, who had tried to find salvation in the arms of a loving and forgiving God, found only torment, self-doubt, and depression. Eventually turned away from the priesthood, as being unworthy, and in a dark, dirty alley, not far from the church where he had tried in vain to find forgiveness and salvation, Mike Atkins, formerly of the United States Army and a reject from the priesthood, was found dead; a dirty syringe firmly implanted in his vein. Mike Atkins had injected himself with an overdose of morality.

51

Ж Ж Ж

LCDR ESTHER COLGATE ASKED HER SKIPPER for some personal time. It was not　leave, but time away from the rigors of the job to get her priorities in order. She packed her B4 bag, took her Tomcat, and went home. She flew up the coast to Dover. There she rented a car and drove the twenty-six miles to her parents' home. It was important she talk with her mom. Only another woman would understand what she was going through, and her mom was her best friend.

It was time Esther got her priorities in order. Her life had taken a sudden and dramatic turn downwards. She was deeply in love, but her man was missing. Desperate to know, she had called Shirley and asked for help. The next day, Shirley had returned her call and told her that Steele was missing and presumed dead.

Funny thing though, she had not cried when Shirley told her this. Call it woman's intuition or extra-sensory perception, whatever it was; Steele was still alive in her mind and in her heart. She could feel him standing next to her. In fact, she remembered one time when Steele had pulled her close and kissed her neck, sending shivers down her back and giving her goose bumps. He had looked into her eyes, smiled and said, "Honey, if I'm lost and suddenly a soft, gentle, summer breeze crosses your cheek when the air is still and you begin to shiver with goose bumps appearing on your arms, please do not be afraid, Esther, for it will be me kissing you from beyond the grave." That was the closest Steele had ever come to telling her he loved her. It was an understanding that whatever happened they would be together.

It had been over two weeks now and no gentle breeze had crossed her face. *Steele is out there somewhere and I can feel him in my heart. He is waiting for something and then he will send for me,* she thought, not really knowing how she knew, but just accepting it.

Ж Ж Ж

Steele did not know how long he had been unconscious. When he came to his senses, he was lying in a grass hammock with two, old village women fanning him and keeping him cool. He was nude and though his watch was still around his wrist, it was broken. Slowly He tried to rise, but found himself unable, collapsing back into hammock. His head throbbed and he was dizzy.

Vaguely he remembered being surprised, by someone who had clubbed him. His groin hurt and both shoulders and his back were sore. Feebly he motioned to the old woman for some water. She gave a near toothless grin and handed him his canteen. He drank long and hard, almost emptying his canteen. The remaining water he poured over his head in an attempt to clear his mind.

Although dizzy, Steele did recognize the tribal chief approaching him, only because the old boy was still wearing the watch he had traded for Renee. This time the chief had a gift for *him*. The shrunken head of Mendoza tied to a small stick by his long hair.

Seeing Mendoza's doll-sized face caused his memory to begin returning in small segments. He remembered looking down on the body of the man who had attacked him and knowing it was Mendoza. Another memory was smiling, showing his pleasure to his diminutive friends. Then somehow, through hand gestures, he was able to convey to the chief what he wanted the warriors to do with the money, jewels, gold, and silver. He had not known how much money was there, nor did he care. He knew he wanted the money hidden, and just he and his friends knew where it was.

I have two immediate problems: How to remove the vast wealth from the jungle and how to transport it to Argentina... Those were the last conscious thoughts before succumbing to his injuries.

The tribe had worked for two days, not including the day of the attack, to remove Steele's treasure from Mendoza's compound.

The chief bowed to him, and Steele smiled, motioning for him to come closer. Not that he wanted to see the shrunken head, but to look at the chief's watch, so he could see the date.

ЖЖЖ

Generals Gonzales and Leon were basking in the limelight of the news media. The networks were giving them credit for destroying Mendoza and his evil cartel. However, the reason for the attack was not nationalistic pride or political advantage but simple robbery. Moreover, if Pablo and his cousin Alano had to kill in order to get Mendoza's money, then that was just the cost of doing business.

Pablo had come up with the idea of killing Mendoza, and robbing him, months ago. However, he had to wait biding his time for the perfect vehicle to strike and Mendoza's anger and paranoia was that vehicle.

In his heart, and mind, Pablo knew McBride had turned Mendoza against him, and he simply played along. Using the army to arrest, and disrupt Mendoza's operations, had all been a ploy to rob Mendoza, and bankrupt him. Pablo had called his cousin, General Alano Leon, and asked him if he wanted to be rich and famous. Alano answered, "Who doesn't!"

Well, now they were famous and in a few days, by using the helicopters so aptly supplied by the Americans, they would be rich.

ж ж ж

After looking at his watch on the chief's wrist, Steele figured, he had been unconscious for a week, and if you counted the day of the attack, plus the two days before he passed out, then it had been ten days since he had reported to HQ. He knew what that meant. By now the military would have declared him "missing in action, presumed dead".

As he lay in the hammock, he thought, *subsequently according to the Army, I am now dead, and yet I am alive and have millions and millions of dollars.*

Weak, he continued to lie in the hammock, and began to chuckle to himself. After a few seconds, he gave a small laugh, which finally erupted into a huge, belly laugh. This in turn caused his long, and very exposed male member to shake and vibrate, which created a stir among the tribal elders. Observing this phenomenon, they pointed at it and began to laugh, joining the great and powerful El Jaguar in his merriment, but not knowing or understanding why.

卐 卐 卐

Steele awakened from a deep sleep by the sounds of drums and trumpet blasts. Looking at his broken watch, he remembered. Off in the distance he could hear the unmistakable whap, whap sound that only helicopter blades make as they slice through the air.

Steele recognized the helicopter sound as that of a Chinook, or as the Marines called them, "Jolly Greens". They were large and very powerful choppers. Looking through the trees, he saw enough to know the markings were not American, but Columbian. Now Steele's curiosity was piqued.

The drums and trumpets got louder, as if the noise they produced could scare off the Jolly Green, and make it fly away. It passed directly overhead, the noise scaring the women and children and sending them into the jungle to hide.

Despite his weakness, Steele grabbed his pants, and boots, and went into the brush to dress. Looking around he found his weapons, and checked them, his instincts telling him that danger was fast approaching. Still unsteady he set off through the jungle, following the green monster, instinctively knowing where the chopper was headed. His friends grabbed their bows, arrows, and blowguns, and followed their war god to do battle once again.

卐 卐 卐

The young pilot flew over the remains of the compound searching for a safe landing spot. Not seeing an adequate space, he turned the Chinook to the northwest where he spotted a clearing that provided a safe landing area. He maneuvered the chopper into position and gently lowered the green monster to the ground. Reaching over, the pilot cut off the battery switch and cut the throttles, killing both engines. Turning to his passengers, he gave them the thumbs-up signal. Both generals nodded and stood up, waiting for the crew chief to lower the tailgate. This allowed them to walk off the helicopter, instead of jumping off.

General Gonzales was the first off the Jolly Green. Looking around, to get his bearings, General Gonzales did not really need to, as the sky was full of buzzards feeding on the dead. All the generals needed to do was follow the smoke, and the stench.

Reaching into his pocket, General Gonzales pulled out a small, blue jar. He opened the jar and taking his finger, dabbed some of the white paste under his nose.

"Here, Alano, take some camphor. It will help kill the stench," Pablo said, handing his cousin the little blue jar.

Alano did as his cousin suggested, his stomach was already reacting to the stench being carried by the wind.

The pilot, co-pilot, and crew chief walked off the chopper carrying an odd assortment of weapons.

"Sir, what is that?" the worried pilot asked his general. The sound of the drums and trumpets were disconcerting to the young men.

"Obviously we are being watched and may even be attacked by cannibals," General Gonzales said, checking his pistol and looking all around.

General Leon handed the camphor back to his cousin, his eyes surveying the surrounding jungle, as he looked for the cannibals.

"Relax, Alano, I seriously doubt they will attack us. They are just curious, that's all," Pablo said, handing the camphor to the others. "I think we will leave the pilot here to guard the helicopter. The rest of us will go and investigate the remains of the mighty Julio Mendoza's cartel.

Here—I want you to take pictures", Pablo said, handing his digital camera to the young co-pilot. Then pointing to the young crew chief he said, "Now, son, you lead the way!"

Ж Ж Ж

Steele watched the chopper, as it circled low over the remains of Mendoza's compound. The large blades of the Chinook created powerful down drafts, causing the smoldering embers, to re-ignite little fires. He noticed that the buzzards were not flying; they just hopped around, flapping their large wings and screeching their displeasure at being disturbed while they feasted.

Watching the helicopter as it moved away, Steele headed back across the river, paying particular attention when the big green machine hovered, then slowly descended only yards from his old camp. Hearing the chopper's engines begin to slow, he knew that whoever, was in the damn helicopter would be coming. He suspected they were here for Mendoza's limitless wealth. *Too bad, assholes, I got it,* he thought.

Steele was sure that whoever, was in charge would leave a guard, probably the pilot, because if there was any trouble, the pilot could start the green monster, and he and his companions could haul ass out of there. Steele reached for his spyglass surveying the situation. He counted four men and when one turned, he recognized him as General Pablo Gonzales. A young kid carrying an M-16 led the way. Closing his spyglass, he figured it would take them an hour, maybe longer, as they did not know the shortcut. However, because the river was no longer a river, but a lake, the shortcut might be underwater anyway. Slipping the spyglass into his pocket, he found the pack of cigarettes he had liberated from the two dead men. Pulling out a cigarette, he lit it, inhaling the smoke, and then blowing it through his nose, which fascinated his little friends. They began pointing at him, watching him, studying him, as he continued blowing the smoke out his nose.

Deep in thought, Steele was oblivious of his friend's inquisitiveness. He was so lost in thought that he did not hear the crack of the rifle shot that echoed and re-echoed, causing the monkeys to scream their extreme displeasure.

He became aware that something had happened when he saw the Amarekaire chief pointing off in the distance towards the trail that ran down the mountain towards the river. Another crack from a rifle, and then another, until the canyon reverberated with the sounds of automatic rifle fire. Pulling out his spyglass and pointing it in the direction of the gunfire, he could plainly see the four men standing back to back, forming a human box. Each man was protecting the other from an enemy they, could not see.

Shaking his hand back and forth in front of his face, Steele smiled, as he pointed to the four intruders, indicating the four men were scared. Picking up his trumpet, he began to blow, sending a long, high-pitched tone into the air. Other trumpets began to answer, followed by the insistent and melodious sound of drums. Adding to the mayhem were the wild screams of the monkeys, and deafening screeches of the macaws. This added to the panic of the four men, who walked into the jungle, following a trail that had been booby-trapped.

Steele watched, and the four men pretending to be soldiers, and it was his experienced opinion, that two, if not all four of these men who shot at imaginary targets, and screaming monkeys, would be dead within the hour. Pablo and the others were arrogant, and stupid, thinking their rank, and the advantage of automatic rifles could scare off the Amarekaire warriors.

To be honest, Steele had to admit that in a fair fight the guns would win. However, the Amarekaire warriors did not know about fighting fair. They did not understand the rules of war. All they understood was that these men were a threat to them, and would be dealt with in their own way.

Ж Ж Ж

Pablo and Alano were laughing, and joking, as they entered the darkness of the jungle. Although the sun was high in the sky, the dense leaves of the large trees formed a large, canopy that shaded the jungle floor. What the little sun that did manage to peek through the canopy cast eerie shadows, causing the four men to shoot their shotguns, and rifles at anything that moved, resulting in the senseless deaths of countless monkeys and macaws.

The intrepid four began laughing, masking their fear with false bravado, as they emptied their weapons into the tree leaves above, supposedly to allow more light onto the jungle floor below.

His rifle empty, the young crew chief stopped to reload. He stepped off the path, allowing the two generals to pass him, and take the lead.

Though he tried to reestablish the lead once his gun was loaded, he held back, choosing caution in lieu of bravado. The darkness, and narrowness, of the path ahead frightened him. The young corporal who had led the group, now found himself last. He began lagging behind the others; not because he was scared,—which he was—but because he was passing gas, something he always did when he sensed danger.

ЖЖЖ

Though weary, and weak, Steele knew he had to keep his wits about him, as he realized never would he have an opportunity like this again. It was precisely the right moment in time, with precisely the right piece of equipment. His only problem was he did not know how to fly the damn Chinook; something the army had not taught him. Now his only recourse was to capture the Jolly Green, along with the pilot and force him at gunpoint to fly him and his treasure to Argentina—for a nice reward, of course.

ЖЖЖ

The words they should have honed in on should have been Caution: death approaching. However, the generals had lost their caution. Like two, drunken old men who had the military hardware to issue death sentences to innocent monkeys, and beautiful birds, the generals had become blind to their surroundings, and the environment that was anything, but friendly.

With each step, they took, into the dark and dank jungle, shooting their weapons, and blaspheming womanhood, and God, they walked closer to meeting their deaths. The four men shot blindly into the jungle, failing to see the old Amarekaire warriors buried among the leaf bundles high above the jungle floor. They failed to notice the low hanging vines pulled taunt covered with Spanish moss, or the manmade, sharpened, wooden spikes attached to the soft, supple limb of a young oak.

Jax, the young co-pilot, and the youngest son of General Alano Leon, was doing, as he had been told—taking pictures. Resting his gun in the crook of his arm, he stopped to turn on the camera. Not being familiar with the camera, he studied the various settings, selecting flash, two-second delay, and a magnification of two-X. He did not know what that meant, but when he pointed the camera up and looked through the viewfinder, he saw what would became his very last view on this earth.

He snapped the little silver button that activated the shutter and flash, he glimpsed at the funny, little multi-colored man, as he puffed into a hollow tube. Jax felt the bee sting on his throat.

Puzzled, he stood silent, as if in disbelief, unable to speak. He could not swallow, nor could he feel any air coming into his lungs. Sinking to his knees, he pitched forward, still cradling the camera against him. Lieutenant Jax Leon of the Columbian Air Force was dead.

The generals did not see, nor hear the young man, as he died, not twenty feet behind them. General Pablo Gonzales and his cousin General Alano Leon had troubles of their own.

Pablo, thinking he was so sure-footed, did not pay attention when he stepped onto a small rock on the trail that tripped a string that pulled a vine, that released the tree, which in turn pulled the snare, and captured Pablo by his feet pulling him straight up so fast that it snapped his spine. The great and soon to be late General Pablo Gonzales was literally up a tree, dangling high above the jungle floor, unable to speak, or move of his own accord, staring face-to-face with an Amarekaire warrior who smiled, and licked his lips.

Startled, by the sudden disappearance of his cousin, Alano panicked losing his balance he Grabbed the first thing to help stabilize him He grabbed the Spanish moss covered vine. The only sound Alano heard was the gurgling coming from his lungs, as he drowned in his own blood. He had been impaled on wooden spikes, made by little men who could not read, nor write, and did not know the meaning of the word "greed".

52

Ж Ж Ж

CAPTAIN ALEJANDRO MEDINA HEARD THE GUN-SHOTS, and then the echoing of screams around him. He closed the large tailgate locking it. Knowing that would be one less thing that had to be done if, and when he needed to take off, in a hurry.

Alejandro was a third generation air force man, but the first to be an officer and pilot. For the most part, he enjoyed it, but unlike his father, he was not planning to make the air force his life's work. He had plans, big plans, and all he needed was money.

Inside the Jolly Green, he was uneasy. He checked his pistols, and armed the two Gatling guns. Not knowing what was going on, he was not going to take any chances. His idea of things were simple enough the generals planned to play solider, check out the ruins, confirm the body count, then Jax would call him on the radio, and he would start the BUFF and helo over to the ruins, and away they would go.

The men often called the Chinook "BUFF". It stood for Big, Ugly, Fat, Friend. Alejandro had other names for the Jolly Green and they were not nice. Looking at his watch, he saw that an hour had passed. The once noisy jungle was now quiet. *Too, damn quiet h*e thought. Pulling a smoke from his pocket he lit the cigarette, knowing that smoking was not permitted in, or around these flying gas cans.

Ж Ж Ж

Flipping his cigarette into the air, Steele walked back towards the camp. The old chief had made a temporary camp behind the mountain rubble along the river's edge. Somehow, the old boy had known not to move him, when he was hurt, and needed rest. El- Jaguar had destroyed his enemies and with his magic wand caused the mountain to move. Because of him, the tribe had actually moved their location, now they had more food, water and better shelter because El Jaguar had killed all their enemies and the jungle was safe again.

Steele put on his boots, bloused his pants, and strapped his knife to his leg. He had no tee shirt, as he had used it for sweatbands. Steele grabbed his shotgun, and pistol, now properly attired he was ready for more killing. His intention was to capture the helicopter, along with its pilot, something he had never done before.

Ж Ж Ж

Jorge Vargas had joined the Columbian Air force to escape poverty. He was not the best at anything, nor did he consider himself the worst. However, when it came to maintaining his helicopter, Corporal Jorge

Vargas was the best. The pilots knew it, and would often take him along on missions, because if anything went wrong with the aircraft, Corporal Vargas could fix it.

Vargas was fifty yards behind the other three men on the trail. His dark brown eyes were constantly moving from side to side and up and down surveying everything. He did not hear the laughing, or cursing anymore. It was his assumption the generals were reloading their weapons and maybe taking a smoke break. Not wanting to be alone, he picked up his pace listening for voices and sounds. However, the only sound he could hear was his flatulence, as he was so scared he was shaking.

Being that the trail was dark and gloomy, Corporal Vargas did not see Lieutenant Leon's body until he tripped over him. Vargas saw the lieutenant's eyes were open, as was his mouth, the general's camera still clutched in his hands. Never seeing a dead man before, the young corporal's mind had trouble processing the fact that he had been talking to Lieutenant Leon just minutes ago. Now the lieutenant was dead and he was completely alone.

Jorge reached over and took the general's camera from Jax, also liberating the lieutenant's rifle and pistol. Taking out his penknife, he cut off the lieutenant's ID tags putting them in his pocket. He searched the lieutenant's pockets finding his smokes, lighter, wallet, which he opened removing the bills.

Finished with the lieutenant's body Vargas gathered all of Jax's, personal effects, knowing Jax would not be spending, or using them anytime soon. He stood up and proceeded down the path not towards the safety of the helicopter, but towards the generals. Jorge was not a particularly brave man; however, if he did a brave thing like saving a general's life, he figured he would get medals, and a big promotion, maybe to sergeant. Corporal Jorge Vargas's bravery was motivated by greed, and power, not by patriotism, or ones devotion to duty, and country.

Corporal Vargas walked down the same path the generals had walked five minutes before. He had gone ten meters when came upon a slippery incline that made a sharp turn left hiding whatever, lay before him. There for the second time in his life he saw another body. He saw the blood-soaked body of General Leon father of Jax.

General Leon's shotgun was lying on the ground. Jorge's hands did not tremble, as he cut the general's ID tags from around his neck along with his Saint Christopher medallion. Purely for greed, Jorge grabbed the general's wallet helping himself to the money. Picking up the shotgun, He slung it over his shoulder wondering about the other general. Glancing in all directions, he saw nothing, and not wanting to tempt fate, Jorge started to walk away, but then thought maybe he should prove his story. He stepped back, and took a picture of General Leon. As he passed by Lieutenant Jax's body, he took a couple pictures of Jax, especially his face. He was standing, looking down at the body of his once fearless lieutenant, who now lay dead at his feet. The lieutenant's father, the general, was standing not ten yards away, impaled by large sharp stakes that were supporting him, a look of surprise forever, etched upon his face. Jorge asked himself the question: *Where is the other asshole general? The one who had told them the cannibals would not attack.*

Taking a deep drag on his cigarette, the corporal surveyed his surroundings. A creepy feeling came over him, excluding the bodies of the general, and his son. Vargas was not alone he was being watched.

Making a quick decision, Jorge Vargas did not run. As scared as he was, Jorge held his composure and began to walk back down the path towards his helicopter, each step emitting a strong and purposeful sound.

Ж Ж Ж

Having decided on the best way to sneak up on the Jolly Green, Steele took a dugout and paddled across the new lake. On the other side, he pulled the canoe onto the bank and walked up the hill, keeping the shadows of the jungle at his back, and the jungle foliage and fauna in front of him. He stopped periodically to check on the helicopter guard, his mind trying to figure out just how he could commandeer the Jolly Green.

Steele's concentration was broken when he noticed, out of the corner of his eye, a young man walking out of the jungle, heading for the helicopter. Slung over his left shoulder was a shotgun, over his right an M-16. In his hands, he carried another M-16 at the ready.

Sizing up the situation, Steele knew by the young man's walk, and the fact he carried extra weapons, that no one else was behind him. Not waiting further, Zack seized the moment and ran towards the helicopter, keeping it between him and the young man. If possible, he did not want to kill him, but instead use him and if necessary bribe him.

Just short of the Chinook, Corporal Vargas stopped and pulled out Jax's radio, keying the mike. "Hello, Captain Medina. This is Corporal Vargas requesting permission to come aboard."

"Permission granted", came the terse reply.

Ж Ж Ж

Steele had managed to get to the Jolly Green unseen. He slid his body underneath the mammoth helicopter, and waited, for whatever came next. He anticipated the pilot would open the side door nearest him. Sure enough, Steele had guessed correctly. He heard the latch turn and the door slide open. From his vantage point, he watched the legs of the young man walk towards the small portal nearest the cockpit.

Carefully Steele slithered his body backs towards the tires, making sure to keep the large tires between him and the young man. The young fellow walked past the tires, Steele slid out from under the helicopter coming up behind the young corporal. Steele shoved him into the doorway, his shotgun immediately in the face of the startled pilot.

"Don't shoot!" screamed the pilot in perfect English, as he backed away from the door, his hands held up above his head.

Pushing the young man back away from the doorway, Steele motioned for the pilot to come out of the helicopter. While watching the pilot, Steele removed the weapons from the young corporal placing them on the ground. Steele could see no fear in the pilot's eyes, just questions, while the young airman was scared shitless.

With his head, Steele motioned for the corporal to come closer. Not knowing what was about to happen, the corporal let loose with one of the longest, and loudest fart, either Steele or the pilot had ever heard. Suddenly, the air became putrid with the boy's gaseous emission, causing the other two men to wave their hands in front of their faces and step backwards. Then both men began to laugh, as did the corporal.

Steele turned to the pilot, using the international hand signal, he asked for a cigarette. The pilot laughingly obliged, taking one out for him, as well and offering one to the corporal. The captain took out his lighter lighting Steele's cigarette for him before lighting his own.

Looking at his unexpected guess, the pilot pointed at Steele, and in his best English asked, "Green Beret?"

Steel exhaled the smoke drifting away, asking himself the question, *"What do I do now"?* He went with his instincts nodding to the pilot, acknowledging his question.

The pilot turned to the young corporal, and proceeded to explain to him what this man that stood before them was. In perfect English, the young corporal turned, pointed, and replied, "No Shit!"

Both men burst out laughing at the young corporal's expletive. Steele began to relax, figuring he was in no real danger. Not sure exactly what it was, there was something about the pilot that he liked.

"Sir, what are you going to do with us, now that you have us?" asked the pilot.

"What is your name?' Steele asked.

"My name, sir, is Alejandro Medina of the Columbian Air Force."

"Well, Alejandro, I'm not going to kill you or the corporal unless he farts again. And you can tell him that."

Alejandro did, as instructed instantly the fear was gone from the corporal's face.

"I need you both to help me, and I'm willing to pay you very well," Steele said, taking another drag on his cigarette.

"You want me to fly you to Bogotá?" asked the captain.

"No, Alejandro, not Bogotá. I want you to fly me to Argentina, Buenos Aires to be exact," Steele said.

Alejandro began to laugh, "Oh is that all you want? You want me to fly you to Buenos Aires in this?" he said, pointing with his thumb at the Jolly Green. "What I'll do is fly you to Bogotá. From there you can take a commercial airplane to wherever you want," Alejandro said, nonchalantly walking over to where the weapons were lying on the ground.

Alejandro froze in place when he heard the unmistakable sound of Steele's 12-gauge shotgun being cocked.

"Sorry Steele", Alejandro said, "I wasn't thinking".

Steele did not return Alejandro's smile.

"We were discussing getting me to Argentina." Steele said.

"Look, Steele, let me explain it this way. This helicopter, fully loaded with fuel, and traveling at cruising speed can go maybe five hundred miles. Buenos Aires is thousands of miles from here. By commercial jet it takes six hours, and that's at five hundred miles an hour." Alejandro said lighting another cigarette.

Steele did not respond to Alejandro's explanation. Instead, he motioned with the shotgun, pushing Alejandro away from the weapons. "Sit down, both of you," he ordered, as he motioned to the ground with his shotgun to enforce his order.

Walking over to the weapons, Steele gathered them in his arms. Turning, he walked over to the open portal placing each weapon, one at a time, side by side, methodically removing all the shells, and bullets, rendering them harmless. He did it on purpose removing any harmful intentions against him while keeping both the Columbians alive.

Finished with his task, Steele turned and conversationally asked the two men, "Do you know of another way to get me to Argentina?"

"Sir, why must you get to Argentina?" Corporal Vargas asked.

The simplicity and directness of the question took Steele by surprise. The "why" he could understand; it was the "where" he did not understand. He had known that by stealing Mendoza's fortune he had to hide, and that had to be somewhere where, if he was found, the United

States could not come after him for any reason. No longer did he have any real ties to the United States. His family was all deceased; the only one he cared about was Esther. Now he was not sure about her.

Thinking a moment he then said, "Tell me, Alejandro, if you had millions of dollars and nobody knew you had the money, where would you go to hide?"

"That is an easy question to answer," Alejandro said as he stood up and walked towards Steele.

"Let me have my map case," Alejandro said, pointing to the black leather bag resting on the floor behind the pilot's seat.

Steele turned and reached for the case. He noticed a cooler, and pulled that towards him.

"Yeah, yeah," Alejandro said, pointing to the cooler.

When Steele handed the leather bag to the anxious pilot, Alejandro handed it to the corporal who was now standing behind his captain.

Steele pulled the cooler until the handle was clearly visible, the pilot then reached over and grabbed both handles, lifting the cooler and placing it at Steele's feet. Alejandro backed away from the cooler, allowing Steele the honor of opening it.

Inside the cooler were fruit, water, canned beer and some sandwiches. Steele picked up and threw a bottle of water and an apple to the young corporal. Next, he tossed a beer to Alejandro and he took a beer for himself.

"Ok, amigo, show me where you would hide with millions of dollars," Steele said, popping the beer cap.

"Here, in Brazil," Alejandro said, pointing to a city named Belem.

"Why there? Why not here in Natal?" Steele asked, pointing to a small dot on a very large map.

"Because, Steele, I can reach Belem, and they have an airport, where you can take a commercial flight to Argentina." Alejandro replied taking a sip of beer.

Processing Alejandro's remarks, Steele answered, "Ok, here's the deal…"

With the meeting concluded, and hands shaken Steele stood up and waved his arms, signaling to the Amarekaire that all was well.

"What are you doing?" Alejandro asked, standing up looking for something to happen.

"I'm going to save your lives." Steele replied.

"From what," Alejandro asked, looking around, not seeing anything.

"From them," Steele replied. Pointing all around, as the warriors stepped out of the jungle shade, and bushes.

Corporal Vargas jumped to his feet, belching farts, as he scampered towards Steele's protection. The tribal elders gasped waiving their hands in front of their noses. The old chief pushed Julio's shrunken head towards Vargas, lifting his war club pointing it at Vargas, and back to the shrunken head. The meaning was clear if Vargas farted again, the old chief would shrink his head. Vargas jumped into the Helicopter.

"Steele please tell me who are these people?' Alejandro asked smiling attempting to show no fear.

"They are my friends." Steele replied, bending down removing ice cubes from the cooler, and passing them around.

Five pallets stacked high with Columbian and Mexican pesos, and Australian dollars, were placed to the side. Steele motioned both, Alejandro and Corporal Vargas over to the pallets.

"Alejandro, when I along with my money, have been safely deposited in Brazil, you and Vargas can return and take these five pallets, no harm will come to you. However, in return, neither of you are to tell anyone about the Amarekaire Indians, and the money. Remember, this is for *your* safety." Alejandro and Vargas extended their hands, shaking on the deal.

How much money the two men would get? Probably millions, but he did not care. He had what he wanted—enough money to live a thousand lifetimes, and would never need worry about being hungry or cold again. Right now, his immediate problems were his identity and clothing. If he could manage to get to his apartment in Bogotá, he could bathe, and shave, change into his civilian clothes, pack a suitcase, grab his passports and fly to Brazil where he could set up an international banking account. After that, he would fly to Rio, or Buenos Aires, using his new identity given to him by General Pablo Gonzales now deceased. The Columbian Government for escape purposes had given the original seven men false identities.

The original seven—of whom, he definitely was one—had been given foolproof identities. That was until Pablo had sold them out. Now that Pablo was dead, Steele felt safe in assuming the identity selected for him by Pablo: Dante Alvarez, a rich, Columbian Industrialist.

53

ЖЖЖ

"AMIGO, WHAT IS WRONG?" ALEJANDRO ASKED, handing Steele a beer.

"Well, Alejandro, I have two very serious problems. One is establishing a new identity. I have identity papers in my apartment in Bogotá, but no way to get there. Also, I need decent clothes, a bath, and a shave."

"Yes, amigo, you need a bath," Alejandro said, laughing and then taking a sip of beer. "I have an idea, Steele. Vargas and I also live in Bogotá. My car is parked at the El Dorado terminal. How about the three of us fly into the Bogotá airport and land close to the terminal? I will request a fuel truck be standing by when we land. Vargas will fuel the helicopter and check the oil. When he is done, the three of us will calmly walk out the side gate and get into my car. I will drive you to your apartment. Taking out a cigarette and handing it to Steele, Alejandro waited.

"Oh, just like that, we will fly a military helicopter that's a city block long into an international airport, where you will calmly land and ask for fuel. Then we will just walk away, leaving millions of dollars unguarded. Oh, yeah, amigo let us not forget me. I kind of stick out in a crowd," Steele said sarcastically, as Alejandro lit his cigarette.

Jorge and Alejandro began to laugh at, but Steele was not amused. Both men backed away from Steele, giving him his space.

Alejandro motioned for Steele to come over where he and Vargas were standing. Steele cocked his head, giving the two men a funny look, as he moved towards them. Come, come," Alejandro said, motioning with his hand for Steele to hurry up.

When Steele walked into the huddle, he did not know how to react when Alejandro grabbed his arm firmly, and spun him around.

"Look there, you see those numbers?" Alejandro asked, pointing to the rear rotor tower of the Chinook.

"Ok, I see a number with a bunch of zero's, so what?" Steele said, looking at both men questioningly.

"The last three numbers are zeros, or as you say in your country, triple nuts. This helicopter belongs to the general. Everyone knows it, and everyone knows that his helicopter is guarded. The corporal will service the helicopter; I will be standing next to the open door talking to you. The fuel truck driver will know that you are the guard. Vargas will tell the driver to ask people to stay away, or they will be shot it's that Simple!"

"Besa mi asno," Steele said, pissing both combatants off.

"Joda LE!" Alejandro yelled, getting into Steele's face.

Quicker than the eye could see, the Columbian captain was on the ground, a shotgun stuffed between his eyes.

"No senor Steele", came the desperate cry of the young corporal pleading for his captain's life. "What Captain Medina says is true. No one will come near."

Backing away a few steps, Steele allowed the shaken captain room to stand and gain his dignity.

"Steele, let me try and explain it this way", Alejandro said, his voice softer, and more respectful, after his near-death experience. "With this load we will reach our destination, but Corporal Vargas, and I will not have the fuel to return to get our money. We must stop and deposit our money in my brother-in-law's bank. My brother-in-law is the bank manager of the largest bank in Cartagena. I will call him, and tell him to rent a van, and meet us somewhere where we can off-load the money. He will take a small percentage for his trouble and of course, for my sister, and her children. Then Corporal Vargas and I must fly to Camp Larandia, which is about forty miles from Bogotá, and report the very sad story of how three dedicated men gave their lives so that the corporal and I could escape. If you want, Steele, I could ask my brother-in-law Hugo about you?"

Steele took a puff of his borrowed smoke, and dropped it to the ground, stamping it with his boot. He did not speak, as the smoke he had just inhaled began escaping through his nose drifting away with the wind. Neither Vargas nor Medina spoke, preferring to let the final decision rest with Steele.

"You know, Medina, you would make a great used-car salesman," Steele said, extending his hand in friendship. Then in an uncharacteristic show of trust, he emptied his shotgun, expelling each shell for both men to see. Now they were equals.

Ж Ж Ж

The razor stung Steele's face as it dragged across his sandpaper beard; adding more insult to his head; his burning tongue, and mouth had already been treated to a thorough treatment of toothpaste. He looked in the mirror, he could recognize himself, and when he splashed on his aftershave Steele actually gave out a yell. He was back in the human world.

As he walked out of the bathroom, he heard Alejandro talking to someone. Steele figured it was Hugo the bloodsucking, money-grubbing, butt fucking, brother-in-law, Alejandro's exact words. Going into the kitchen, he noticed Jorge was missing, as were the car keys. He remembered Jorge had asked if he was hungry apparently, Jorge had gone for food.

Steele walked back into the living room, and took a seat, listening, as Alejandro negotiated with Hugo. Between the cursing and the hand gestures, Steele was able to ascertain that Hugo wanted a flat ten percent of everything.

Steele did not like the tone of the negotiations figuring Hugo was trying to extort money from Alejandro, and if Hugo would do that to his family, what would Hugo want from him? Steele decided to end the bickering. He waved his hand catching Alejandro's attention and motioned for the cell phone. Alejandro stopped talking in mid-sentence, and handed the phone to his new amigo. With a smile, Steele flipped the phone closed, instantly stopping all negotiations.

Shocked, Alejandro threw his hands in the air in disgust. Steele began laughing, and then Alejandro's momentary anger gave way to laughter. Why Steele was laughing, Alejandro had no idea, but if Steele laughed, then he must surely know something.

"We will wait for Hugo to call back," Steele said, handing the phone back to Alejandro. When he does, tell him you will give him one million U. S. dollars, no questions asked. If he begins to complain, say "Sorry, Hugo', and hang up."

Shaking his head, Alejandro smiled, thinking that a million dollars split three ways was a cheap price to pay for a lifetime of comfort.

On the kitchen table was a roadmap of Columbia that Steele had been studying earlier, before the Alejandro vs. Hugo negotiations had diverted his attention. His concentration was interrupted again, when he heard a noise that quickly grew into a rapid-fire kind of tapping, and then a series of long, hard knocks coming from the back door. Opening the door, Steele was eye to eye with a wet pissed off corporal. Vargas had been caught in the rain while carrying the two large pizzas, a six-pack of beer, and bags of junk food.

Jorge could hear his captain singing and began to chuckle, as did Steele. Taking a cold beer from the young corporal, Steele stood up and walked back to the bedroom where he found Alejandro dancing nude, as he dried himself off. Steele just shook his head handing Alejandro the beer. Then walked over to the chest of drawers, and pulled out some clean underwear, for his guest.

"Jorge is here with the food; We will eat, and wait for him to shower, then we will make our final decision, as to where we go if Hugo doesn't call us." Steele said walking out of the bedroom.

Noticing the clock on the microwave, only six hours had elapsed since he had made the acquaintance of Alejandro and Jorge. True, at first the meeting had not been on the best of terms. In fact, a person might have called it contentious. Now he was drinking beer, eating pizza and discussing ideas on where to deposit their fortunes.

Young Jorge came up with the idea of renting a private airplane, and flying the money to Argentina.

"Hmm, can we do that, Alejandro? Can we simply rent a cargo plane, and fly our fortunes into Argentina instead of Brazil?" Steele asked.

Alejandro stopped eating and placed his pizza back into the box. He took a sip of beer to clear his throat, and smiled. "Yes, we can and it would not cost us a million dollars either."

Steele stood up, and walked over to the kitchen cabinet above the refrigerator pulling out a phone book. He handed it to Alejandro and patted Jorge on his back. "Good idea, Jorge", Steele said, reaching for another slice of pizza.

"Alejandro Medina, Captain in the Columbian Air Force calling. I want to talk with Manuel Garza."

Steele and Jorge looked at each other. As if anticipating Steele's question, Jorge shrugged his shoulders.

"Hello, Manuel, it's Alejandro, I need a big favor. I need a fast cargo plane that can carry two, maybe three metal security containers. I cannot tell you any more than that as the mission is top-secret," Alejandro said, smiling into the phone.

Manuel Garza had been Alejandro's flight instructor when he had joined the air force. A few years ago, Manuel had since retired and opened a flight school, aircraft rental, and charter service. He was good, reliable, and could keep his mouth shut.

"Ah, yes, Alejandro, I have just the aircraft. However, it is very expensive. It is a two-engine turbo prop with two outside ramjets. Can you fly such an airplane?"

Alejandro laughed, "You mean that old KC 127 that is parked across the field from your hangar?"

"Yes, that is the aircraft, Alejandro."

"Manuel, what is the airplane's cruising speed and range?" Alejandro asked, giving his two partners the thumbs up. Fine, do the necessary inspections and fuel the tanks. Then taxi it over next to General Leon's helicopter. I will also, need three large cargo containers, and a fork-lift. Oh Manuel, you will be paid in cash, and nobody must know. Understand, amigo?"

"Yes Alejandro, I understand, and yes, I will tell nobody", Manuel promised and hung up.

"We have our plane. It will get us to Argentina with no problem," Alejandro said, turning his attention to the young corporal. "Corporal Vargas, we will help you load the airplane. Then I want you to check over the airplane, especially the engines and fuel. Do a visual check of the fuel tanks and all the flight controls, especially the cables and do not forget the oil. Do you understand, corporal?"

"Yes sir!"

"Once unloaded, Steele and I will take the helicopter back to the base. If everything goes well, we should be gone two hours, maybe three. I forgot to tell you something Steele. Manuel had a son named Miguel, who worked for some hombre named Juan Carlos who was Julio Mendoza's chief lieutenant. General Leon is the one who killed his son in that vicious bomb attack on Mendoza's compound. I now believe that attack was nothing more than murder to obtain Mendoza's fortune and that is why we flew there. It was to obtain the money that you already had…"

Alejandro's voice dropped an octave and his eyes became small needlepoints, as they bored into Steele's eyes. "It was you! You are the one who killed all those people! Not General Leon or Gonzales, I thought the damage looked too severe for our bombs," Alejandro said, turning his body towards Steele.

Steele held up his hands, palms out. "Alejandro, Jorge, nothing has changed between us. What happened back there happened for a reason. I said nothing because what those generals did was a brave thing and I respect bravery. So give them their honor, Alejandro, and we shall take the spoils of war."

Alejandro smiled and nodded his head in agreement.

54

ЖЖЖ

I T WAS EARLY IN THE MORNING when the Bogotá tower gave its permission to take off. Corporal Vargas had dutifully inspected and re-inspected the airplane, finding only two major discrepancies. The hydraulic reservoir used to raise and lower the landing gear was nearly empty, as someone had deliberately cut the hydraulic line. The other discrepancy was a little more devious. One of the thrust attenuator link pins had been removed. Upon landing, the pilot extends the attenuators, which in turn will reduce the engine's thrust, but does not reduce the engine's rpms. This is a method of braking to help control the airplane.

Captain Medina would have automatically engaged the attenuators upon landing and with only one attenuator, working the plane would have skidded sideways. Everyone knows airplanes do not do well when they land sideways.

Both these discrepancies had been deliberate, just as Captain Medina had suspected they might.

⚜ ⚜ ⚜

Alejandro looked at his watch. Figuring average cruising speed, divided by distance, it would take about nine hours to reach Argentina. The airplane would cost about a thousand dollars an hour. Whatever time it took, it was still cheaper than a million dollars, or the ten percent Hugo wanted.

Jorge is a genius, Alejandro thought, as he chuckled to himself. *Arrival time would be around nine in the morning. Corporal Vargas would service the aircraft while Steele using his fake passport would make arrangements with Argentina Customs Authorities. Then the three of them would get a bite to eat, hire a car, and find the closest branch of any Bank of Argentina.*

The plan was for Steele to stay in Argentina while he and Jorge returned to Columbia. Then when the time was right, they would return to Argentina, and start a new life, doing whatever they wanted to do with more money than either man, could possibly earn in ten lifetimes.

⚜ ⚜ ⚜

When the Argentinean Customs Agent asked Jorge for the cargo manifest, only one word was written on it: Money. The agent looked at the three containers and asked Jorge to open the middle box.

Jorge looked at Steele as if asking him, "Do I dare?" Steele smiled and nodded his head and the young, soon to be very rich corporal nodded to the agent and opened the box. The agent stamped the form and walked off the airplane.

With that, the three men walked across the tarmac towards the cargo terminal. It was finished accept for one thing.

Ж Ж Ж

ESTER WAS IN BED, staring at the ceiling, waiting for sleep to come, She was listening to the rain, as it hit her bedroom windows. She had not been sleeping well, and now had the early morning vomiting. She knew with certainty that it was not the flu. What she had was a baby on board.

She knew it was her fault, as she had been careless that one time, when she had grabbed him so tightly with her arms, and legs, that he hadn't been able to pull out—because she wouldn't let him—even though he had twice told her he was about to explode.

For comfort, she was wearing his army-issued green tee shirt. She had planned to wash it, but liked the way the shirt smelled. It smelled of Steele.

She had decided to give up the Navy, and move home with her mom and dad. They would be ecstatic to have a grandchild. God had granted them their fondest wish, while all she wished for was a tall, stubborn man named Zachary Steele to return from, wherever he was and come home to her.

The soft jingle of her cell phone startled her. Glancing at the clock, she saw it was after midnight. Warily she flipped her phone open and said, "Hello?"

That deep, masculine voice belonged to only one man: Her man. She began to cry.

Ж Ж Ж

It had been over a month since Esther had heard his voice that rainy night, and now as the Boeing 747 slowly started its descent into Rio, she would be reunited with Steele. It did not matter to her what his new name was or why the government had made him change it. Esther Colgate did not know that she would become Senora Esther Alvarez, the wealthiest woman in Argentina and one of the richest women in the world. She would never know how her two "lost kitties" had made it all possible.

The End

www.ingramcontent.com/pod-product-compliance
Lightning Source LLC
Chambersburg PA
CBHW062027170626
46813CB00001B/312